Praise for the authors of

A Western Christmas Homecoming

LYNNA BANNING

"Banning's talent for crafting warm, delightful tales once again wins fan devotion."

—*RT Book Reviews* on
Miss Murray on the Cattle Trail

LAURI ROBINSON

"Well written, dramatic and complete with a cast of beloved townsfolk. Readers will laugh, cry and rejoice."

—*RT Book Reviews* on *In the Sheriff's Protection*

KATHRYN ALBRIGHT

"Well-paced, sweet romance [...] For Western fans, Albright's Americana tale will be an entertaining read."

—*RT Book Reviews* on *The Prairie Doctor's Bride*

Lynna Banning combined a lifelong love of history and literature into a satisfying career as a writer. Born in Oregon, she graduated from Scripps College and embarked on a career as an editor and technical writer and later as a high school English teacher. She enjoys hearing from her readers. You may write to her directly at PO Box 324, Felton, CA 95018, USA, email her at carowoolston@att.net or visit Lynna's website at lynnabanning.net.

A lover of fairy tales and cowboy boots,
Lauri Robinson can't imagine a better profession than penning happily-ever-after stories about men—and women—who pull on a pair of boots before riding off into the sunset...or kick them off for other reasons. Lauri and her husband raised three sons in their rural Minnesota home and are now getting their just rewards by spoiling their grandchildren. Visit laurirobinson.blogspot.com, Facebook.com/lauri.robinson1 or Twitter.com/laurir.

Kathryn Albright writes American-set historical romance for Harlequin. From her first breath, she has had a passion for stories that celebrate the goodness in people. She combines her love of history and her love of story to write novels of inspiration, endurance and hope. Visit her at kathrynalbright.com and on Facebook.

A WESTERN
Christmas
HOMECOMING

Lynna Banning
Lauri Robinson
Kathryn Albright

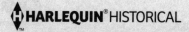

H HARLEQUIN® HISTORICAL

ISBN-13: 978-1-335-05180-6

A Western Christmas Homecoming

Copyright © 2018 by Harlequin Books S.A.

The publisher acknowledges the copyright holders
of the individual works as follows:

Christmas Day Wedding Bells
Copyright © 2018 by The Woolston Family Trust

Snowbound in Big Springs
Copyright © 2018 by Lauri Robinson

Christmas with the Outlaw
Copyright © 2018 by Kathryn Leigh Albright

Recycling programs
for this product may
not exist in your area.

This edition published by arrangement with Harlequin Books S.A.

For questions and comments about the quality of this book,
please contact us at CustomerService@Harlequin.com.

® and ™ are trademarks of Harlequin Enterprises Limited or its
corporate affiliates. Trademarks indicated with ® are registered in the
United States Patent and Trademark Office, the Canadian Intellectual
Property Office and in other countries.

Printed in U.S.A.

CONTENTS

CHRISTMAS DAY WEDDING BELLS

Lynna Banning

Dear Reader,

To me, what is important about Christmas is the spirit of the season. Christmas is a time for wishing those we care about health and happiness and happy endings. And I wish the same to all of you.

Lynna

Dedication

For David Woolston and Yvonne Mandarino Woolston who exemplify the best in kindness, caring and love.

Chapter One

Alice watched the leather-bound volume of Keats skitter off the counter and slide across the library floor. "I beg your pardon, what did you say?"

The young deputy's face looked somber. "The sheriff wants to see you, Miss Alice," he puffed. "Wants you to come over to his office right away. Said it was real important."

What on earth could be so important that Sheriff Rivera would send his deputy to summon her in the middle of her peaceful October afternoon at the Smoke River library?

"Sandy, did he say *why* he wants to see me?"

"No, ma'am. Just said for me to get the lead—uh…to hurry and not take no for an answer."

Alice retrieved her wide-brimmed sun hat and her beaded reticule, locked the library door and followed the deputy down Main Street to Sheriff Rivera's office. When she entered, the lawman shifted his feet off the desk and jackknifed to attention.

"Miss Alice, good morning." He wasn't smiling, and that made her uneasy. Hawk Rivera smiled at all the girls. Or, to be more accurate, all the girls smiled at *him*.

"What have I done, Sheriff?"

"Alice, I want to introduce you to US Marshal Randell Logan. He's brought some news you need to hear. It's about your sister, Dorothy."

For the first time she noticed the tall, lean man standing in one corner of the small sheriff's office next to a bulletin board plastered with yellowing Wanted posters. He gave her a brief nod. "Miss Montgomery. I'm afraid it's bad news."

He was very tan, she thought irrationally. With dark hair and a mustache over his unsmiling mouth. He took a step toward her. "Maybe you'd better sit down, Miss."

Oh, God. She sank onto the hard-backed chair across from the sheriff and clasped her hands in her lap. "Tell me," she whispered.

The marshal cleared his throat. "It concerns your sister, Dorothy Coleman. As you know she's been living in a mining camp in Idaho."

"Yes, I know that. Silver City. Dottie owns an assay company she inherited from her husband when he died. Does your news concern the business?"

She watched his gaze flick to Sheriff Rivera and then return to her face. His eyes were an unusual color. As she studied him, those eyes went from hard jade to mossy green.

"I'm sorry to tell you this has nothing to do with the assay business, Miss Montgomery. It's about your sister herself."

Alice clenched her hands into fists. "I haven't heard from Dottie in some weeks. What about her?"

To her surprise the marshal knelt in front of her. "I'm afraid your sister is dead, Miss."

Alice cried out. "But she can't be! Dottie's only twenty. She's younger than I am, my little sister. She can't be dead."

Marshal Logan waited without speaking.

"H-how did she die? Typhoid? Cholera?"

He let out a long breath. "She was killed, Miss."

"An accident? A mining accident? But she never went into the mines. She hated dark places and—" She broke off, wondering why Sheriff Rivera was pouring whiskey into a shot glass on his desk.

The marshal hesitated. "Your sister Dorothy was murdered."

Unable to utter a sound, Alice sat without moving. The marshal reached for the whiskey and held the glass out to her.

"It's not true," she said. "I don't believe you. Everyone loves Dottie! No one would want to hurt her."

"Alice." Sheriff Rivera's voice. "It's hard to accept something like this, so just take your time."

She drew in a shaky breath and pushed aside the whiskey the marshal held out. "I d-don't drink spirits," she said in a ragged voice.

"Maybe not," he said. "Might make an exception today, Miss." He folded her fingers around the glass.

She took a tentative sip. It burned all the way down her throat and brought tears stinging into her eyes. She coughed, then took another, bigger swallow.

The marshal was still kneeling in front of her. "What did you say your name was?" she said, her voice hoarse.

"Logan, Miss. Randell Logan."

"How do you know about my—my sister? Were you there?"

"No, ma'am, I wasn't. I'm a US Marshal out of Colorado Territory. I was called in by the Owyhee County sheriff to investigate your sister's death. Actually, I'm working for Pinkerton on this case."

Alice began to feel disconnected from what was going on around her. "Pinkerton? How was Dottie killed? I mean, was she stabbed or…?"

"She was shot," the marshal said quietly. "If it's any comfort to you, the sheriff in Silver City said she died instantly."

"Oh. Oh, my God. Murdered… *Oh, my God.*" She gripped the whiskey glass and began to rock back and forth. Everything felt unreal, as if she were dreaming. Some of the whiskey splashed down the front of her shirtwaist, and she felt the marshal's hand on her shoulder.

"You gonna faint?"

"No. I n-never faint. I just feel…numb."

Then Sheriff Rivera was standing beside her, lifting the whiskey out of her hand. "Alice, do you think you can walk? I want you to go back to your boardinghouse and lie down."

She nodded but kept on rocking.

Rand saw that her eyes were shut. Something about the small hand clenched in her lap made his belly tighten.

Sheriff Rivera tipped his head toward her. "Rand, could you…?"

"Sure." He rose and reached under her armpits to help her stand. "Come on, Miss Montgomery. I'm gonna walk you home."

"She lives at Rose Cottage," the sheriff said. "Over on Maple Street. Take a right off Main about two blocks down." He tossed back the rest of the whiskey, then sent Rand an inquiring look. "Want a shot?"

He did, but not until he got Miss Alice over to her boardinghouse. "Later, Hawk."

"I'll be at the Golden Pheasant in an hour."

"Yeah."

Miss Montgomery moved unsteadily toward the door. Rand kept his arm around her shoulders and guided her out onto the street. She walked slowly past the mercantile and the hotel, but when she got to the saloon, she bobbled a step. He slipped his arm around her waist to steady her and she grabbed on to his forearm.

A fresh-faced kid shot around the corner. "Hiya, Miss Montgomery."

She raised a listless hand as he skipped by.

"You a schoolteacher?" Rand asked.

She shook her head. "I am the librarian." Late-afternoon sunlight fell across her face, but she didn't seem to notice. Her straw sun hat was still clutched in her hand.

At the front gate of Rose Cottage she paused to pick a yellow rose from the tumble of blooms along the fence.

"Dottie loved roses," she murmured. "Especially yellow ones."

As he moved her up the walk, a grizzled older man rose from the porch swing. "Alice?" Frowning, he clumped down the front steps. "Alice, are you all right?"

"Yes, Rooney," she murmured. "Just…tired."

The man took a closer look at her face, tramped back up onto the porch and banged through the screen door. "Sarah! Got trouble!"

Rand sat Alice down in the swing just as a handsome older woman bustled out the door. "Alice! Child, whatever is the matter?"

He took the woman and her husband aside, identified himself and explained the situation. "Oh, no," Sarah moaned. "Oh, Alice, honey, I'm so sorry." She sank down beside Alice, folded her into her arms and began to rock her back and forth.

"Gol-dang-it," the older man, Rooney, swore. "How come it's the good 'uns that get stomped on?"

Rand had no answer for that. It was something he'd often asked himself over the years.

"Life sure never gets any easier," Rooney said with a sidelong glance at Alice. "Fightin' Indians is lots easier than watchin' something like this."

Sarah stood and helped Alice move toward the screen door. "You'll stay to supper, Marshal Logan?"

He hesitated. He'd been in the saddle since mid-August, sleeping on the ground and eating canned beans and bacon. He hadn't had a home-cooked meal in over a month.

Rooney laid a hand on his arm. "Look, Marshal, I used to scout for Wash Halliday, so I know what it's like, bein' a lawman. Every so often ya need to kick back and take a night off. 'Specially if there's a fine-tastin' supper involved. Besides, my Sarah would be highly insulted if you walked off her front porch without acceptin' her hospitality."

Rand thought about sharing a drink with Sheriff Rivera

at the Golden Pheasant, then weighed it against explaining the rest of his mission to Alice. Alice won.

"Okay, Rooney, sounds good. Thanks." He would tell Alice the rest after supper.

Chapter Two

Alice came downstairs to supper feeling as if a freight train had smashed her flat. She had tried to sleep for an hour, but every time she closed her eyes Dottie's face rose before her. She was so numb she couldn't cry, but her entire body ached, and when she thought about her sister her heart pounded erratically. She felt like screaming.

On top of everything else, one of her blind headaches was coming on. If Sarah had not insisted, she would not be coming down for supper but crawling into bed with a cold cloth over her eyes.

Voices drifted from the dining room. She recognized Rooney's low rumble and old Mrs. DuPont's quavering soprano. Doc Graham never said much. Sarah's grandson, Mark, rarely spoke during a meal, but tonight he was rapid-firing questions at someone. His nine-year-old voice broke when he got excited, and apparently the answers were exciting; one minute he was a soprano, the next he was a baritone.

When she reached the table, the marshal, Randell Logan, rose to his feet, followed by Rooney, Doc Graham and young Mark. Iris DuPont clucked at her sympathetically, and Alice gritted her teeth. If anyone said one single word about Dottie or how sorry they were she would lose control. Better to pretend it was a perfectly normal fall evening in Smoke River and nothing was wrong.

She took her seat and automatically unfolded the napkin lying beside the blue-flowered plate. The marshal rested his gaze on her for a long moment, and then resumed speaking to Mark. "Actually, Mark, a young man must be at least eighteen to become a United States Marshal."

Mark groaned. "How old were you, Marshal Logan?"

He shot Alice a glance and quickly returned his gaze to Mark. "I was well over eighteen when I joined up. Actually, I was twenty-seven."

"Golly, what took you so long?"

The marshal laughed. "Just living, mostly."

Alice realized the marshal sensed how shaky she was feeling and was purposely carrying on this conversation with Mark to keep attention focused away from her.

Mark's blue eyes snapped with interest. "Didja fight Injuns, like Rooney?"

"Yep."

"With the army?"

"Yep." Rand reached for the ceramic bowl of mashed potatoes.

Mark leaned toward him. "Didja have a girl?" he whispered.

Rand drew in a slow breath. "Yes, son, I did."

"Didja marry her?"

Rooney's wife, Sarah, saved him by plunking down a platter of fried chicken and nudging her grandson's shoulder. "Mark, we don't ask our guests such personal questions."

"Sorry, Gran." But the minute she returned to the kitchen, Mark hitched his chair closer to him. "Well, didja?" he whispered.

"Mark!" Sarah called. "Shut your mouth. Or maybe you fancy washing up the supper dishes tonight?"

"No, Gran." The boy hung his head. "Sorry, Marshal," he muttered.

Rand worked to hide a smile. He was relieved to see Alice's plate was filling up with chicken and mashed potatoes and gravy. Then he realized it was Rooney who was spooning food onto it, not Alice.

She picked at the potatoes, but ate only a few bites. Her

face looked white and set, and she kept her gaze focused on the tablecloth. Her sister's death was hitting her pretty hard. He couldn't blame her, but it would sure make the rest of his job more difficult. This was why an assignment like this one was so hard—the price innocent people had to pay.

The older woman, Mrs. DuPont, and the doctor ate their fried chicken and mashed potatoes in silence, though Doc Graham paid close attention to the talk about soldiering and scouting that bounced back and forth between Rooney and himself.

Young Mark listened avidly, while Alice compulsively pressed the fingers of one hand over the ruffles at the neck of her blue shirtwaist. She had elegant hands, Rand noted. Real lady hands. Well, she said she was a librarian.

He groaned inside. Librarian Alice Montgomery wouldn't have the guts to help him.

"Mr. Logan," his hostess inquired. "Would you care for seconds?" She urged more chicken on him, and then third helpings of everything, and finally she began clearing the dishes.

"Marshal, why don't you take your dessert and coffee out on the front porch where it's cooler? You, too, Alice," she added.

"And me?" Mark piped.

His grandmother shook her head. "I need you in the kitchen, Mark."

"Aw, Gran…"

That brought a half smile to Alice's white face. She pushed back her chair and accepted a tray from Sarah with two thick slices of apple pie and two cups of coffee. Rand stood, lifted it out of her hands and ushered her through the screen door.

He prayed the coffee would make the next hour less difficult.

Chapter Three

Alice sank onto the porch swing and lifted a cup of coffee from the tray the marshal set on the railing. "Cream?" he asked.

She shook her head.

"Sugar?" Again she refused, then watched him load his cup with two heaping spoonfuls. *Aha.* The man had a sweet tooth!

He made short work of his apple pie, and when she offered her own piece, he downed that, too. Apparently he hadn't eaten well recently. Was he married as Mark had asked? Probably not, if his appetite was any indication.

He settled onto the swing beside her, nudged it into motion and stretched his long legs out in front of him. Marshals wore jeans like everybody else, she noted. The only thing that told her he was a marshal was the funny-shaped badge pinned to his leather vest and the gun belt around his waist.

"Alice, is there anything else you want to know about your sister's death?"

"Yes," she breathed. "When did she die?"

"She died instantly, as I told you at the sheriff's office."

She set her cup onto the saucer with a sharp click. "No, I meant how long ago was it?"

He gave the swing another shove. "Three weeks ago."

"What took you so long to notify me?"

An expression crossed his face she couldn't identify. "It's not just a death, is it?" she said.

His face changed again.

"Is it?" she pursued.

"No, Alice, it's not. It was a murder. I told you that."

"Who did it? Do you know? Have they caught him?"

He released a breath and gulped down some coffee. "Nobody has been arrested yet. And no, we don't know who did it."

"Why not?"

He hesitated. "Alice, there's something else I need to tell you."

"I thought so," she said. "Your voice gets quiet when you're hiding something."

He turned toward her, surprise written all over him. "Well, I… That is…"

She had to smile. "You know, Marshal Logan, people think of a librarian as someone with her nose always buried in a book. Actually, librarians are quite observant."

"Obviously," he murmured.

"So I ask you again. What took you almost three weeks to notify me? And why not just send me a telegram?"

"I…wanted to tell you in person."

"What else is it you need to tell me, Marshal? And who is 'we'?"

"You sure you want to talk about this so soon after you got the news?"

She bit her lip. "Yes, I am quite sure. Tell me."

He jolted out of the swing and moved to lean against the porch railing. "'We' is the sheriff of Owyhee County, Idaho, and me. And the Pinkerton Agency in Colorado. As for what else I need to tell you, it's this. The sheriff is stumped. He sent for a US Marshal, and that marshal happens to work for Pinkerton."

"Why did you really come to see me, Marshal? It wasn't just to tell me about Dottie, was it?" When he said nothing, she went on.

"Why is Dottie's death of interest to a US Marshal and

the Pinkerton Agency? Exactly why are you here, Marshal Logan?"

Rand stood and began to stack the empty pie plates on the tray. "No, it wasn't just to tell you about your sister. We... That is, I need your help."

"I thought so," she breathed.

"It's like this, Alice. Your sister lived in this little town that's mostly a tent community of Idaho miners, and they're tighter than ticks about sharing any information with outsiders."

"I would be an outsider," she pointed out quietly.

"You would be, yes. But we... I...think you might be able to succeed where the sheriff has failed."

"Why?"

"Because..." He looked everywhere except at her. "Because you're a woman," he said at last.

"I see."

"I tried to talk Pinkerton out of even mentioning it to you. I knew you'd need time to get over the shock, time to grieve. I wired the sheriff in Idaho that I wasn't going to ask you because it wouldn't be fair. That you wouldn't want to do it no matter what."

Alice took a deep breath. "Right now I would do anything to catch my sister's murderer."

Rand stared at her, a proper, delicate-looking girl whose face was still white with shock. My God, a woman could be tougher than he'd ever imagined. Suddenly he didn't want to go any further with this. She wasn't ready. She might even get hurt.

Then she surprised him again. "What is 'it'?" she asked.

Oh, hell, here it comes. She wouldn't even speak to him after he'd asked what he'd come four hundred miles to ask, much less sit in a porch swing with him. He opened his mouth, then shut it again.

"Marshal?" She looked up at him, and all at once he noticed how blue her eyes were, how downright pretty she was.

"Marshal, what is it you need me for? You might as well spit it out before I lose interest," she said with a soft laugh.

He resumed his place on the swing beside her. "Okay, Alice, here it is. Silver City miners are suspicious of strangers and they're tight-lipped about everything, especially a killing. But they might open up to a woman. Someone who could work undercover."

"Work undercover as what?"

"We figure they wouldn't be suspicious of a, well, of a saloon girl."

He waited for her cry of outrage. It didn't come. Instead, she sat motionless beside him, her eyes searching his face.

"A saloon girl," she echoed. "Do I look like a saloon girl to you?"

"Definitely not," he said quickly.

"A saloon girl who would wear a low-necked gown and fishnet stockings?"

"Yeah, I reckon so. I know it's a real far-fetched idea. Pinkerton came up with it as a last-ditch—"

"I'll do it," she said calmly.

He almost choked. "What? Alice, are you serious?"

She bit her lip. "Believe me, I have never been more serious in my life."

"Miss Montgomery… Alice, I have to warn you it could be dangerous. It's a long, hard trip just getting to Silver City, and a mining camp is a really rough place for a…" He swallowed. "For a librarian." Unbelievably, he heard himself trying to talk her out of it.

She said nothing, just looked at him with a tired smile.

"Alice, I…"

She pushed the swing into motion. "When do we leave?"

Rand could scarcely believe his ears. Never in a hundred years did he think a woman like Alice would agree to such a scheme. He guessed he had a lot to learn about librarians. "Tomorrow."

"I have one question for you," she said. "I won't go alone. Will you be with me?"

"Yeah, I'll be with you."

"Do you promise?"

He blinked. "Well, sure, Alice. You can count on that."

She nodded and pushed the swing again. "Then it's settled. I will be ready in the morning."

He managed not to let his mouth fall open. After a long minute he risked his final question. "Now I have something else to ask you."

She sent him an expectant look and waited.

Rand watched her face and crossed his fingers.

"Can you sing?"

Chapter Four

Rand spent a sleepless night at the Smoke River hotel, and after a breakfast of steak and eggs he made his way to the livery stable. He chose a gentle mare for Alice, certain that no librarian would be an experienced rider, and at eight o'clock he walked over to Alice's boardinghouse and got an unexpected shock.

Alice was seated in the porch swing, waiting for him. "Good morning, Marshal," she called.

He climbed the steps and stood before her. Once more he found himself surprised by Alice Montgomery. Not only was she obviously wide-awake, she was dressed in traveling clothes and a small tapestry bag sat at her feet.

"Before we leave, I must visit the dressmaker."

"The dressmaker? Alice, I don't think—"

She sent him a smile that dried up his words. Yesterday Sheriff Rivera said he thought highly of Miss Alice. Rand had figured it was a man's admiration for a pretty girl, but now he was beginning to wonder.

"If I understand your need of me, Marshal, I will need a…how shall I put it…a 'saloon girl' outfit. Something sinfully silky with an extremely revealing neckline. And fishnet stockings."

Rand bit back a laugh. This girl was no ordinary librarian. In fact, he was beginning to realize that Alice Montgomery was not ordinary in any way.

Sarah Rose stepped out onto the porch. "Marshal, have you had breakfast?"

"Yes, thank you, Mrs. Rose."

Alice stood up. "Mark has a dozen more questions for you, Marshal. While he keeps you busy with the answers, I am going to the dressmaker's."

"Come on in, Marshal Logan," Sarah invited. "Mark can entertain you while he eats his breakfast." She disappeared into the house.

At the doorway, Rand turned to watch Alice make her way down the porch steps and start up the shady, tree-lined street. She was wearing something he'd never seen before, a sort of cutoff skirt that was split up the middle. Blue denim, if he wasn't mistaken, with what looked like one of young Mark's red plaid shirts. And polished leather riding boots.

Inside the boardinghouse, he joined the residents in the dining room, and while they ate flapjacks and bacon he consumed two cups of Sarah's excellent coffee. Mark peppered him with more questions about his life as a US Marshal, and that helped to keep his mind off Alice and what was coming. She'd looked calm and determined this morning. He wondered if she was feeling a bit apprehensive on the inside, but if she was, it sure didn't show.

At the end of the meal, Rooney invited him out to the front porch and sat him down in the swing. "Marshal Logan, I want you to know something. Alice is real special to Sarah and me, and I don't think her sashayin' off with you is a good idea. I told her I don't want her settin' off on this harebrained scheme of yours, and she—you know what she said?"

Rand shook his head.

"It's the first time she's ever talked back to me in all the years I've knowed her," Rooney continued. "She said to mind my own business! That it was *her* sister and *her* life. Kinda hurt my feelin's."

"Mr. Cloudman, there's a big part of me that doesn't want to take Alice to a scruffy mining camp in Idaho. But I'm a United States Marshal, and those are my orders."

"Yeah, I get that, Rand. Shore am glad it ain't me walkin' into a mess like you told me about. I'm gettin' too old."

"Sometimes I get to feeling too old, too," Rand admitted. "I get tired of folks misbehaving and wish I could find some pretty little place and forget all about the law and justice and all that other stuff I swore to uphold."

"Our Alice," Rooney said with a catch in his voice, "she's a whole lot more'n just a librarian, Rand. And you better not forget it, you hear?"

Rand nodded.

"Keep her safe if you can," the older man said.

"You can count on that, Mr. Cloudman. If anything happens to Alice, you'll know that I'm already dead."

Rooney snorted. "Well, hell, mister, that's what I'm afraid of!"

Dressmaker Verena Forester gasped, and the bolt of blue gingham in her arms tumbled onto the floor. "You want a *what*? Say that again, Alice?"

"I want a fancy dress like a saloon girl wears. You know, with lots of ruffles and a really low neckline. Red, maybe. With sequins."

The dressmaker stared at her. "I suppose you've got some harebrained reason, Alice, but I don't guess you're going to tell me what it is."

"I'm taking a job. I'll be working undercover for the Pinkerton Agency, and I need a disguise."

Verena's mouth sagged open. "Pinkerton! Whatever for? You have a perfectly respectable job here in Smoke River as our librarian."

But she no longer had her sister. Alice had spent most of last night mulling over what was worth doing in life. She *did* have a respectable job as the librarian. She had a perfectly respectable life in a perfectly respectable town. Maybe that was the problem.

Maybe she could ease the ache in her chest by helping to catch her sister's killer.

"Do you have any satin, Verena? Red satin?"

The dressmaker pointed at a bolt of fabric halfway up a tall display shelf. "Scandalous color. When do you need this creation?"

"This morning."

Verena gave a strangled cry. "Today? Why, I can't cobble up a dress in that length of time. It takes real effort to sew on a lot of ruffles and sequins. That'll take some doing. And besides, it's gonna be Christmas pretty soon, and every woman in Smoke River's wantin' something new."

Alice smiled at her. "Oh. Well, Verena, I can always go over to the mercantile and buy a ready-made dress."

"Huh!" the dressmaker scoffed. "Carl Ness wouldn't have such a shameless garment in his store. Nobody in town wears such things."

"Except for the girls down at Sally's," Alice said calmly.

"Sally's! How do you know about—?" The dressmaker recovered quickly. "The girls at Sally's order custom-made gowns, and they give a body plenty of time to sew them."

"Verena, please. Could you try? I am pressed for time."

The dressmaker suddenly noticed the distress in Alice's eyes and wilted like an unwatered houseplant. "All right, I'll do it. Red satin and ruffles…it will be so outrageous you'll be embarrassed to be seen in it."

"Oh, I do hope so," Alice murmured. "I need to be as un-librarian-like as possible."

Verena rolled her eyes. "Give me until noon." Then she shooed Alice out of the shop.

Alice went from the dressmaker's to Ness's Mercantile, where she bought a bottle of cologne, a boy's wide-brimmed black Stetson, a lethal-looking six-inch hatpin, a gaudy pink satin garter, and a derringer pistol and a box of cartridges. Then she stopped at the sheriff's office and talked Sandy, the deputy, into showing her how to load and fire the pistol.

Keeping busy helped ease the pain in her chest, but she finally ran out of errands. When she returned to Rose Cottage, Rooney and Marshal Logan were sitting on the porch swing and Mark was perched at their feet. Apparently he still hadn't run out of questions because he posed another one as she came up the front walk.

"How come you don't have a fancy uniform like a colonel or somethin'?"

Rand laughed. "Because it's easier to sneak up on a criminal if you don't look conspicuous."

Even Rooney laughed at that.

"What's 'spicuous?"

"Conspicuous is what a man wears when he wants to get noticed, maybe by a girl he's interested in."

Mark shot him a curious look. "Are you interested in a girl?"

"Nope." At least he wasn't before he laid eyes on Alice Montgomery. Now he wasn't so sure. In fact, at the sight of her in that swingy blue skirt and the boy's shirt that revealed she was very obviously *not* a boy, he felt a tug of awareness he hadn't felt in years.

"Before we leave," Alice announced, "I have some parcels to pick up at the mercantile and the dressmaker's."

"Whadja buy, Alice?" Mark inquired. "Any caramel drops?"

Alice smiled at him. "No caramel drops, I'm afraid. I bought a dress. Some smelly cologne. A hat like yours. And a pink garter." She saw no need to mention the derringer.

"Just dumb girl stuff," Mark muttered. "No caramels?"

"No caramels."

Rand rose and offered the seat next to Rooney on the swing.

"A pink garter, huh?" Rooney muttered. "Just what are ya thinkin' of doin' with a pink garter?"

She grinned and slid closer to him. "Rooney, I don't think I should explain in front of Mark."

Rand, however, very much wanted to hear the explanation.

Rooney draped his arm around Alice's shoulders. "Honey-girl, I don't mind tellin' ya that I don't like this idea one bit. Not one bit."

Alice sent him a smile. "I know, Rooney. You've been saying that since six o'clock this morning."

Mark hunched his thin frame closer to her knees and gazed up at her. "Golly, Alice, it sounds real neat, 'specially if Rooney doesn't like it. Kin I come along?"

At noon, Rand picked up Alice's travel bag and walked her over to the livery stable, then to the mercantile and the dressmaker to pick up her parcels. The dressmaker package was bulky, and Rand noticed a sprinkling of tiny sparkly circles escaping from one corner where the twine tie had slipped off-center. Saloon girl sequins, he gathered. Red ones. Another niggle of apprehension crawled up his spine.

They loaded the saddlebags on his bay gelding and her chestnut mare and then on their way out of town they stopped at Rose Cottage.

The porch was empty. Alice dismounted and went inside, and after a long ten minutes she came out red-eyed and stiff-lipped, climbed back on her mare and reined away without a word.

They rode side by side in silence until the town dwindled off into the occasional house and wide meadows of yellow dandelions and lavender desert parsley. The air smelled of pine trees and smoke.

They followed the slow-moving river bordered by cottonwoods and gray-green willows, and when the river split, they followed the branch flowing north and headed for the hazy purple mountains looming in the distance. The sun overhead was hot, even for October.

Alice hadn't said a single word since leaving town, and

Rand was starting to wonder why. He slowed his bay until she caught up.

"Alice, are you all right?"

"Yes. At least I think so. I had to leave the key to the library with Sarah. This is the first time since the library was built six years ago that I won't be there in the morning to open it up. It feels strange."

Rand did a quick calculation. If her sister Dorothy was the "little" sister at twenty, that meant Alice was probably around twenty-two. Had she been in Smoke River all her life?

"You been a librarian a long time?"

"Ever since I turned eighteen. It's all I ever wanted to do, be around books."

Aha. That would make her maybe twenty-four or twenty-five. Before he could ask, she volunteered a piece of information about herself he hadn't expected.

"I am a spinster, Marshal. I have nothing in my life but my library, so I have nothing to lose by going with you to a mining camp in Idaho to find my sister's killer."

"Forgive me for saying so, but that's not smart thinking. I'm a lot older than you, and I figure I've got a helluva lot to lose."

"How much older?"

"I'm thirty-four."

"What will *you* lose if you don't live through this trip?"

Rand blinked. She sure kept surprising him with her questions.

"You mean besides my life?" he said drily. "Well…" He waved an arm at the field of white clover and dogbane they were riding through. "I'd miss seeing meadows like this one. And I'd miss the smell of woodsmoke and mint. And roses. By the way, what kind of scent did you buy at the mercantile?"

She gave a soft laugh. "Why, I don't even know! I didn't smell it. I just picked out a pretty-shaped bottle."

"Not very 'saloon girlie' of you, Miss Montgomery."

"No, I suppose it isn't. I'm going to need some practice in the 'saloon girl' area."

Rand kept his face impassive. Was it possible she was unaware of how attractive she was? Nah. No girl as pretty as Alice would be blind to her effect on the male population. But her remark made him wonder.

Something else puzzled him, too. She hadn't asked one question about the journey to Silver City, how many miles away it was. How many days of travel it would take. And nights.

Maybe she didn't care. But if that was true, he wondered *why* didn't she care?

"Alice, do you know anything about Idaho?"

"Oh, yes. When Dottie first married Jim, her husband, and went away to Silver City, I read all about Idaho. I learned about mining camps and silver assaying. The library has lots of information on such subjects."

He chuckled. "Then you probably know more than I do. I've never set foot in Idaho Territory."

She turned toward him, a surprised look on her face. He couldn't see her eyes under that black Stetson she wore, but her lips rounded into a soft, raspberry-tinted O. "You mean you've never been where we are going?"

"Nope. Does that make you uneasy?"

"Nope," she shot back.

Rand laughed. He liked her quick humor. He liked a lot of things about Alice Montgomery.

But he didn't plan to pay much attention to them. This was a damned dangerous mission, so he'd best keep his mind on the problem at hand.

Chapter Five

The campsite Rand chose for their first night was nestled in a grove of pine trees and protected by a half circle of large gray boulders. A shallow, gurgling stream meandered nearby.

After more than eight hours in the saddle, Alice's derriere was numb and her thigh muscles felt hot and jumpy. Never in her life had she ridden a horse for more than an hour at a time; she never dreamed she could be this tired. She slid off the chestnut mare and had to grab on to the saddle to keep her legs from collapsing.

The marshal surveyed her from the fire pit he was digging. "You've had a long ride," he remarked. "Want some of my liniment?"

When she nodded, he rummaged in his saddlebag and thrust a bottle of brown liquid into her hand. It smelled like the furniture polish Sarah used on the dining table at the boardinghouse. Maybe it *was* furniture polish.

She stumbled down to the stream, dropped her skirt and her under-drawers and sloshed some of the smelly stuff onto her aching backside. When she returned he had built a campfire and was digging a frying pan and some bacon out of his saddlebag.

"Hungry?" he asked without looking up.

"That is a rhetorical question, Marshal. Of course I am hungry."

"And tired, too, I bet."

"And crabby," she admitted.

He didn't answer, just sliced off some bacon and laid it in

the pan. When the bacon was crisp he dumped in a can of chili beans, and that was supper. She wasn't complaining. She was so tired and hungry she would eat anything, even a bear if it lumbered into camp. She shivered at the thought.

He dished up the mess into two tin plates and handed her a spoon, and for the next half hour they ate without talking. Whatever he called this concoction, it tasted wonderful! She gobbled it down, and when her plate was empty she unrolled her blankets and sat staring into the fire while Rand tramped off to the stream to wash the plates.

When he returned a mug of coffee appeared at her elbow.

"You sure don't talk much," he said, settling himself beside her.

"Neither do you," she retorted.

"I guess that's because I usually travel alone. I do talk to my horse sometimes, though."

"And since I'm a librarian, I talk to my books."

He laughed at that, and then answered the question she hadn't asked yet. "Three days. It'll take three days of riding to reach Silver City."

"You mean I cannot bathe for three whole days? By then I will smell to high heaven!"

He bit back a smile. "Nah, you won't. First of all, you've got a bottle of fancy-smelling stuff in your saddlebag. And second…" He paused to toss the dregs of his coffee into the fire. "There are lots of streams and rivers between here and Silver City where you can take a bath. As long as you don't mind cold water," he added with a grin.

"How do you know that, Marshal? About the rivers and streams, I mean?"

"Maps," he said with a chuckle. "Books are full of 'em. I should think you'd know that, being a librarian."

She studied him in the firelight. It was too dark to see his face, but his voice was full of laughter. Thank the Lord! There would be nothing worse than traveling for three days with a man who was dull in the head.

Suddenly she remembered why she was riding into the wilderness with the marshal and she sucked in her breath. Tears stung under her eyelids at the thought of her sister. Deliberately she turned her attention to something else.

Her traveling companion, Marshal Logan, for instance. He was a puzzle of a man in many ways. Well-mannered. Considerate. Knowledgeable. And obviously a dedicated lawman. And, she had discovered, he was a passable cook.

And yet she sensed a streak of something hard and unyielding in him; he was like a bar of iron wrapped in something soft, like velvet. She liked the way he listened to her, as if what she said mattered. But she was constantly aware of that core of inner toughness.

Something *tu-whooed* in a nearby pine tree and she jerked. "What was that?"

"Owl."

She pointed at something rustling in the shrubbery behind them. "And that?"

"Don't know. Probably something that's more scared of us than we are of it."

"That," she said with a shudder, "is cold comfort. Do you think it's something big, like a...mountain lion?"

"Nope. Probably the rabbit that owl is after. Alice, you've been cool and collected for the last ten hours. How come you're so skittery all of a sudden?"

"Maybe because I just realized how alone we are way out here in the middle of nowhere. No lights. No sheriff. No...help."

"Alone is good. A smart traveler is always wary of company on the trail. Besides, I'm a marshal, remember?"

His voice sounded overpatient. Surely she wasn't being a trial. For the last twenty-four hours she had worked hard to appear calm and rational and brave. She couldn't lose control now. She just couldn't.

"Alice? Is something wrong?"

"No. Well, yes. I am—I am a bit frightened." A little laugh escaped her. "Actually, I am a *lot* frightened!"

"That's a relief," he said. "I was beginning to think you were more stone statue than flesh-and-blood girl."

"Oh." His voice was not accusing; it was understanding, which was a relief. "I assure you, Marshal, I am quite human."

Rand turned toward her. "For God's sake, Alice, could you call me Rand instead of 'Marshal'?"

She flinched, and Rand was instantly sorry he'd snapped at her.

"Of course," she said quietly.

He strode off to the stream, and when he returned she was rolled up in her blankets like a sausage, her body curled close to the dying fire. He stood looking down at her for a long time, thinking how the firelight made everything look soft until it faded into blackness. And then he noticed the blanket was shaking.

She was crying. He couldn't hear her, but he knew. He dragged his own bedroll from behind the saddle, shucked his boots and stuffed his Colt under the saddle at his head. Then he crawled next to her, wrapped himself in his bedroll and pulled the shuddering bundle into his arms.

"Alice, I'm sorry. Guess I'm tired, but I didn't mean to snap at you."

The blanket covered her face, but he could hear her still crying. Of all the things that he hated in life, hearing a woman cry was the worst.

"Alice."

"I—I'm not crying because of anything you s-said, Mar—Rand. I'm crying b-because I'm exhausted and saddlesore and s-scared."

Relief surged through him. "Alice, if you weren't scared, you'd be crazy."

She gave a choked laugh. "Well, then, it would appear I am most certainly not crazy."

"I've been scared plenty of times, Alice. Once on an army patrol we ran into a bunch of outlaws holed up in a canyon. It was my first campaign, and I was plenty scared. We managed to capture all but two of them, and I was scared the whole time."

"What happened to the two you didn't capture?"

He hesitated. "I shot them."

"Were you frightened then?"

"The fear was there all the time. I just tried to move through it and keep going."

She nodded and he heard a ragged sigh. "Thank you, Rand."

He lay for a long time with his arms around her blanket-wrapped form. Finally her breathing evened out and he figured she'd fallen asleep. Just as he started to ease his arm out from under her, the blanket fell away and she opened her eyes and tried to smile.

"I have had a really terrible time since you told me about my sister. Most of the time I feel like screaming."

"You want to give it up? Go back to Smoke River?"

There was a long silence. "No," she said at last. "I want to keep on. I want to find whoever killed my sister."

They rode east, toward Idaho Territory, and the landscape turned brown and dry and hot. Tiny stinging insects swarmed around Alice's face, and no matter how much she swatted and flailed at them, they got caught in her hair. The streams grew narrower, and the shallow rivers they rode across flowed green and lazy. She desperately wanted a bath.

To occupy her mind, she studied Rand Logan. He was interesting in a lawman sort of way, with his rifle nestled in a saddle scabbard and a worn leather gun belt strapped low on his hip. His leather boots had spurs, which chinged when he walked, but she never saw him touch his horse with the rowels. Maybe the spurs were just for show.

Except that Marshal Logan didn't seem to care about appearances. This morning he'd shaved hastily and sloppily, and the dark mustache over his upper lip looked a little raggedy. She liked his eyes, green as jade and always watchful. He certainly didn't talk much, but when he did speak she paid attention. She *had* to pay attention, she acknowledged. This was the most frightening thing she had ever done.

As a librarian she'd led a very circumspect life. No bumps or surprises, just nice, quiet books in a nice, quiet building in a nice, quiet town. Books were her life, her reason for living. The printed word made sense of the world around her, of things she couldn't control, like wars and floods and hunger and suffering.

And murder. She knew the only way she could help find Dottie's murderer was to follow this man into God knows what, and that made her more than a little bit uneasy.

Halfway through the afternoon they turned north, toward the mountains. Now, instead of riding straight into the sun, its rays came from her right, and she quickly learned to keep her hat tilted and the shirtsleeve on that side rolled down to avoid sunburn.

But by midafternoon, the hot October sun was burning her skin right through the fabric.

Rand rode with his gray Stetson tipped down so far she wondered how he could see the trail ahead. Occasionally she glanced over at him, but he didn't notice. Or didn't seem to notice. He studied the trail ahead, his right hand always resting on the butt of his revolver. Force of habit, she guessed.

Hour after uneventful hour passed, but he still watched everything, even her. And she couldn't help studying him when he wasn't looking. His hair was overlong, just brushing his earlobes. And the hand holding his reins was lean and long-fingered. A surgeon's hands. Why had he chosen to become a US Marshal rather than a doctor?

She flicked the chestnut's reins and drew ahead of him, then waited for him to catch up.

"In a hurry?" he called.

"I get restless just plodding along with nothing to do but think."

"If you want your horse to last in this heat, you'll go slow."

"Slow is hot," she said.

"I figure there's a stream a couple of miles ahead. We can stop there."

"How could you possibly know that?"

"Trees." He tipped his head. "Look yonder. Cottonwoods grow where it's wet. Willows, too."

Sure enough, a fuzz of green leafy growth appeared on the horizon. She couldn't wait for the stream; just thinking about water made her thirsty. She uncapped the canteen hanging on her cantle and shook it. Empty. Rand unhooked his own canteen and passed it to her.

"Why am I out of water when you're not?" she wondered aloud.

"Maybe because you're greedy?" He phrased it as a question, but she got the message. She shouldn't guzzle water just because she was thirsty; she should ration it out. She took a single swallow of the warm, metal-flavored water and handed the canteen back to him.

She was completely out of her element out here. This wilderness was so far removed from her peaceful, quiet library she might as well be on the moon.

Another hour brought them to a little trickle of a stream, just enough to water the horses and refill the canteens. There was barely enough to splash over her sweaty face and neck.

"Still got a couple hours of daylight left, Alice. Are you okay with going on?"

She laughed. "You mean I could hurry up the sunset if I wanted to stop for the night? Librarians are smart, but they're not *that* smart."

He turned his head to grin at her and she noticed something. One side of his face was darker than the other. He must have been riding north before he arrived in Smoke River and his sunburn had turned his skin tan.

"Rand, where were you coming from when you reached Smoke River?"

"How do you know I didn't come in on the train?"

"I just know. Librarians are—"

"Observant," he finished with a chuckle. "I was coming from Colorado Territory. Denver City."

"Colorado! That's hundreds of miles from Oregon."

"Sure is. Why do you think I was so hungry at supper that first night?"

"Why didn't you take the train from Denver City instead of riding all that way?"

He didn't answer for a long while. "Because I needed the time," he said finally.

"Time for what?"

"Time to work out a plan. And," he added, "I didn't want to load Sinbad on a freight car." He bent to pat his horse's neck.

For the next hour Alice thought about his answer. So he needed to think up a plan. And he cared about his horse. Interesting.

By the time they made camp next to a pretty, shaded river in the foothills, she had run out of questions. She watched him loosen the cinch and rub his bay down with a handful of dry grass, then do the same for her chestnut mare. Finally he dropped both saddles at her feet and strode off to the river. When he returned, his hair was dripping wet.

"I'll put some supper together while you take a bath if you want. There's a little pool behind that scrubby willow, and I didn't leave any soapsuds floating in the water."

Soapsuds! She didn't have any soap that would make suds. She had forgotten to purchase soap at the mercantile, so she had only a sliver of Sarah's yellow laundry soap.

"Think you're gonna be scared tonight?" he asked.

"What an odd question. I expect I will be scared every night until...until this is over. Why do you ask?"

"Just wanted to know how close to lay our bedrolls."

She eyed the two saddles he'd dropped at her feet. "Close," she said. "You are the experienced one with a gun."

As it turned out, Rand regretted sleeping close to her. All day he had been reviewing his plan for catching her sister's killer, deciding who to interview and what premises to inspect. He was also worrying about how to keep Alice safe in an untamed mining camp.

He was continually surprised by the woman riding with him. She wasn't frightened by the things that *should* frighten her, like trapping a killer. Instead she jumped at rustling in the underbrush, at buzzard calls, at things that were no threat, like a chicken hawk swooping off a tree limb or a rabbit scuttling away under a huckleberry bush.

But she had no idea how rough the frontier outside a small peaceful town like Smoke River could be. And she had a lot to learn about open country. He knew he could keep her safe in countryside like this, where there was clearly identifiable danger. But what about in a rough mining town?

He'd noted that Alice could be a bit headstrong, somewhat impulsive in making decisions and stubborn when it came to defending them. He figured Rooney hadn't had a prayer in hell of dissuading her from accompanying him. But Alice knew nothing outside of her genteel, civilized life as a librarian. He was apprehensive about her getting hurt.

They spent an uneventful night rolled up in their blankets beside the campfire, and while Alice said she wasn't frightened, Rand still worried.

The next morning his worst fear played out. After a breakfast of coffee and biscuits he had mixed up and baked on a hot rock, he packed up the saddlebags and they started into the hills. They followed a barely discernible trail that wound up through dry scrub and stands of sugar pine and alder trees, and they had just come around a bend when they ran smack into a surprise.

A seedy-looking character in frayed Levi's and a rumpled shirt was perched on a flat rock with a rifle trained on them.

Rand drew rein.

The man's bloodshot eyes studied his horse for a long minute. "Where ya goin', mister? And missus," he added.

Rand prayed to God Alice would keep her mouth shut. Casually he crossed his hands over the saddle horn and bent toward the man. "Goin' to Boise City, friend. I own the saloon next to the hotel."

Behind him he heard Alice give a little squeak.

"Ya do, huh? How come I never seen you there?"

"Guess that's because I've been traveling for the last month."

"Oh, yeah? Where to?"

"Eastern Idaho. Little town called Broken Toe."

"Broken Toe, huh? Never heard of it."

"I'm not surprised," Rand said easily. "Hardly more'n a wide spot in the trail."

The man eased his bulk off the rock and clumped down close enough to poke his rifle barrel into Sinbad's neck. "Whatcha doin' in Broken Toe?"

"Gettin' married," Rand said quickly.

Alice gave another squeak.

"Yeah?" The bloodshot eyes lifted to Alice. "She yer wife, is she?"

"Yep. Name's Oliver," Rand volunteered. "George Winston Oliver. My wife's called Bess."

"Well, now, Bess. Whaddya got to say fer herself?"

"I say that I am eager to see the new house George has purchased in Boise City," Alice said smoothly.

The man gave her a lingering look. "Say, you're a right pretty gal!"

Rand held his breath.

Alice cleared her throat. "I was voted the belle of Broken Toe when I was a girl," she said.

"Were ya, now?" The man took two unsteady steps forward. "Ya still don't look more'n a girl, honey."

Rand spotted a saddled horse almost hidden among the trees. Unobtrusively he moved his hand toward his holstered Colt.

"George," Alice called. She moved her horse forward and reined to a stop on Rand's right, shielding his gun hand from view. "You said your father is expecting us, and he never likes anyone to be late. And you told me how impatient he is, being the sheriff."

"Huh?" Scruffy sent her a sharp look. "What's in them saddlebags, Miz Oliver?"

"Pots," Alice said instantly. "And my mama's best iron skillet. She gave it to us for a wedding present."

"Got any money?" He took a step closer and Rand thumbed off the safety on his revolver.

Alice's laughter rang out. "Money! You can't be serious. Ever since we left Broken Toe, George has been complaining about how much our wedding cost him. And now…" She reached over and playfully slapped his arm. "We have nothing left to set up housekeeping with except my mama's iron frying pan and some old pots."

"Got any liquor?"

Alice drew herself up so stiff Rand thought she might pop the buttons off her red plaid shirt. "Sir! I am a good Christian, raised in St. Joseph's United Methodist Church in Broken Toe. I will have you know I never, ever touch spirits! And," she added with a sidelong look at Rand, "now that we're married, George doesn't touch spirits, either."

Rand unclenched his jaw and choked back a snort of laughter. Alice was as inventive as she was pretty.

The man groaned and began to back away. "Oh, hell, I'm wastin' my time on you two." He staggered off into the trees for his horse, and clumsily pulled his bulk into the saddle.

"Adios!" he called. Rand watched the man wheel his mount, crash through the brush and disappear. He waited until the hoofbeats faded away, then thumbed the safety back on.

"Is—is he gone?" Alice whispered. He noticed the hand holding her reins was shaking.

"Yeah. Pretty quick thinking, *Miz Oliver*. Very creative."

She gave a nervous laugh. "Really? I was petrified!"

He chuckled. "You been reading books on acting in your library?"

She was silent. He stepped Sinbad forward. "Come on, *Miz Oliver*. We've got hours of riding ahead of us."

Chapter Six

By the time Rand indicated where they would camp for the night and drew rein, Alice had managed to stop shaking.

"You okay?" he asked.

She nodded.

He sent her a curious but admiring look. "Whatever were you thinking to spin such an outlandish tale?"

"You started it," she pointed out. "You invented George… what was his name? Oliver? And the town of Broken Toe. Where did that come from?"

"I sure as heck don't know," he confessed. He couldn't seem to stop looking at her. "But you came up with the part about the wife and the expensive wedding and the frying pan."

"Maybe *you* have been reading books on acting," she quipped. She lifted her bedroll out of the saddlebag and tossed it near the circle of stones Rand was gathering to make a fire pit.

"We have to decide some things about Silver City," he said. He pared dry twig shavings with his pocketknife and arranged leaves and small branches over them. "I don't want to make up our story on the fly."

"Very well. I am a saloon girl and you are…?"

"Your bodyguard. George Winston Oliver. Pick a name for yourself, Alice."

"Martha."

"Nah, too grandmotherly."

"Suzannah, then."

"Too Southern. You don't sound Southern. You sound Northern. Yankee-refined."

"What about—?"

"Lolly," he supplied. "Lolly…Maguire. If you're Irish you'll be forgiven for a bit of blarney if you make a mistake."

"Lolly," she murmured. "Rand, I have never set foot in a saloon. What does a saloon girl do, exactly?"

He tramped twice around the fire pit, stopping to extract a tin of corn and another of beans from his saddlebag. Using his jackknife, he jimmied the beans open and set the can on a flat rock near the fire. Then he sat back on his heels and looked up at her to answer the question.

"A saloon girl dances with the patrons. Gets them to buy her drinks. Flirts. Maybe she sings a bit."

"Sings? Sings what? The only songs I know are hymns."

He laughed. "Then it looks like I'm gonna have to teach you some bawdy songs."

That piqued her interest. "What would be the lyrics to a bawdy song?"

Alice Montgomery, you should be ashamed of your interest in such things.

But she wasn't ashamed. She was curious. In fact, she felt a bit daring, venturing to delve into the mysteries of the seamy side of life like the girls down at Sally's, the ones Verena Forester sewed fancy dresses for.

"Are you going to share a bawdy song with me?" she asked.

Rand busied himself spooning corn and beans into a blackened kettle and set it near the fire. "A bawdy song," he murmured. "Let me think." After a long pause, he turned toward her.

"Here's one. 'A pretty girl from Abilene, tall with hair of red, she waltzed a gent and talked so sweet, he forgot his wife, took her to—'"

He broke off. "Well, you can guess the rest."

Alice's cheeks felt hot. Songs with words like those certainly did *not* appear in library books!

She stared at him. "Where on earth did you learn a song like that?"

"In a saloon," he said drily. He busied himself stirring the corn and bean mixture in the pot, then dumped a handful of coffee beans in the small wooden mill and rattled the handle around and around. Alice thought his cheeks looked a bit pink, but it was getting dark so she couldn't be sure.

She did wonder about him, though.

"Have you spent a lot of time in saloons?" she asked.

"Nope." He set the coffeepot over the fire and spooned some of the corn and bean mixture onto a tin plate and handed it to her.

"You mean you just made up that song?"

"Sure. Kinda like you coming up with that wild tale about your mama's frying pan and the Boise City sheriff."

"And tomorrow I will have to pretend to be Lolly Maguire, a saloon girl."

"Yeah," Rand said. He shot her a glance. "Think you can manage it?"

Oh, my, Alice thought. What would someone called Lolly Maguire say to a man? Especially one in a saloon?

"I will try," she said. "I might turn out to be such a convincing Lolly Maguire you may be quite smitten!"

Instantly she dropped the spoon onto her tin plate with a clank.

Where had that thought come from?

Rand gave her a long look and without a word poured a mug of coffee and set it on the ground near her elbow.

"Smitten, huh? Alice," he said with a chuckle, "it's the miners you're supposed to charm, not me."

Chapter Seven

When they reached Silver City they reined up on the hill overlooking the canvas structures and flimsy-looking buildings of the town spread below them. "It's a mining camp, like I told you," Rand said. "Looks kinda impermanent."

"It looks like a sea of gray canvas." Alice pointed to a large green-gray canvas structure with a white-painted wooden cross over the entrance. "Even the church is a tent!"

Rand turned to her. "Are you ready for this?"

"Yes, I am ready." Her heart thumped under her plaid shirt as she followed Rand's bay, guiding her mare down to Silver City. The narrow road into what passed for a town was oozy with thick mud that squished under their horses' hooves.

They picked their way down the tent-clogged street until they reached the two-story red-painted Excelsior Hotel, which, thank God, was made of wood. But red? Such a bold color for a hotel!

Next door to the hotel was another wooden building, the Golden Nugget saloon. That seemed strange in a town named for its silver mine. There must be other wooden buildings, but all she could see were tents and more tents. Big ones. Little ones. Some more ragged than others.

Oh, poor Dottie. Could her sister really have been happy here in this temporary-looking place?

The desk clerk at the hotel, a bent gray-haired man with thick spectacles and a wrinkled shirt that had once been white, flipped open the register and stood poised with his pen.

"Name?" he said in a weary voice.

"George Oliver."

"This your wife, Mr. Oliver?"

Rand turned to her. "This is Miss Lolly Maguire."

"Separate rooms, then," the clerk muttered.

Rand laid his hand across the register. "One room. Miss Maguire is a well-known entertainer, and I work as her bodyguard. Where she goes, I go."

The clerk's salt-and-pepper eyebrows waggled. "Even to her hotel room?"

"*Our* hotel room," Rand said evenly. "Like I said, Miss Maguire doesn't go anywhere without her bodyguard. Where she goes—"

"I go," the clerk finished. "Oh, well." He sighed. "It's not the first time two crazy people came through town."

"We're not going 'through' town. Miss Maguire is staying. As am I."

The graying eyebrows lowered into a frown. "That'll be two dollars a night, Mister Oliver. In advance."

Rand slapped a fistful of silver dollars onto the counter, and the clerk pounced on them. "Let's see, now…" He counted them with his forefinger and slid them off into his palm. "That'll get you five nights at the Excelsior."

"Six," Rand challenged. "You miscounted."

There was a long minute during which no one spoke. Finally the clerk heaved another sigh. "All right, six nights." He snatched a key from the row of hooks on the wall behind him and laid it in Rand's outstretched palm. "Second floor, third door on your left. Number seven."

The small room overlooked the street below and beyond that was a view of the hills surrounding the town. Two narrow beds were shoved together against one wall, and a tall oak armoire and a white-painted chest of drawers sat against the other. Rand started to stow the saddlebags in the armoire, but Alice stopped him.

"Wait. I want my saloon girl dress."

"Now?"

"Yes, now. I need to hang it up. And I will need a bath before...before I make my debut."

Rand went back downstairs to order her bath, and while he was gone Alice watched the goings-on in the street below. Horses. Wagons. Filthy-looking miners covered with white dust slogged through the mud. Only one or two women. And no children. The town felt raw. Unfinished.

But it was certainly busy. *Seething* would be a more accurate term. Everyone looked like they were in a hurry, even on this scorching October day, and they all walked with their heads down, as if thinking intently about something.

Rand returned ten minutes later, along with a Mexican man lugging a metal bathtub and two giggling girls who dumped in bucket after bucket of steaming water. When they were finished, they left folded towels and a bar of sweet-smelling soap beside the tub.

Alice eyed the tub of steaming water and then noticed that Rand was eyeing it, too. "Isn't there something you need to do, Rand? Visit the barbershop or the sheriff or something?"

"Nope. I'm staying right here. Like I said, I'm not letting you out of my sight."

"Well, I hardly think—"

"Alice, don't think. My orders are to protect you and find your sister's killer, and that's exactly what I'm going to do. The killer could be anybody, so I'm sticking close."

"But, Rand, I want to take a bath!"

"Good idea. I'll turn my back."

She gave him a long look, then studied the steaming tub that beckoned. This was highly improper, sharing a room with Rand, and now... She gulped. Now she would be taking a bath with him standing right there? This was the most scandalous thing she'd ever done in her life!

But instinctively she knew he wouldn't be talked out of staying, so she shrugged, shook out the petticoat and the corset and lacy camisole she'd brought in her saddlebag and hung them up to air with her red dress. Then, with a surreptitious glance at Rand she began to unbutton her denim riding skirt.

"Rand?"

"Yeah?"

"I am waiting for you to turn around."

"Oh. Yeah." He pivoted toward the window and stood with his back to her.

Rand didn't watch her, exactly. But he could sure hear her. Every little splash and sigh set his imagination on fire, and finally he cracked. He half turned away from the window, and out of the corner of his eye he caught a glimpse of the bathtub. And her.

Big mistake. Big damn mistake.

By the time she finished smoothing that cake of soap all over her skin he was rock-hard. Miss Lolly-Alice was changing his mind about everything—librarians, Pinkerton assignments, even celibacy. When she reached for a towel to dry herself off, he knew he had to escape.

"Alice," he said, his voice hoarse. "I'm going to talk to the sheriff after all. Don't let anyone in, even someone who wants to take away the bathtub."

"The bathwater is still warm, Rand. Wouldn't you like to use it? It will be cold when you get back."

"A cold bath will suit me just fine." If he was honest with himself, a cold bath was exactly what he needed.

He sidled past the tub, locked the door behind him and headed out onto the street to find Sheriff Lipscomb.

Silver City had exactly seven wooden structures. In addition to the Excelsior Hotel and the Golden Nugget saloon, there was the Silver City National Bank, the Coleman's Assay Office, the run-down livery stable, the tiny sheriff's office, which looked like a made-over chicken coop, and a large, well-maintained stamp mill, where mined rocks were smashed into bits to extract the silver. Everything else, two mercantiles, a dressmaker, a barber shop, a bathhouse and four eating establishments, one of which served nothing but pie, conducted business in tents. Even the physician-coroner and the funeral parlor did business in tents. One stiff wind would flatten the entire town.

Rand found the sheriff's office, lifted the tent flap and stepped over the threshold. The fleshy lawman sat with his boots propped up on a desk littered with Wanted posters, sipping from a glass of what looked suspiciously like whiskey. That, Rand thought with annoyance, might explain why the murder investigation had stalled.

"Sheriff Lipscomb?"

"Yep, that's me. Who's askin'?"

"Rand Logan. I wired you ten days ago."

"Oh, yeah? Sorry, don't recall that."

"Randell Logan," Rand clarified. "United States Marshal."

The sheriff shot to his feet, scattering posters all over the floor of the tent. "Oh, yessir, Marshal Logan, now I remember. You're investigatin' Miss Dorothy's murder."

"I am, yes. Do you have any new information to report?"

"Uh…cain't say that I have, no. Talkin' to those miners is like conversin' with a clammed-up clamshell."

"Has the coroner made a report?"

"Nope."

"Have any witnesses come forward?"

"Nope."

"You hear any rumors or scuttlebutt around town about the killing?"

"Nope."

Rand gritted his teeth. Looked like miners weren't the only closed-up clams in this town. "Sheriff Lipscomb, would you care to accompany me to visit the coroner?"

"You mean now?"

Rand nodded. "Now."

The sheriff set his whiskey on an uncluttered corner of his desk. "Well, shore, Marshal. Doc Arnold's a friend of mine. His office is just around the corner on Jasmine Street."

Jasmine Street smelled like rotting garbage, not like anything remotely floral, but Dr. Arnold's office smelled better, like antiseptic.

Sheriff Lipscomb barged into the coroner's tent. "Doc, this here is Marshal Randell Logan."

Rand shook the man's hastily extended hand. "Dr. Harvey Arnold," the physician muttered. The sheriff plopped onto a canvas folding chair and ran two fingers through his thinning hair.

"Jeremiah," the physician intoned, "you want a drink?"

"What? Uh…no, thanks, Harve. I'm on duty."

For a split second a look of confusion crossed Dr. Arnold's lined face, and Rand nodded in comprehension. During the day Sheriff Lipscomb drank. A lot. Rand clenched his teeth so hard his jaw hurt. That might explain why Dorothy Coleman's killer hadn't been apprehended; the sheriff was probably drunk by noon. Sheriffs were elected. How did this man ever get voted into office?

He cleared his throat. "Gentlemen, I am investigating the death of Dorothy Coleman."

Dr. Arnold jerked. "Oh, yes, I remember. Murder, as I recall. Gunshot."

"You recover any bullets from her body?"

"I dug one out of her back," the physician said in an almost inaudible voice. "The other one was embedded too deep in her brain to retrieve without…you know, damaging her looks."

"Are you saying she was shot twice? Once in the back and once in the temple?"

Doc Arnold nodded and turned to a tall cabinet in the corner. He scrabbled through three file drawers and finally dropped a bit of metal into Rand's hand. A thirty-two-caliber bullet, Rand noted.

"Any other injuries on her body?"

The physician exhaled heavily. "Other than a slight abrasion on one elbow, Miss Dorothy looked as pretty as she always did." His voice died away, and he dropped his eyes to study the stack of medical reports on his desk.

The doctor was behind in his paperwork, Rand noted. He also noted how inappropriate the physician's observation was.

"Was a funeral held?"

"Oh, sure, Marshal Logan," Dr. Arnold assured him. "Half the population of Silver City turned out, all of 'em crying and carrying on like it was the end of the world. Miss Dorothy's buried up on the hill, behind the stamp mill."

"Is that the town cemetery?"

"Not exactly," Sheriff Lipscomb said. "But Miss Dorothy was awful partial to the Lady Luck mine, and that's as close as we could get to dig her grave."

Rand nodded. "If either of you think of anything else that might help the investigation, you'll find me at the hotel. I'm registered as George Oliver, for reasons that should be obvious."

The sheriff and Dr. Arnold exchanged a puzzled look. "Pinkerton sent you, isn't that right?" the sheriff asked.

"Yes, that's right. But I'm working this case undercover."

Both men looked at each other and nodded, and Rand took his leave. "Gentlemen, stay in touch."

He headed back to the hotel with a sinking feeling in his gut. The sheriff liked whiskey. The coroner was almost obscene in his admiration for Alice's sister, Dorothy Coleman. And if either one of them knew anything of significance, they weren't saying. This investigation was going to be uphill all the way.

Chapter Eight

"Lolly? Open up, it's me, uh… George."

Alice removed the chair she'd pushed under the doorknob and slid back the dead bolt as he unlocked the door. "Rand!" She swung the door open. "Did you talk to the sheriff?"

"I…" The words died on his lips. Standing before him was a stunningly attractive woman in a shiny red satin gown with a neckline so low it would make a shady lady blush.

"Say something, Rand. Do I look the part? Like a saloon girl?"

"You do," he said tersely. "And I want you to take it off."

"What? What do you mean, take it off?"

"I—I've changed my mind, Alice. I don't want you to go anywhere dressed like that."

"But it was your idea," she protested. "This was your plan, you said so yourself."

Rand nodded. "Yeah, I did. Now I wish I hadn't."

Alice propped her hands on her hips. "But you can't have changed your mind! You said I was just what you wanted, an undercover saloon girl. The dressmaker made this gown especially for me."

Rand settled himself heavily onto the bed closest to the door. She was right. But he was so shocked at seeing her all dolled up like that, all red sparkles and creamy bosom, that for a minute his mind wasn't working right. Lolly-Alice had sneaked up on him.

"Rand?"

"Give me a minute, Alice." He tried to calm his racing pulse by reminding himself of the assignment he'd taken on. Pinkerton wanted… Oh, hell, Pinkerton wanted him to use Alice as bait. He'd thought it was a good idea before he saw her in that sparkly red getup. Now he wasn't so sure.

She settled on the bed beside him. "Whatever is the matter? Is my dress not daring enough? Don't you like it?"

He stifled a groan. Her skirt rustled and he smelled the unmistakable scent of violets. "Yeah, I like it fine, Alice. You look very…fetching."

You look so damn beautiful it makes my mouth water.

"Rand?" she said, a tentative note in her voice. "You are looking at me most oddly. Is something wrong?"

"No," he lied. *Everything is wrong!* "I'm just surprised at your…disguise."

She stood up and twirled in place, making her skirt bell out, then sent him a look of pure girlish pride. He almost choked.

"I find dressing up as Lolly Maguire has made me quite ravenous," she announced. "Are you hungry?"

Hungry! He bit back a groan and considered stripping and plunging into the tub of cold bathwater still sitting in the middle of the room. He reached to unbutton his leather vest, then caught himself. He wouldn't mind taking his clothes off in front of her, but he *would* mind revealing his engorged groin.

He swallowed hard. "Yeah, I'm hungry, Alice. I think we should go down to the dining room and eat some supper before you go into action at the Golden Nugget."

"Oh, good." She peeked in the mirror over the dresser and pinched her cheeks into a shade of raspberry that made his mouth water.

"I want a great big thick steak," she said with obvious relish. "With mashed potatoes and lots of thick gravy. What do you want, Rand?"

She sent him a definitely un-librarian-like smile, and all his thoughts about librarians and undercover operations and incompetent sheriffs winged their way out of his head. He closed his eyes and clenched both hands into fists.

"Ice cream," he answered. "That's what I want. Something cooling." Something to erase the image of Alice in that red satin dress.

Walking into the hotel restaurant caused a minor sensation. The entire room full of diners, almost all of them male, stopped talking and stared at Alice. Embarrassed, she tugged the red wool shawl she wore tighter around her shoulders to cover the revealing neckline and chose a chair facing the wall with her back to the patrons.

When conversation around them resumed, they placed their supper orders with the waiter, and Rand told her what he had discovered from Sheriff Lipscomb and Dr. Arnold, the coroner. Alice listened without interrupting, her mouth pressed into a thin line and her eyes filling with tears.

"You mean Dottie's not even buried in a proper cemetery? That's simply awful!"

"There's more," Rand said heavily. He waited until the waiter had set their plates down in front of them and retreated.

Alice ignored her supper and leaned toward him. "What 'more'? Tell me."

He reached for his steak knife. "Your sister was apparently very well liked in Silver City. Dr. Arnold said most of the people in town came to her funeral."

He sliced off a bite of meat. "And," he continued, "she was shot with a thirty-two-caliber bullet."

"But you already knew she was shot, Rand." She loaded her fork up with mashed potatoes, lifted it to her mouth and then lowered it without tasting it. Her lips, Rand noted, looked redder than usual. Rouged, maybe. Something inside him tightened. A large part of him didn't want Alice to turn into Lolly Maguire.

"You already knew my sister had been shot," she repeated.

"Yeah, but I didn't know she'd been shot twice."

Alice's already shiny eyes widened into two pools of dark blue ink. "What? I don't understand."

He leaned across the table and lowered his voice. "The coroner told me your sister was shot twice. He recovered one bullet from her back, but the other one—" He stopped at her stricken look.

She laid her fork down beside her uneaten steak, her face white as milk. "What does that mean, that she was shot twice? Two different killers? Or did the same person fire twice?"

"I don't know what it means. But you can bet I'm going to find out."

She drew in three deep breaths before she picked up her fork again. "While I am…um…entertaining the gentlemen at the Golden Nugget tonight, what will you be doing?" Her voice was shaky.

"Watching you."

"Oh." Her cheeks turned pink.

"There's a killer somewhere here in Silver City, Alice. I'm not letting you out of my sight."

"How do you know he's still here? Or would it be a *she*?"

He thought about how to phrase his answer. "Because the sheriff in Owyhee County said it wasn't a robbery. Your sister's murder was very deliberate, not something done in haste. Whoever shot your sister meant to kill her and he, or she, took a good deal of care in doing it."

Alice studied her plate of uneaten food. "Very well," she said slowly. "I think it is time to go to work."

Chapter Nine

The air in the Golden Nugget was blue with smoke and sour with the smell of liquor and old cigars. The minute Rand and Alice walked in, the place went silent except for the piano player, who went on pounding out "Clementine."

Rand escorted Alice up to the bar, feeling the gaze of every male in the place following them. Or rather following Alice. Any red-blooded male would look his fill and he wouldn't blame them one bit.

The bartender, a burly red-haired man with sharp blue eyes, swiped his greasy rag over the polished mahogany counter and then planted both elbows on it.

"You'll be wantin' something, I'm bettin'." It wasn't a question. Rand opened his mouth to order a beer when Alice spoke up.

"I'm wantin' a job, sir." She let her shawl drop just enough to show some cleavage. "I'm known as Lolly Maguire back in Chicago."

The bartender's eyes dropped to her chest. "Maguire, huh?"

"Sure and it is," Alice said, her voice low and sultry.

Rand blinked.

"I want you to know that I can be quite friendly in the right company," she said softly.

He blinked again.

"Oho," the bartender said. "An' what's the right company, if it's not too much to ask?"

"I am partial to the Irish," she purred. "Irish men in particular."

"Well, now, girlie—"

"Lolly," Alice reminded. "Maguire. I haven't been called 'girlie' since I was five years old back in County Clare, Mr....?"

"Donnell. Lefty Donnell. And what'll ye be havin' this fine night, Lolly Maguire?"

"Beer," Rand said shortly.

Alice rested two fingers on the bartender's beefy hand. "And I would like a chat with your piano player, if you please."

Lefty Donnell's red-blond eyebrows rose. "Hey, Samson!" he yelled. "Lady here wants to talk to ya."

Alice sent Rand a quick look, stepped away from the bar and glided toward the piano against the far wall. Ignoring the tall glass of beer the bartender slid toward him, Rand couldn't help but watch.

She spoke to the piano player, Samson, no more than a minute before he swiveled his stool around to the keyboard and placed his fingers on the yellowed keys. He looked to be Chinese, Rand thought. Short and compact, with jet-black hair and very white hands. He rippled out a cascade of notes, and Alice turned to face the patrons.

The piano sounded a chord and she began to recite. "'"T'was Robin of Locksley and Little John, in Sherwood Forest hiding…"'"

She'd added an Irish lilt to the words; it sounded like poetry spoken out loud.

Another rippling chord, followed by a pause.

"'"When King John came riding through the thick green woods…"'"

More chords. Patrons began shushing their companions as Alice's voice rose. Rand gulped down a swallow of his beer.

"'"…and spied a gleam of silver there…"'"

By now the entire saloon full of miners sat as if spellbound. Even Rand listened, scarcely breathing. Where had *this* come from? he wondered. Was it something she had memorized? Or was she making it up as she went along?

Her voice rose and fell like dusky smoke, with a slight Irish lilt. "'All soft among the greenwood trees…'"

Mouths hung open and drinks were forgotten as the men listened with rapt attention. And, Rand knew, every one of them looked at Alice, swaying provocatively at the piano, with hungry eyes.

As the poem wound on and on, she began to move about the room, stopping at each table to smile at her goggle-eyed listeners. She ended up back at the piano, and when she brought her recitation to a close, she briefly touched Samson's shoulder. Instantly he began pounding out a waltz.

Alice sashayed up to a paunchy miner and held out her arms in invitation. When he lurched to his feet, Rand gulped two more quick swallows of beer and dropped his hand to the Colt at his hip.

Alice and the miner whirled around and around the smoke-filled saloon while Rand gritted his teeth. And then he noticed that the miner was talking a mile a minute, and Alice was nodding her head and listening.

Chester, he said his name was. He smelled rank, but Alice pasted on a smile and asked another question in as sultry a voice as she could manage.

"Oh, sure, Miss Lolly. I know ever'body in town almost. Been a miner at the Lady Luck for thirty years. Not much ever gets by ol' Chester."

"Thirty years! Why, how very interesting. Tell me more."

Gradually she brought the conversation around to Coleman's Assay Office, and then to her sister.

"Yep, I knowed Miss Dorothy. She was a real fine lady, she was. Always had a kind word when we came in with our diggins'. I was real sorry when she died."

"Oh? How did she die?"

"Don't rightly know, Miss Lolly. Sheriff hushed it right up, and three days later we was buryin' her out behind the stamp mill. She always liked the Lady Luck mine. Said it was makin' her and ever'body else here in Silver City rich."

For the rest of the night Alice danced and questioned and filed away information while Rand nursed his beer and Lefty the bartender wiped down the counter and poured out shots of bourbon and rye. Finally he clanged a cowbell he pulled from behind the bar.

"Closing time, gents. Drink up, pay up, and go home and sleep it off."

Alice appeared at Rand's elbow, reached for his beer glass, downed a big swallow and made a face. "Oh, my, that tastes perfectly awful!"

"You prefer whiskey?" he inquired with a grin.

"I prefer plain water or lemonade, but my throat is parched from talking. And, oh, my goodness, Ra— Um… George," she whispered. "I learned some very interesting things tonight."

He rescued his beer glass and shook his head at her. "Later," he murmured. He took her arm and steered her out into the chilly night air, then guided her along the board sidewalk to the Excelsior Hotel and up the staircase to Room Seven. Only when the door was locked and carefully bolted behind them did he turn to her.

"What did you learn tonight, Alice?"

She draped her red shawl on the armoire door handle and walked to the window. "I learned that Jim, Dorothy's husband, died from a gunshot wound, too. That was two years ago. And after Dottie was widowed, all the men in town swarmed around her like honeybees."

She focused her gaze on the street below, where two unkempt-looking men lurched down the street after a well-dressed gentleman riding a horse.

"You know," she said in a puzzled tone, "since we arrived in this town I have seen only four women, and two of those were hotel maids. I find that very strange."

Rand frowned. "Why is that strange?"

"Well, it does explain why the men at the Golden Nugget are so eager to talk to me. They must be starved for female companionship."

Rand suppressed a groan. "The men at the Golden Nugget talk to you because you're damned good-looking," he blurted out. "And every single one of them would like to do more than just talk!"

She turned from the window with an odd expression in her eyes. "Oh, I hardly think—"

"Alice."

"Yes, Rand?"

"You are a very beautiful woman. And it's not because of that silky red dress with all the sparkles and that low neckline that shows your—uh…that low neckline. You are probably the most enticing female they've ever seen."

"Oh, I never thought of that."

He rolled his eyes. "How can you be unaware of how attractive you are?"

She said nothing for so long he wondered if she was insulted by what he'd said.

"Alice?"

She turned back to the window. "When Dottie and I were growing up, she was always the pretty one. I was the smart one, more interested in books than dresses or ribbons or how to curl my hair."

"What did your mother tell you? Or your father?"

She bit her lip and studied the carpet. "Mama and Papa were both killed when we were little. Dottie was three, I was seven. Papa's sister brought us to Smoke River to live, and then she disappeared."

"You mean your aunt abandoned you?"

"Yes, I suppose so. One day she just wasn't there anymore. Dottie and I used to make up stories about what happened to Aunt Frances, about how she was really a famous opera singer and had to return to Paris for a concert, or that she was really a Russian princess in disguise and had traveled to Smoke River incognito. Dottie believed everything. I didn't really believe the stories we made up, but I couldn't stand to hear my sister cry at night, so I went on making them up."

Rand coughed to clear his throat. "How did you end up at the boardinghouse with Sarah and Rooney?"

Alice gave a little half laugh. "Sarah and Rooney found us, really. When I started to go to school, the teacher found out that Dottie and I were living in old Mr. Cooper's bunkhouse, out on his ranch. Nobody had lived there for years, so after Aunt Frances left we just sort of moved in. When Sarah heard about it she drove out in a wagon and got us and brought us back to Rose Cottage. They adopted us, really. Later, when Dottie grew up and married Jim Coleman, Rooney was best man."

Rand made a mental note of that, then asked another question, this time about Dorothy's husband, Jim Coleman.

"Dottie was married when she turned sixteen. Jim had an assay business in Idaho, so they moved away to Silver City."

"And you stayed in Smoke River with Sarah and Rooney."

"Yes. By then, though, I had already been working at the library for a couple of years. When they built the library in town, the man who gave all the money, Mr. Normanson, asked me to choose all the books. And then he hired me to be the librarian. Reading all those wonderful books is probably where I get my taste for wild stories and tall tales."

"Like Robin Hood and Little John," he said quietly.

She spun away from the window. "Did you like that story, Rand? It's one of my favorites."

He couldn't stop looking at her. She'd worn her hair down tonight, and suddenly he wanted to gather up a handful of the dark, glossy waves tumbling about her shoulders and bury his nose in it. What Alice had just told him about her childhood and the library didn't explain half of what this woman was.

He smoothed one finger across his mustache and tried to think. He couldn't afford to let himself get distracted in the middle of a murder investigation. He hadn't been interested

in a woman since his Texas Ranger days, and when she'd
been killed he'd sworn he'd never allow another female he
cared about into his life.

But it was growing harder and harder to keep his mind
off Alice Montgomery. Especially when she was playing
Lolly Maguire.

"Rand? Please say something."

"Yeah, I liked your Robin Hood story. You. Everything."

She must have heard something in his voice because she
walked over and sat down on the bed beside him. Instantly
he stood up and moved away. He didn't trust himself anywhere near her.

Lordy, he needed a drink!

Huh! He was no better than weak-willed Sheriff Lipscomb, drinking on duty. God in heaven, it was going to
be a long night.

"Rand, what is the matter? Did I say something wrong?"
Her eyes looked hurt and a little frightened.

He crumbled. "Alice, dammit, I—"

She rose slowly and moved toward him, her face pale.
"What?" she breathed.

He reached out to touch her shoulder. "Hell and damn,
I'm half in love with Lolly Maguire and you're not even
real! I'm trying to investigate this killing, and I don't need
any distraction!"

To his surprise, she laughed. "Oh, thank goodness. I
thought there was something *really* wrong!"

"Alice, what in the hell do you think *this* is?"

She looked up at him with the most puzzling look he'd
ever seen on a woman's face. "Oh, Rand, it's very simple,
really."

"Simple? It doesn't seem simple to me. Why don't you
explain?"

"It's simple because…" She stretched up on tiptoe and
brushed her lips against his cheek. "Lolly Maguire is just a
pretend person, and you're just a pretend George Winston

Oliver. It's only these pretend people who are attracted to each other, not you and me."

He jerked as if she'd shot him. "*What? Are you crazy?*"

She laughed again, more softly. "It's just Lolly and George," she repeated.

"No!" he said brusquely. "Lolly or not, or Alice, or whoever you are, I can't fall—and you can't. We have work to do."

"Yes, I know," she said with a little catch in her voice. "We have to find out who murdered my sister."

"Yeah. I just wanted to remind you that's why we're here."

"Together," she said.

"In this hotel room."

"Together," she said again.

"Alice." He curved his fingers around her shoulders and purposefully set her aside. "If you stay here one more minute, I'm going to kiss you, and I won't want to stop. Do you understand?"

"Oh," she breathed.

"Alice?"

"I never, ever thought this would happen to me," she whispered. "And I…I have a confession to make."

His heart dropped into his stomach. "Yeah?"

"I have never kissed a man. I mean *really* kissed a man. Not unless you count the boys out behind the barn at dances."

Rand couldn't decide whether to laugh or cheer. Alice was the most unexpected, most surprising, most puzzling, most maddeningly attractive female he'd ever encountered. He prayed he could get through the next few days until he'd solved the murder without compromising her.

He glanced over her head at the two beds in the room, shoved together to make a wide, almost double sleeping arrangement against one wall. He could separate them, pull them far apart from each other. But he'd been sleeping at just an arm's length from Alice for the past three nights. Why stop now?

Because, you idiot, because now you're falling in love with her and you're an honorable man. Or you used to be.

The answer to this dilemma was simple, he decided. Just *stop* falling in love with her.

Her voice startled him. "What will we do tomorrow, Rand?"

The question jolted him out of his mental rambling. "Tomorrow? Well, we—*I* will visit your sister's assay office, talk to the people who work there and look through the business records. Then I'll look up Dorothy's attorney, find out whether she had a will."

"Oh, good. I was getting a bit bored talking to the miners at the Golden Nugget."

"You're not coming with me."

"Oh, but I am, Rand." She pressed her lips together. "Dottie was my sister, and I am your undercover assistant. You need me."

"You'll have to be Lolly Maguire," he warned.

She laughed. "I am growing fond of Lolly Maguire. She's like my secret self, someone I could never be in real life, just in a pretend world."

"It could be dangerous," he warned. "A killer is a killer. He'll be ruthless in covering up his crime."

"Well, of course, Rand. I knew that all along."

He just looked at her. Alice was not just surprising, she was shocking. She was brave. Foolishly brave. And, right in character, her next question surprised him.

"Do you think the dining room is still open? I find I am most dreadfully hungry."

Chapter Ten

That night Rand couldn't sleep. Neither could Alice, as far as he could tell. He couldn't hear her breathing, and he suspected she was lying awake four feet away from him, wondering whether *he* was asleep. Being in a hotel room with her wasn't like sleeping rolled up in blankets beside a campfire; this was far more dangerous.

The problem was he had surreptitiously watched her peel off that red dress and a silky-sounding petticoat, and then he'd kept right on watching right down to her lacy camisole and frilly drawers. By the time she crawled under the blue quilt covering her bed, his groin was swollen and he was plenty hard.

This is just plain damn crazy.

Now he lay awake, aching and feeling lonelier than he'd ever been in his life. He realized suddenly that nothing was going to help until two things happened. First, Dorothy's murderer was caught. And second, he could hold Alice in his arms and kiss her for as long as he wanted.

But God knew that might never happen. Not the catching the murderer part, but the Alice part. He was sure of his ability to apprehend a killer; he was less sure about Alice. Lolly Maguire might want him to kiss her, but what about Alice Montgomery? What would Alice want?

He flopped over and closed his eyes again.

Alice listened to Rand toss and turn for another hour until all at once she couldn't stand it one more minute. "Rand!"

He sat straight up in bed. "Yeah? What's wrong?"

"Nothing. Everything."

"Well, which is it, 'nothing' or 'everything'? Or maybe it's just 'something,' huh?"

She twisted to face him. "Rand, you are absolutely no help in a crisis."

"What crisis? What are you talking about? We've barely started to solve your sister's murder… *What* crisis are you referring to?"

"I'm…worried. And I can't sleep."

"Maybe you're hungry."

She had no answer to that. At midnight he had conducted her downstairs to the dining room, where she had devoured fried chicken and mashed potatoes and he had downed a platter of dry scrambled eggs and bacon.

"Actually," she said hesitantly, "feeling hungry isn't the problem."

"But?" His voice sounded both sleepy and exasperated.

She couldn't answer. She lay still for a long time, wondering what was wrong. She was feeling hungry for something, but it wasn't food.

"I don't know what's wrong, Rand. Something is nagging at the back of my mind, but I don't know what it is."

"And this is your crisis, is it?" he said in a tired voice. "Something 'nagging'?"

"Well, yes. I'm feeling restless and upset and confused, and I'm starting to realize how alone I am now that Dottie is gone. I feel lost, Rand."

He groaned, and the next thing he knew she started to cry and he was sitting on the bed beside her. He pulled her upright and held her tight against him.

"Alice," he breathed.

"Don't talk, Rand. Just hold me and listen. All of a sudden I'm frightened. Not about play-acting as Lolly Maguire, I know I can ferret out information from the miners at the Golden Nugget that you can use to catch Dottie's murderer. It's something else, something I've never felt before."

"Want to try to put it into words?"

"No. It's too unsettling."

"Try, Alice. You might feel better if you talk about it. Sometimes that cuts things down to size."

She hesitated, then drew in an uneven breath. "Dottie's death has brought my own life into clear focus, made me wonder about things I never thought about before."

She stopped and mopped the tears off her cheeks. Rand gave her a little shake. "What things? Seems to me you've done a good deal of thinking up until now. What's puzzling you?"

"Well… Oh, Rand, it's hard to admit this but deep down underneath I am frightened, *really* frightened, for the first time in my life. And I am surprised at how much I enjoy pretending to be Lolly Maguire."

"Yeah," he said drily. "I'm surprised, too." He could feel her body trembling and it brought out all his protective instincts. "And?" he prompted.

"And it makes me wonder who I am. I mean who I *really* am inside. Am I a librarian who is play-acting at being a seductive siren? Or am I a siren play-acting as a librarian?"

He tried not to laugh at that, but she went on without pausing.

"And then I start wondering what is my life worth, really? What is worth doing in life?"

"Alice, I don't want you to be frightened. And I sure as hell don't want you to get hurt. Maybe we should give up on this plan?"

She twisted to face him. "No. I want to find the killer. If he shot Dottie, he could kill someone else."

He stared at her for a long moment, then without thinking he bent his head and kissed her. She was warm and tentative and unknowingly inviting, and he was lost the instant his lips touched hers. After a moment he realized her mouth was opening under his, soft and inviting, and…

He broke away, his breathing ragged. For a long moment

she didn't utter a word, and then she shocked the stuffing out of him.

"Thank you," she whispered. "I will never forget that."

He blinked. "I shouldn't have done that."

"Yes," she said, her voice trembling, "maybe you should have."

"No. We've got a lot of things ahead of us before…" He pressed her head into the curve of his shoulder and whispered against her hair, "Before we can think about other things besides Pinkerton and being a US Marshal."

"Rand, I think—"

He clamped his jaws together. "Don't think, Alice. Go to sleep."

In the morning Rand woke before it was fully light and lay staring at the lump under the quilt next to him. His mind felt bruised. What had happened last night to make him crazy enough to kiss her? Guess he'd better knock off the beer at the Golden Nugget!

Jumping jennies, he wanted to knock off *everything*, the murder investigation, his undercover plan…

And Alice. Most of all, Alice.

But he knew he couldn't. He was a sworn US Marshal and his duty was clear. The way forward had nothing to do with how scrambled up his insides felt. It had to do with Lolly Maguire and her clever ways of prying information out of half-drunk miners at the Golden Nugget.

"Alice. Wake up."

"I'm awake," she said, her voice sleepy.

"We have work to do."

"Yes…work," she muttered. She rolled over and curled into a ball under the covers.

"Alice, the sooner we finish what we came to do, the sooner you can get back to Smoke River."

"Mmm-hmm."

"Alice."

She sat up. "Oh, all right," she said. "I was having the loveliest dream, and you spoiled it."

He didn't want to know about her dream. If it was anything like *his* dream, she would still have the quilt pulled over her head and wouldn't speak to him for a week.

"After breakfast we're going to visit your sister's assay office, see what we can uncover."

"Who will I be today, Rand? Lolly or Alice?"

"Lolly."

"Well, Lolly is hungry." She tossed back the quilt and swung her bare legs to the carpeted floor. She'd slept in her drawers and that lace-frosted camisole, and he tried not to look as she padded across to the basin and water pitcher on the bureau to splash water on her face. Then she dug a hairbrush out of her travel bag and began pulling it through her dark hair.

Rand closed his eyes.

"I'm going to have flapjacks for breakfast," she announced. Her voice sounded funny, and he snapped his lids open. Her head was hanging upside down while she brushed away at her hair. He seized the moment and pulled on his jeans and a shirt, buckled the revolver at his hip and buttoned his sheepskin vest across his chest.

When she finished arranging her hair, she donned her petticoat and the sparkly red dress while he tried to focus on the window overlooking the street.

"It is amazing to me," she remarked as they descended the stairs and entered the dining room, "that I could be so hungry after all that late-night food and liquor I drank last night."

"What liquor? The drinks those miners are guzzling are full-strength, but the ones they buy for you are pretty well watered down."

"How do you know that?"

"Because I bribed Lefty Donnell to water them down. He just dribbles a teaspoon of whiskey into your glass.

That's how the Golden Nugget makes money, watering down drinks."

"Why, that's cheating!"

Rand chuckled all the way through his scrambled eggs and two cups of coffee while she ate a big stack of flapjacks and sipped a cup of tea.

After breakfast they stepped out onto the boardwalk and headed up the street.

Chapter Eleven

Already the sun at this mountain elevation was merciless, pouring down like hot honey, wilting Alice's upswept hairdo and dampening the camisole under her red satin dress. She wrinkled her nose. The air smelled like smoke and something oily.

People stared at her. Even though she had knotted the red knitted shawl over her chest and wore the respectable sun hat she had unfolded from her travel bag, it was obvious to everyone that she was a woman with a questionable reputation. A "fancy lady." While there were precious few women on the street to disapprove, there were dozens of men, mostly miners and shopkeepers, who cast admiring glances her way.

The Alice part of her cringed at all that male attention. The Lolly part of her smiled and shamelessly batted her eyes. Rand, she noticed, kept her arm securely drawn through his, and whenever a man ogled her he tightened his hand.

Coleman's Assay Office was housed in a small, neat building painted bright yellow with window boxes of red geraniums attached to the front. Her heart squeezed.

"Just look at that," she murmured. "Dottie loved red geraniums, they were her favorite flower. Jim planted red geraniums for her until the day he died."

Rand conducted her up the walk and onto the wide front porch. When they entered the office a bell over the door tinkled, but there was no one behind the wooden counter. A handsome iron scale sat on one side.

After a moment a smartly dressed woman in her forties stepped forward. "Yes?" Her gray-blonde hair was pulled into a prim bun at her neck, and her crisp brown shirtwaist and brown plaid skirt looked schoolteacher-ish.

"Are you the owner?" Rand asked.

"Who is inquiring?" the woman asked with a frown.

"The name is Logan. I'm a US Marshal, Miss…?"

"Whittaker," she said quickly. "Emmeline Whittaker."

"I understand the original owner, Dorothy Coleman, is recently deceased," Rand pursued. "Are you the current owner?"

The woman bit her lip. "Yes, I am," she said. "And no, I am not." She studied Alice for a long minute and then flicked her gaze back to Rand.

"Would you care to explain, Miss Whittaker?" Rand asked.

"Um. Well, you see, Mrs. Coleman, the owner, left the business to me when she died."

"Oh? Mrs. Coleman had a will?"

"You'll have to ask my attorney about that, Marshal. His name is Jason Meade. Just up the street on the left, past the dressmaker." She ran a disapproving eye over Alice's satin and sequin dress.

"Marshal, how long will you be in town?"

Rand looked straight at her. "For as long as it takes." He touched his hat brim. "Good morning, Miss Whittaker."

"Rand," Alice whispered when they were back on the boardwalk outside. "Aren't you curious about the business records? Why didn't you ask to see the account books?"

"I don't want Miss Whittaker to know I'm interested. I'll get the account books tonight."

"Tonight? How?"

"Steal them," he said shortly.

She stared at him, but he looked away and guided her on down the street. "Rand?"

He shook his head. "Later," he intoned.

Jason Meade's law office turned out to be a small smudged white canvas tent with a painted wooden sign outside. Rand pulled open the entrance flap. "Mr. Meade?"

A skinny, dark-haired man in serge trousers and a gray striped shirt looked up from a desk stacked with thick law books. "That's me, all right." His gaze landed on Alice and he jerked to his feet. "Say, aren't you the gal who sang at the Golden Nugget last night? Lolly something? Lolly Maguire, that's it. I recognize that red dress you're wearing."

Alice smiled at him. "Mr. Meade, I am interested in purchasing the assay office across the street. What can you tell me about it?"

"I'm afraid it's not for sale, Miss Maguire."

"You mean the owner is not interested in selling?"

He cleared his throat and gave Rand a quick glance. "The owner is, uh, deceased, Miss."

"Who owns the property now?"

"Um…well, no one, actually. Miss Emmeline Whittaker is managing the office until the terms of the will are clarified."

"Do you have the will?" Rand asked.

"Well, yessir, I do. But it isn't exactly a public document. Not just anybody off the street can read it."

Rand pulled his vest aside to reveal the revolver. "I'm not just anybody, Mr. Meade. I'd like to see that will."

The lawyer's eyes rounded. "Oh. Well, I'm afraid—"

Rand fished in his shirt pocket and laid his US Marshal's badge on the desk. "Now," he added.

Lawyer Meade blanched, then turned to a small steel safe in the corner, twirled the dial back and forth and swung open the door. "Here it is, Marshal."

Rand scanned the single page of yellowed parchment, then handed it to Alice. "Says here that upon Dorothy Coleman's death, her sister, Alice Montgomery, inherits the assay office."

"Well, yes, that's true, Marshal. We've wired Miss Montgomery a number of times, but there's been no response."

"Who is 'we'?"

"I mean *me*," Meade said quickly. "I wired Miss Montgomery."

"When did you send that telegram to the deceased's sister?"

"Oh, right after Miss Dorothy, that is Mrs. Coleman, passed on. Got no answer. No answer at all."

Rand folded up the will and stashed it in his vest pocket.

"Wait a minute, you can't take that! That's a legal document."

"It sure is," Rand agreed. "If I were you, Mr. Meade, I'd keep trying to contact Miss Montgomery. I am quite sure she will want to know about her sister's bequest."

That afternoon Rand leaned back on his dining chair and sent Alice a grin. "Interesting morning, wouldn't you say?"

Alice finished off her lemonade and he refilled her glass from the pitcher on the table. "Very interesting," she agreed. "Emmeline Whittaker is usurping ownership of Dottie's assay business. Lawyer Meade is lying. And it's all making me terribly thirsty."

"Sheriff Lipscomb was in a real hurry to hush up your sister's murder," Rand said. "And it looks to me like the coroner, Dr. Harvey Arnold, was in on it."

"But none of that is a motive for killing someone, is it?"

"Maybe not. But we're not finished yet. I'm going to get my hands on the assay office account books, and you have another night of sleuthing at the Golden Nugget."

"This undercover business is wearing," Alice breathed.

Rand lifted his glass and touched hers. "More lemonade?"

Chapter Twelve

That night Rand busied himself at the Golden Nugget bar reading a cheap magazine while Lolly Maguire consulted with Samson the piano player and then began circulating among the patrons. Finally she glided over to the piano, and Samson played an introductory arpeggio. Lolly-Alice struck a pose and the room quieted.

At the sound of her voice, Rand looked up from the account ledger he'd concealed under the pages of *Gentlemen's World*. The tune Samson played as an introduction was familiar, something Rand had heard many times before, and when he recognized it, he froze. Good God, it was the folk song "Barbara Allen"! He'd sung it a hundred times when he was growing up.

"'In Scarlet Town, where I was born…'"

Lolly began to sing. But it wasn't "Barbara Allen."

Back in Smoke River that first night he remembered asking Alice if she could sing. She'd said no, but obviously that wasn't true. Her voice had a low, smoky quality that was impossible to ignore. And the words raised his eyebrows.

"'There was a lass from Dublin town, That all the boys from there around, Did want to kiss and take to bed, So… never did she want to wed!'"

Rand choked on his beer, and the miners cheered and stomped their heavy boots on the floor. Where had Alice ever learned such a song? Could she be making up those bawdy lyrics on the fly?

There was more. More suggestive words sung to the tune of the old folk song.

"'There was a girl from Abilene, Oh, she was pure as purest cream, Until she learned that sex was fun, And then… her work was never done!'"

Rand clamped his jaw closed and forced himself to shut out Alice's seductive voice and concentrate on the account ledger. Absently he reached for the shot glass of whiskey Lefty had offered in exchange for a magazine page with girlie pictures, turned over another page of debits and credits and choked.

Something sure didn't add up. He flipped back through the figures for the preceding thirty-six months and began making some comparisons, and all at once things began to fall into place.

Alice turned her face aside to snatch a breath of un-whiskey-saturated breath. What was this miner's name, Charlie? Donald? Jonah, that was it!

"Jonah, you're a very successful miner. Did you ever visit Coleman's Assay Office?"

"Oh, shore, Miss Lolly. But she shore were busy! Miss Dorothy, she allus used to shoo away all them gentlemen, but they jest kept comin' and comin'. Made some of us miners mad cuz we knowed she weren't no loose woman, even if she was a widow."

"I bet you have a good memory for faces, Jonah. Who were these 'gentlemen'?"

"Mostly it was that doctor fella, Doc Arnold. He practically drooled all over hisself whenever Miss Dorothy walked by. And then sometimes there was the sheriff."

"That would be Sheriff Lipscomb?"

"Yes, ma'am. And, lessee, oh, yeah, that lawyer over on Jasmine Street. Jason Meade his name is. Sometimes I'd hear Doc Arnold yellin' at her and then she'd cry and carry on. Dang, it made me mad!"

"Cry and carry on about what?"

"Don't rightly know. But iff'n I was to hazard a guess

it'd be somethin' he wanted her to do that she didn't want to do."

"Something about money, maybe?"

Jonah shook his straggly salt-and-pepper hair out of his eyes. "Nah. Doc's got plenty of money. I'm thinkin' it was something more personal-like."

Alice nodded. What kinds of things would a well-to-do man want a well-to-do woman to do? Lie for him, maybe? Steal for him? Surely not...

She went cold all over and suddenly stopped dancing.

"Gol-darn-it, Miss Lolly, I knowed I shouldn't have told ya nuthin'. Ain't none of my never-mind, anyhow."

"On the contrary, Jonah. You did exactly the right thing. You are a gentleman and a prince."

His leathery cheeks turned bright red. "A prince, huh? Golly, who'd a thunk that about ol' Jonah?"

Jonah tramped off with a gobsmacked expression on his wrinkled face, and Alice found herself in the arms of another beery miner. This one, called Tom, had lots to say about the Coleman's Assay Office. Emmeline Whittaker had never gotten along with Dorothy Coleman, and after Dorothy's death, Emmeline was often seen in the back room of the office, talking with both Sheriff Lipscomb and Jason Meade, the attorney.

She'd heard enough. Alice left Tom in the middle of the floor and headed straight for Rand, sitting at the bar. He glanced up from the magazine he was reading. "You look like a cat who's just lapped up a saucer of cream."

"And you," she said in a low voice, "look like you'd just swallowed a cage full of canaries."

He grinned and leaned close to her. "You'll never guess what I discovered in the assay office accounts," he said quietly.

"Someone was embezzling money from the business?" she asked.

Rand stared at her. "How'd you figure that out?"

"Intuition," she intoned. "And Jonah McCrary and some miner named Tom just told me some equally interesting things."

"About your sister, Dorothy," he guessed.

"And Dr. Arnold. Jonah heard them arguing about something after Jim was killed."

"Money, I bet," Rand supplied. "Interesting."

"Possibly not money," she breathed. "Tom told me something even more interesting."

He gave her a considering look. "Alice, I have an idea. Could you manage some more play-acting tomorrow night?"

Chapter Thirteen

They planned it carefully. Alice made sure she looked the part of the marshal's fancy woman, someone who would lie for a price. Then she made sure all the members of their staged "play" were present in the back room of the assay office—Sheriff Lipscomb, Dr. Arnold, her sister's attorney, Jason Meade, and Emmeline Whittaker, who was now passing herself off as the owner of Coleman's Assay Office.

Before she walked into the office, Alice took a moment to make sure Rand was already hidden in the shadows behind the window curtain. Then she calmed her breathing, twitched her red satin skirt and said a brief prayer.

Please, Lord, let me lie convincingly and not lose my nerve.

Pasting on a smile, she advanced into the back room.

The first person she saw was Emmeline Whittaker. "Good evening, Miss Whittaker," Alice began. "Perhaps I might call you Emmeline? I'm sure we have a great deal in common."

"Oh?" the woman said, her tone frosty. "What could you and I possibly have in common?"

Alice didn't answer. Instead she smiled warmly at the lawyer, who was bouncing from one foot to the other, a worried expression on his narrow face. "Mr. Meade, how nice to see you again. Very shortly I may have need of your services."

She then turned to Sheriff Lipscomb, who had perched his bulky frame uneasily on a straight-backed chair. "Sheriff, I understand you have for many years enjoyed the trust of the miners of Silver City?"

"Why, yes, ma'am. They sure do trust me. Miners are the lifeblood of Silver City."

"As you know," she said in her most silky tone, "I am… How shall I put this delicately…? An acquaintance of Marshal Randell Logan."

"Oh, yes, ma'am," the sheriff blurted out. "That bit of news has got all around town, hasn't it, Jase?" He sent a significant look at Lawyer Meade. "Jase and me, we share a pint now and again and we're on pretty good terms. He told me about you an' the marshal visitin' his office yesterday."

Alice risked a surreptitious glance at the curtain in the shadows where Rand stood. She hoped he was armed.

"And," she continued, "Dr. Arnold, I wanted to include you in our discussion because…" She stepped in close to him and lowered her voice. "I am prone to having fits, and I appreciate havin' a medical professional nearby in times of stress. And," she added in a loud whisper, "I fear our discussion tonight might be…stressful."

"What discussion?" Lawyer Meade queried.

Alice fluttered her eyelashes at him. "Why, my offer to purchase the assay office, of course. The marshal didn't tell you?"

Emmeline Whittaker clutched her bosom. "Purchase the—?"

"Coleman's Assay Office, yes," Alice purred.

The woman's face went white. "What on earth for?"

"Oh, now, Miss Emmeline, surely you can guess? I look at you and I see a respectable businesswoman. I look at myself and I see…well, a less-than-respectable woman. And life moves on, does it not?"

A puzzled look crossed Emmeline's pale face.

"Now," Alice continued, "I have managed to save up a good deal of money over the years, and now that my middle years are fast approachin', I feel I should invest in a respectable business venture for my old age. A business like this one, Coleman's Assay Office."

Emmeline stared at her in dumbfounded silence.

Alice grinned and smoothed her skirt. "I am prepared to make quite a large deposit, and I will have Lawyer Meade here draw up the papers this very night."

Sheriff Lipscomb coughed and sent a significant look to Emmeline Whittaker. "Whaddya need me for, Miss Maguire?"

"Why, Sheriff, I am carryin' a large amount of cash as we speak. I wouldn't feel safe walkin' back to my hotel tonight without an escort."

"What about yer marshal friend? Why cain't he escort you?"

Alice's eyes went as wide as she could make them. "Why, I could not ever, *ever* let Marshal Logan know what I am proposin' to do."

"Why's that?" the sheriff asked.

"Because..." Alice lowered her voice. "The marshal thinks I am returnin' to Chicago with him. He doesn't know I am hankerin' to...well...retire, as it were."

She turned to Emmeline. "You understand, don't you, Miss Emmeline? I need to find another source of income, one that's more, um, steady. And more...respectable."

Emmeline sank onto a wooden chair. "This is all very sudden, Miss Maguire."

"Well, yes," Alice said quickly. "I just found out that Mrs. Coleman had willed the assay business to her sister. But if the sister cannot be located..." She directed a smile at Lawyer Meade. "The business will be taken over by Mrs. Coleman's longtime business assistant, Emmeline Whittaker, here. Isn't that so, Mr. Meade?"

Lawyer Meade nodded and ran his forefinger under his shirt collar. "Just what are you prepared to offer, Miss Maguire?"

"Well..." Alice paused dramatically. "Assuming that this

sister can *never* be located, then Miss Emmeline here will be the owner. Isn't that right, Mr. Meade?"

Again the lawyer nodded, but now he was smiling.

"Then perhaps you could stop lookin' for this sister and allow me to pay you, generously, of course, for your services in, um, drawing up a deed of sale."

A heavy silence fell, during which Emmeline, Sheriff Lipscomb and Lawyer Jason Meade stared at each other. Dr. Arnold looked genuinely puzzled.

In the lull, Alice stepped toward the door. "If you will excuse me, I will withdraw for a few minutes so you can talk over my proposal among yourselves. I have an appointment with the dressmaker down the street. She is expectin' me at eight sharp this evenin', and I see I am almost late."

She knotted her red shawl about her shoulders and sashayed out the front door in a swish of satin and petticoats.

Hidden behind the curtain, Rand held his breath until he heard the door close and knew Alice had left the building. Then he settled in to wait for the sparks to fly.

It didn't take long.

"Emmy," the sheriff said in his gruff voice. "You can't sell the business. And by God you know why."

"You mean then you wouldn't get your payments every month," Emmeline snapped. "That's why you don't want me to sell, isn't it, Jeremiah?"

"What payments?" Lawyer Meade and Dr. Arnold asked simultaneously.

"The ones she's been makin' ever since Jim Coleman was killed," Sheriff Lipscomb answered.

"What? What's he talking about?" Dr. Arnold queried.

"Jeremiah," Emmeline shouted, "you shut your mouth!"

"Hold on just a minute," Dr. Arnold said. "Jim Coleman was shot during a robbery here at the office. At least that's what you told me, Sheriff."

"Well…uh…yes I did, Harve. But it weren't so much a robbery as a—"

"Jeremiah, shut your mouth!" Emmeline screeched.

"Oh, my God," the doctor groaned. "Harve, you've been blackmailing Emmeline, haven't you?"

"Well, yeah," the sheriff said. "See, when Jim Coleman was shot it looked kinda suspicious, like maybe Emmeline had shot him. So when she offered to…uh…well, pay me to keep my mouth shu—"

"I didn't offer, you wretch!" Emmeline shouted. "You said if I didn't make it worth your while, you would arrest me for murder!"

Behind the curtain Rand began to smile. So, Miss Whittaker was blackmailing the sheriff to cover up killing Jim. And she had killed Jim Coleman because he had somehow figured out that she was embezzling funds from the assay business. The proof was right there in the account books.

He strained his ears to hear the continuing conversation.

"Emmeline!" Dr. Arnold said, his tone incredulous. "You mean that bullet I dug out of Jim Coleman's chest came from your revolver? The one I'd given to Dorothy for protection?"

Emmeline said nothing.

"Good Lord," the physician continued in a strangled voice. "You shot Jim?"

"Emmeline," Lawyer Meade interjected. "Don't say anything. You need a lawyer."

Dr. Arnold pinned him with blazing eyes. "She doesn't have to say anything, Jason. The bullet I took out of Jim Coleman matched the one I dug out of Dorothy's back. A thirty-two-caliber bullet from a Remington revolver."

A long silence fell.

"Emmeline," Dr. Arnold said in a low voice, "do you own a revolver?"

"Certainly not!" she insisted.

But Rand knew different. Last night when he had "borrowed" the account books, he'd found the revolver hidden in a secret desk drawer. A thirty-two-caliber Remington revolver.

"You killed Dorothy, didn't you?" the physician whispered. "Why? *Why?*"

"Because," Emmeline said, "after Jim was dead you kept asking Dorothy to marry you. I figured she would, eventually, and then—"

"And then," Lawyer Meade supplied, "the business, the building, everything would belong to Dorothy's sister, this Alice Montgomery. And that would mean your source of funds would disappear. Isn't that right, Emmeline?"

Rand jerked. Lawyer Jason Meade was taking money from Emmeline to keep him from contacting Dorothy's sister about the will.

"You knew what I was doing, Jason," Emmeline snapped. "You knew all along."

"But Emmeline," the lawyer said, "I never dreamed... I just thought you were paying me a bit extra not to find Dorothy's sister. But you...you actually killed her!"

"You shot Dorothy to keep her from marrying me?" the doctor asked, his voice breaking.

Rand closed his eyes. Emmeline Whittaker had killed Jim Coleman, and then with her brazenly stolen funds from the Coleman's Assay Office she had blackmailed the sheriff. And, to keep her source of cash from drying up, Emmeline had murdered Dorothy.

He couldn't wait to get Alice out of this hellhole!

He drew his Colt and stepped out from his hiding place.

"Emmeline Whittaker, you are under arrest for the murders of Jim Coleman and Dorothy Coleman."

Emmeline stared at him, her face pasty.

Rand gestured for Sheriff Lipscomb and Lawyer Meade to raise their hands. "Conspiracy and embezzling are also crimes, gentlemen."

Dumbstruck, Dr. Arnold looked from Sheriff Lipscomb to Lawyer Meade and shook his head.

Rand snapped handcuffs on the wrists of the two men and grasped Emmeline's arm. "Let's go."

Rand locked the three prisoners in adjoining jail cells himself, then wired the US Marshal in Boise City. The following morning he ushered them all aboard the northbound train, and later that day he delivered three prisoners to the sheriff in Owyhee County.

Chapter Fourteen

Alice slept late at the Excelsior Hotel, ate a leisurely breakfast of fried eggs and bacon, and spent the day at the railroad station, waiting for Rand to return. When the southbound locomotive steamed into the depot she rose from the bench, shook out her split riding skirt and waited.

Rand stepped off the train and without saying a word scooped her up into his arms and swung her around and around in a circle. "Pinkerton send their thanks," he said at last. "They want you to know you did them a great service."

"Oh," she breathed. "I can hardly believe it's over."

"And I want you to know that librarians are now my favorite people."

"Not actresses?" she said.

"It's a toss-up," he said with a laugh.

"I have news," she said. Rand stiffened and set her feet on the ground.

"Yeah, what news?"

"Dr. Harvey Arnold offered to buy my lunch today."

Rand sent her a long, searching look. "Ah. And what did you say?"

"I told him I wasn't hungry."

He chuckled. "Are you ready to leave Silver City?"

"I am ready with a capital *R*! I want to go home. I packed all my things, and I took the liberty of loading your saddlebag, as well. I can't wait to leave!"

"What about the assay office? You're the legal owner now."

"I sold it," she said quietly. "To Dr. Arnold."

Rand stared at her. "Alice, you are an endless source of surprise. *That* I would never have expected."

"And you will never guess how I plan to use the money!"

"For a new red dress?" he joked.

She shook her head.

"How about a fancy parasol and a horse and carriage for the trip back to Smoke River?"

"No. I said you would never guess."

"Try me," he said in a weary voice.

"I'm going to buy books! Lots and lots of books. For the Smoke River library."

He laughed aloud. "Books on acting, maybe?"

She snatched off her wide-brimmed felt hat and swatted him with it.

"Come on, Alice, let's go home."

Rand saddled their horses and loaded up the saddlebags, and within half an hour they were riding out of Silver City. He was relieved to be on the trail again. He could not have stood one more night sleeping close enough to Alice to touch her but *not* touching her. He didn't know how she felt about it, and he didn't want to risk asking her. He already cared more about her than he wanted to.

They rode all day, until the sun finally sank behind the pine-covered hills in the west. Alice was unusually quiet. Even when a startled doe and her fawn clattered across the trail in front of them, she merely reined her horse to a stop and sat waiting until the rustling in the underbrush stopped.

Later, when he cobbled together a supper of canned beans and bacon, she took the plate he handed her, set it on the ground beside her and laid her fork on top. Then she leaned forward and pressed her forehead against her bent knees.

Instantly Rand realized something was wrong.

"Alice. Alice, don't cry. It's over now. We caught your sister's killer and it's all over."

She made no answer. He moved her plate out of the way and knelt beside her. "Alice, what's wrong?"

She lifted her head and swiped one hand across her wet cheeks, then swiped it again, but the tears kept spilling down her face.

He touched her shoulder and pulled her into his arms. Her body shook, and her tears turned to gut-wrenching sobs. He held her, rocking her gently to and fro, while she sobbed and he bit his lip and sweated. His chest hurt.

Finally she lifted her head, dug a handkerchief out of her shirt pocket and mopped at her eyes. Then she took a shaky breath, blew her nose and drew in a long, uneven breath of the smoky air.

Her face looked puffy, and her eyes were red and swollen. He felt like a horse had kicked him in the gut.

"I'm s-sorry, Rand. I guess it's all catching up to me now. Before we left I went to visit her grave, and it made me realize Dottie is really, really g-gone, and I'm n-never going to see her again."

Rand nuzzled her head under his chin and tightened his arms around her. A delayed reaction like this wasn't unusual, but it was sure tearing him up inside. He held her until her breathing sounded normal and then he reached out one hand to pick up her supper plate.

"We've been riding all day, Alice. You should eat something." He scooped up a tiny bite of beans and offered it.

Obediently she opened her mouth and he slid the fork past her lips. The next forkful he devoured himself, and then he began alternating, one bite for her and one for him. He broke up the bacon in small pieces and fed them to her the same way.

Something inside him began to ache. When it grew full dark and the fire burned down to coals, he wrapped her blankets around her and she tipped over onto the ground right where she sat.

Rand rinsed the tin plate off in the stream, filled the coffeepot and gathered an armload of deadfall for tomorrow morning's campfire. Finally he rolled himself in his own blanket and stretched out next to her.

He stared at the dying coals, listening to the crickets, until his eyes burned. He thought about the woman sleeping next to him. Eight days ago he'd never laid eyes on Alice Montgomery. Tonight he felt like he'd known her all his life.

And then an unexpected thought slammed into his brain. *Alice is one woman in a million. I don't ever want to be away from her.*

Alice smelled coffee, and when she opened her eyes a steaming mug sat on a low, flat rock next to her. Rand was at the campfire, bent over a skillet of sizzling bacon. She sat up and reached for the mug.

"Good morning," he said without turning around.

"Good morning, Rand. Thank you for the coffee. And for letting me cry it out yesterday."

"No thanks necessary," he said. "Losing someone you love is one of the worst things I can think of."

She sipped her coffee in silence. "Have you ever lost anyone? Someone close to you, I mean?"

He didn't answer.

"Rand?"

He turned away from the skillet and faced her, then turned back to the fire. "I lost my wife," he said, his voice flat.

"Oh, my God, I'm sorry. I'm so sorry, Rand."

He shrugged, but he didn't turn around. "That's why I became a US Marshal."

She waited. He forked over the bacon slices and spoke again, still with his back to her.

"I used to ride with the Texas Rangers," he said, his voice flat. "Had a cattle ranch in Texas, down near the Black Chisos Mountains. One day I came back to the ranch to find my wife had been shot."

"Oh, Rand." Tears started at the back of her eyes.

"I tracked the killers into Arizona Territory, but I had to stop at the Mexican border because Rangers can't operate outside the States. So I quit the Rangers and became a US Marshal."

"Did—did you ever catch whoever did it?"

He lifted the skillet off the fire and forked three slices of bacon onto a tin plate. "I did. Caught them down near Nogales and brought him back to the Chisos and watched them hang."

He dropped a biscuit onto the plate and handed it to her. "Now eat your breakfast."

She could tell he didn't want to talk anymore, so she obeyed, and within an hour they had mounted up and were back on the trail before the sun was barely touching the tops of the sugar pine trees.

All morning she rode with her hat tipped to one side to shield her eyes from the blinding rays, and two hours after their noon stop to water the horses she felt the first warning signs of one of her blind headaches. Her vision blurring, she gritted her teeth and closed her lids against the glare, letting her horse follow Rand on its own.

By evening she was in agony, her right temple pounding with each heartbeat. She slid off the chestnut, dug her blankets out of the saddlebag and lurched over to the fire pit Rand was building.

"Alice, what's the matter?"

"Headache," she said through stiff lips.

"Bad?"

"Yes." She dropped her blankets on the ground and without bending over managed to kick them open. Very gingerly she lay down and closed her eyes. She could tell Rand was standing over her because she could smell his sweaty shirt.

"Alice." He squatted beside her.

"It's all right, Rand. I've had these headaches all my life. First I see strange flashes of light and then it just pounds, mostly on one side. Light hurts, so I keep my eyes shut."

"Migraine," he said. "My mother used to get them. I'll make some coffee."

She winced at the raucous noise the coffee grinder made, then heard the metal pot clank onto the rocks around the campfire. He set another pot down, too. It was full of water, she guessed, because after a short while she heard splashing and then he laid a warm, wet cloth over her closed eyes.

"My mother used to say this eased the pain," he breathed. "And this." With his forefinger he smeared something over her temples. It smelled like mint.

"What is that?" she muttered.

"Peppermint oil. My mother swore by it." He removed the cooling cloth that was over her eyes and replaced it with a warm one.

When the coffee boiled he poured out a cup.

"Caffeine helps, too." He sat down beside her and dribbled the liquid into her mouth one spoonful at a time.

"Thank you," she breathed.

"I'm gonna see to the horses and then make some supper. You just stay quiet."

She laughed, then wished she hadn't because it made her temples throb. "As if I could do anything *but* stay quiet," she managed.

She heard him lift off the saddles, rub down the horses with something scratchy, probably dry grass, and turn them loose to graze. Then he lifted away the cooling cloth and dropped another warm one over her eyes.

He stirred up something for supper, something out of a can. Maybe tomatoes, she guessed from the sloppy sound.

"You hungry?" he asked.

"No," she whispered. She wondered if a "shady lady" like Lolly Maguire ever got headaches.

He sat beside her while he ate, and every so often he spooned another teaspoon of coffee into her mouth.

He kept changing the cloth over her eyes, dropping the cool one into the water pot with a soft plop and wringing out the warm one and laying it across her face. His fingers were gentle. Later she heard him walk off to the creek to wash his supper plate and she tried to sleep.

Finally he spread out his bedroll next to her; she could tell because his blanket brushed against her bare arm.

He smelled good. Like woodsmoke. It made her want to cry.

Chapter Fifteen

In the morning Alice was a bit groggy when she woke up. Her head felt as if it were stuffed full of cotton, but she managed to eat two biscuits and a slice of crisp bacon and drink two cups of coffee. Then she volunteered to wash the tin plates in the creek while Rand packed up the camp and kicked dirt over the fire.

"You must be feeling better if you could eat two of my overdone biscuits," he quipped.

"My head feels like an eggshell, but other than that, I do feel better." She sent him a smile. "I must remember to ask Carl Ness at the mercantile to order some of that peppermint oil. And I can hardly wait to tell Doc Graham about it."

They mounted up and headed into the hills where the late-October leaves on the maple trees were turning scarlet and red-orange. Rand gestured for her to ride in front so she wouldn't have to breathe his dust; besides, he wanted to keep an eye on her. She rode like an Indian, never wasting a motion, and he couldn't help but wonder who had taught her to ride. Rooney Cloudman, maybe.

They rode all day, watering the horses at willow-swathed streams and eventually emerging from the woods into meadows covered with blue chicory. When the sun dropped behind the hills, flaming the sky peach and scarlet, Rand reined to a stop beside a stand of alders.

"We're still some hours from Smoke River. You want to stop and camp here or go on?"

"I want to go on and get home. I'm anxious to have a bath and sleep in a soft bed."

"Okay." He gigged his horse forward.

"I sound terribly overcivilized, don't I? Quite unlike Lolly Maguire."

Rand chuckled. "Not 'overcivilized,'" he pointed out. "Just civilized. I'd be lying if I said I wouldn't like to wash off my trail dust, too."

They rode steadily for another four hours. By the time they reached town, it was pitch-dark and his stomach was rumbling. They unloaded their saddlebags and Alice's travel case, left instructions with the livery attendant for feeding and brushing down the horses and started down the street toward Rose Cottage.

Now that this ordeal was finally at an end, Alice couldn't think of a thing to say. In silence she walked beside Rand beneath the maple trees, past gardens smelling of roses and night-blooming nicotiana, feeling oddly flat. She was returning to Sarah and Rooney and her beloved Smoke River; Why wasn't she feeling the joy she'd expected? Instead of elation she felt tired. And…sad.

She had missed her library, she reminded herself. Her wonderful library with its collection of exciting books about everything under the sun. And now she was back and she could enjoy them again. Still, something was different. Was it Dottie? She caught her breath. She missed her sister. She would always miss her.

Then all at once she knew what it was. *She* was different. This whole ordeal had changed her in some way.

No, it was Rand who had changed her.

And he was leaving in the morning.

Her steps faltered and he slowed and turned to her. "Alice?"

She looked up at him. "Don't go," she whispered.

"Alice, I have to go, you know that. Pinkerton already has another mission for me."

"Yes," she breathed. "I know. It doesn't seem possible

that in less than two weeks my whole life has been turned upside-down."

He tipped her face up to his. "You know I'm in love with you, don't you? It's taken half my life to find you. I don't want to let you go."

"Never in a million years did I expect to feel this way about a man," she whispered. "It hurts."

"I could send for you," he said, his voice hoarse. "We could be married in Denver City."

She hesitated and finally released a long breath. "I can't, Rand. This has all happened so…so fast I don't trust it. I guess I'm not ready. Not yet."

He wrapped his arms around her and caught her mouth under his. After a long, long minute, he lifted his head. "All right," he murmured against her lips. "I understand. I don't like it, but I understand."

Alice stepped out of his embrace and they turned back to the street. "Come on," she said. "We're both hungry. Sarah will have something for us to eat."

He heaved a sigh and they walked on.

At the boardinghouse, Sarah and Rooney were rocking in the porch swing while young Mark sat at their feet playing pick-up sticks. "Well, my stars!" Sarah exclaimed. She rushed down the steps and pulled Alice into a hug, then planted a kiss on Rand's bristly jaw. "Welcome back! Are you hungry?" she said in the same breath.

Rand laughed. "Yes!" Alice sang. "We're starving."

"Then come on into the house, you two. There's cold chicken and potato salad, and I just took an apricot pie out of the oven."

Mark climbed to his feet. "Didja shoot anybody, Marshal?"

"Nope. Came close, though." He ruffled the boy's hair as he climbed the porch steps.

Rooney caught Mark's arm and propelled him through

the screen door and into the house. "How close?" he intoned to Rand.

"Close enough. Double murder and embezzling. Alice…" He sent an admiring look at her. "Alice was instrumental in catching three criminals."

Rooney rolled his eyes. "Don't let on to Sarah, or she won't let Alice out of her sight till Christmas."

Mark slapped back through the screen door. "I wanna know about what Alice did."

Rand shot a quick look at the woman who had made his undercover plan work. She sent him a subtle shake of her head, and he quickly modified what he was about to say.

"Well, one night Miss Alice got dressed up real pretty in a red dress with a real low—uh…with sequins all over—"

"Sequins!" Sarah yelped. "Red sequins? Well, I never!"

Rooney caught his eye. "Bet she looked real fetchin', didn't she?"

"Oh, yes, sir," he breathed. "She looked like a walking burst of fireworks."

"Thought so," the older man said with a grin.

"Tell me 'bout what Alice did!" Mark insisted.

Sarah ushered them all into the dining room. "Clean up," she ordered. She pointed into the kitchen.

Alice went first. Then, while Mark danced at his side, Rand managed to lather up at the sink and accept the slightly damp towel Alice handed him. "Tell Mark about the miners," she breathed.

Sarah shouldered her way past them with a platter of fried chicken. "Mark, bring that bowl of potato salad in the cooler."

"Aw, Gran, I wanna hear 'bout Alice and the miners!"

"I want to hear about that, too," Sarah said in a determined tone. "So, you two sit down. Eat. And…" She sent Alice a significant look. "Talk!"

Rand helped himself to a crispy chicken breast and a double spoonful of salad. "Okay, about those miners…"

"And Alice!" Mark crowed. "Tell about Alice!"

Rand swallowed a bite of cold chicken. "Well…" He sent Alice a quick smile. "Alice got to know some of the miners, and—"

"How'd she do that?" Mark interrupted. "Did she go down in a mine?"

"Um…well, she found a place that had a piano player, and she…um…danced with them."

Sarah's fork clattered onto her plate.

"What kinda place?" Mark queried.

"A saloon, no doubt," Sarah said through thinned lips.

"There was a nice Chinese piano player who played waltzes," Alice said quickly. "So I danced with the miners, and I talked to them."

"We call it 'gathering evidence,'" Rand explained.

"That's not what *I'd* call it!" Sarah grumbled.

Rand swallowed. "So," he continued, "Alice worked undercover, getting the miners to share information with her."

"Like what?" Mark pursued. Rooney laid his hand on the boy's arm.

Rand caught the older man's eye. "Like who's who in town and who had enemies, that sort of thing."

"In a red dress with sequins," Sarah spluttered. "Really, Alice. I am shocked."

"Alice was very proper," Rand said quickly. "And very clever. And I watched over her every single minute."

Sarah harrumphed and flounced into the kitchen to start a pot of coffee. When she returned she set a golden-brown deep-dish apricot pie in front of him. "Ice cream?" she barked.

Rand couldn't help laughing. And so did Rooney and Alice and, finally, even Sarah.

"Oh, all right, I forgive you," the older woman said. "But you surely gave this old heart of mine a turn."

"And then what happened?" Rooney and Mark said in one voice.

"Then," Alice supplied, "we devised a plan to get our quarry to admit what they had done without letting them know Rand was listening."

"What's a 'quarry'?" Mark asked.

"Bad hombres," Rand said.

"My sister's murderer," Alice added.

Sarah rose. "I don't even want to know what that plan was, Alice. Coffee?" Then she sank back onto her chair and leaned toward Alice. "On second thought, I *do* want to know."

"I'll get the coffee," Rand volunteered, laying his napkin on the table.

"The cups are in the hutch, Mark," Rooney said, giving the boy a nudge.

Sarah pinned Alice with sharp blue eyes. "So, what was this clever plan you came up with?" She kept her gaze on Alice's face.

Alice explained about her theatrical performance at the assay office. As she talked Mark's eyes got bigger and rounder and Sarah's mouth got smaller and tighter.

"Young man," she said when Rand emerged from the kitchen with the coffeepot, "I don't want you and Alice to take any more of these trips together. Is that understood?"

"I brought the ice cream, too," Rand said blandly, "in case anyone wanted…"

Mark applauded, and Alice couldn't stop smiling at him.

When the pie and ice cream had disappeared, Sarah emerged from the kitchen, her apron in one hand, and sent Rand a long, considering look. "Marshal Logan, you might as well use the guest bedroom tonight, seein' as how you're half asleep already and the hotel's probably full up. And," she added, "I'm heating bathwater, if anybody's interested."

With a quick twist of her wrist she wound the apron ties around her waist and marched back into the kitchen.

Chapter Sixteen

Alice lay wide-awake, watching the fat, silvery moon drift across the sky and drop behind the branches of the pepper tree in the front yard. For the first time in days she was squeaky clean and wearing a long, lace-trimmed nightgown. She should be feeling calm and civilized after so many hot, dusty days on horseback.

But she wasn't. Instead she lay on her bed feeling something so shocking she tried to brush it out of her mind.

Hours passed, and still she lay sleepless and overwarm until a soft click brought her up on one elbow. Her bedroom door opened, and a shadow slipped inside.

Rand.

Thank God. Tears stung under her eyelids.

Without a word he walked to the bed and stretched out beside her. With a start she realized he wore only his drawers, and with another start she realized three things. First, that she wasn't surprised that he was here with her. Second, that she didn't care what he wore, or didn't wear. And third, that she wished she had the courage to strip off her nightgown.

Next time.

But there might not be a next time.

"Rand," she whispered. "I thought you might not come."

"You're not wrong too often, Alice," he murmured. "Maybe you should trust your instincts."

She turned into his arms.

"Oh, honey, don't cry. Please don't cry." He smoothed

one hand up and down her back, and after a moment he pressed his lips against her forehead. "You smell like roses."

"You smell like...pine trees."

He chuckled. "Rooney's soap."

"I want to remember your sweat-and-woodsmoke smell." She squeezed her lids shut to stop the tears.

"Alice," he said, his voice low and serious. "Alice, don't."

"Kiss me," she whispered.

He touched his mouth to hers, deepened it until he thought he would explode, and then he just lay quietly and held her in his arms.

When the sky started to lighten, he kissed her one last time, rolled off the bed and left.

It was the hardest thing he'd ever done.

Chapter Seventeen

Usually Alice loved Christmastime. School was out for the holidays and youngsters of all ages flocked to her library, from little Manette Nicolet, who devoured every book she could find about insects, to oh-so-grown-up Adam Lynford, who had just discovered the laws of physics. Annamarie Panovsky asked for works by Dickens and Shakespeare, while Molly Bruhn, whose mother had just purchased a new Windsor piano, read about the great composers, Beethoven and Schubert and Brahms.

As Christmas drew closer, bands of carolers roamed the town singing "O Come All Ye Faithful" and "Joy to the World" for rewards of gingerbread and hot spiced cider. The annual tree-decorating competition, sponsored by Poletti's Barbershop, got under way, and children all over town made paper chains and popped corn to string on the tree branches. Peter and Roberta Jensen hosted a big winter barn dance where box lunches were auctioned off to raise money to buy new music for the community choir.

Alice was invited to all the holiday events. Even though she didn't feel the least bit like celebrating this year, she put in an appearance at most of them. There were whist parties and taffy pulls and Christmas sing-alongs and quilting bees, and she made endless batches of divinity and fudge for Sarah's afternoon teas.

But mostly she tended to her library, ordering the new books she could now afford with money from the sale of Coleman's Assay Company in Silver City.

She heaved a sigh. Activities in Smoke River during

Christmas could be exhausting. In the evenings she knit socks with Sarah on the front porch of Rose Cottage and tutored Mark in mathematics. And late one night she sat bundled up and rocking in the swing next to Rooney and confessed how empty it all felt.

"Honey-girl, lemme tell you somethin' I learned from an old *vaquero* way back when I was scoutin' for Colonel Wash Halliday. Goes like this. 'Don't promise anythin' when yer happy. Don't reply to anythin' when yer angry. And don't decide nuthin' when yer sad.'"

"Oh, Rooney, the last time I was happy was the night Rand was here eating Sarah's apricot pie and ice cream."

"Yeah," he said. "I know. Takes time to get over it when yer heart's broke."

"I've never felt quite this empty and unhappy, not even when Dottie died."

"Then, like the *vaquero* says, don't decide nuthin'. Jes' pull up yer socks and go on as best you can."

And so she went on. Christmas drew closer. Frost tipped the branches of the Douglas fir trees, and schoolchildren did extra chores for their parents and tried to be extra-good.

With each day that passed the library grew quieter and quieter, and Alice grew more and more despondent.

And then one afternoon, just when she thought she had pulled her socks up about as far as they could go, she sat alone in her empty library, her head down, reading a thick volume of Chaucer's *Canterbury Tales*, when a patron stopped by her desk and presented a book to be checked out.

She was so absorbed in *The Wife of Bath's Tale* she didn't even look up. "Do you want to take the book home?" she asked.

There was a pause, and then a familiar voice said, "No. I want to take the *librarian* home."

She looked up, and Chaucer and the vase of red poinsettias on her desk went flying. "Rand!"

"Miss Alice."

He stepped over the scattered blooms and the volume on the floor, caught her in his arms and swung her around and around.

"Rand," she said breathlessly, "where did you come from?"

"Colorado," he said simply. "From the Pinkerton Agency."

"Oh!" He was covered with a light dusting of snow, obviously weary, his cheeks bristly and his gray-green eyes questioning.

He kissed her forehead and both cheeks before he finally found her mouth. Then he did it in reverse.

"I'm not going back," he said when he finally lifted his head. "Pinkerton agreed that I can work from Oregon as well as Colorado. From Smoke River, in fact."

He kissed her again, and this time it lasted so long she thought she might faint. When he released her she stood staring at him while outside somewhere a winter sparrow started to trill.

"Miss Alice," he said at last. "I have come to invite you to a wedding."

She gaped at him. "A w-wedding?"

Now he was smiling at her. "That's what I said, Alice. A wedding." His smile worked itself into a grin. "In Broken Toe, Idaho."

Passersby that afternoon looked at each other in wonderment. From the library, where Miss Alice Montgomery had always, *always* insisted on absolute quiet, floated the sound of laughter. A man's and a woman's prolonged, unrestrained, joyous laughter.

The wedding was held on Christmas day in the parlor at Rose Cottage. In the middle of all the cake and champagne and congratulatory wishes the couple slipped off to the livery stable, climbed on their horses and rode out of town.

Heading for Broken Toe, Idaho, of course.

* * * * *

SNOWBOUND
IN BIG SPRINGS

Lauri Robinson

Dear Reader,

Christmas is often referred to as the time of year when miracles abound. Though I believe miracles abound year-round, I do enjoy writing stories set during the holidays and of course love happy endings that might be a bit miraculous. I hope you enjoy Welles and Sophie, and their Christmas journey!

Blessings,

Lauri

Dedication

To our grandson Connor, who has made life a wonderful adventure from the moment he was born. Love you!

Chapter One

This was the last place he wanted to be. The last thing he wanted to do. Trudging through knee-deep snow during a blizzard in Eastern Colorado was for men who didn't want the finer things in life. He did. He wanted good card games, strong whiskey and pretty women.

"I'm not even dressed for this kind of weather!" Welles Carmichael shouted. Not that it did any good. The howling wind swallowed up his words faster than he'd said them. The same wind that was making icicles form on his eyelashes. Yes, his eyelashes. He could feel the frozen crystals. See them every time he blinked.

Blinking didn't do any good, either. He couldn't see a foot in front of his face. The only thing he had to tell him he was heading in the right direction was the long wooden pole the conductor had given him to poke into the snow and hit the iron rails to make sure he stayed on the railroad tracks. The ones that led into Big Springs. A place he'd left five years ago, and had only missed a few things about it.

"Not the wind!" he shouted. "Didn't miss this!" Every part of him was cold. Frozen. Stiff.

He'd missed Gramps. The chance to say hi was the reason he'd been on the westbound train that was stuck in the snow a good two miles behind him. At least he hoped it was two miles behind him because that would mean he only had another mile to go.

Another mile ahead should be the little wooden sign, letting people know they were rolling into the Big Springs depot. The town hadn't been much five years ago, and

Welles wasn't optimistic enough to believe it had grown into some sort of metropolis.

He might not even be optimistic enough to believe he'd already walked two miles in this blinding snow, but he sure hoped that was the case. The bitter cold had seeped all the way into his bones, making it harder and harder to lift his legs high enough to take a step, and his fingers were so burningly cold, holding on to the pole was growing difficult. Any part of his body he could feel was shivering.

The only thing that seemed to be unaffected by the blizzard was his mind, the part that held memories. And dreams. He'd imagined himself stepping off the train at the Big Springs depot in his new three-piece tailored suit— black with a white shirt and sky blue vest—and black boots, completely unscuffed and still shining like brand-new.

The boots were new. Not even a week old, and he'd lost feeling in his toes shortly after leaving the train. He still had on the suit, too, but it was covered with the quilt he'd tied around himself. And his new hat, well, the brim wouldn't still have the steamed curled edges, because he had a woman's knitted scarf tied beneath his chin, holding his hat on and keeping his ears warm.

It wasn't working. His ears probably had more icicles hanging off them than his eyelashes did.

Deep in the midst of feeling sorry for himself, freezing to death as he was, Welles almost missed the sign he'd been hoping to see for miles. He stumbled to a stop, squinting to see through the millions of swirling white flakes of snow. A heated flash of excitement raced through him, but cautious, because he'd learned to be that way. He used the pole to help him take a couple more steps, until he was close enough to wipe away the snow stuck to the flat board with one sock-covered hand.

Big Springs.

He'd made it.

If he had the energy he might have laughed or gave out a

triumphant shout. As it was, it took a good amount of his energy to shake the snow off his hand and turn left. If nothing had changed in the past five years, which he highly doubted, all he had to do was cross the road, which he couldn't see, of course, then he'd be on Gramps's property.

The livery stable, the big barn he'd helped build nearly ten years ago when he'd been fifteen and thought he knew all there was to know about horses and was overly excited to be working with them, would be first. Then, no more than fifty yards from there would be the house.

Warm and cozy and smelling like coffee. Gramps drank pots of coffee. Morning, noon and night.

Welles used the pole, poking it into the snow just as he had while following the tracks. Without the iron rails to keep him walking straight, he could easily get turned around in the wind, end up walking back in the direction he'd just come, or veer off one way or the other. He'd miss the stable if he did that.

As if someone overhead had finally decided he could use a guardian angel, a hole appeared for a split second in the swirling snow. It didn't reveal much, but he saw red. Red. The color of the Big Springs livery barn.

His feet were too cold, too numb, to lift over the snow as he slogged onward, using the pole to pull him forward, shaking harder with every step.

Another sense of euphoria filled him when he stumbled into the stable, but by the time he made it around the building, even shuffling his feet through the snow had become nearly impossible. He fell, several times, while crossing the yard between the livery and the house, and though he wanted to rest, if only for a moment or two, he found the wherewithal to get up, try again. Had to. If he didn't make it, a train full of people wouldn't, either.

The thud on the front porch had Sophie George looking across the table at Chester, who was spooning soup into his mouth with one hand and holding a slice of bread, ready to bite into, in his other hand.

"Did you hear that?" she asked.

Chester swallowed before he nodded. "The wind."

The blizzard had grown stronger all morning. When she'd crossed the yard to the livery after breakfast, there had only been a few flakes, but less than an hour later, she'd barely been able to see the house through the blowing snow. She set her spoon down as another thud sounded. "That was more than the wind."

Chester, who liked the entire world to believe he was a grumpy old man—which he could be at times but she knew the real Chester Carmichael—huffed out a breath as he pushed his chair away from the table the same time she did. The uneven thud of his cane followed her into the front room.

She pulled apart the curtains on the window, not wanting to open the door and let in the cold if not necessary. Frost had collected in the corners, and peering through the glass was like looking at a wall of white. Sophie was still in the midst of trying to see beyond the swirling snow when Chester pulled open the door, letting in a blast of cold air.

"Someone's there!" he shouted.

The wind was doing more than whistling; it was howling and filling the house with snow. Sophie hurried around him. "Who would be out in—" She gasped at the sight of a snow-covered person staggering up the steps and rushed forward. "Hold the door open while I get them inside!"

It wasn't until she and Chester had the man propped against the wall next to the parlor stove and had peeled away the snow-crusted quilt and the thickly knit scarf that was frozen stiff, that Sophie realized who it was.

So did Chester.

"It's Welles," Chester said gravely, taking in his grandson's condition. "Glory be! Why didn't he write to let us know he was coming home?"

Sophie pulled the socks, which were stiff, off Welles's hands, hoping his fingers weren't blue, or black, meaning they'd been frozen beyond repair. "If we don't get him warmed up, he'll freeze to death before we get a chance to find out."

She rubbed Welles's hands, one then the other, between hers, thankful they were red, but she didn't like how icy they were. Her heart was missing every other beat. At one time Welles was the only person in this town she'd considered her friend, until he'd run off with Colleen Sanders, and every penny Chester had to his name. "Go get a quilt while I get his boots off."

His face was just as red as his hands, and Sophie wondered if his eyes were frozen shut. Not even his lashes fluttered as she pulled his boots and socks off. When Chester returned with the quilt, she tucked it around Welles and then stood. "Watch him. I'll get some coffee."

She added a couple of logs to the parlor stove, stirring up the coals so the logs would catch flame, and then went to the kitchen, where she wrung her shaking hands together.

Welles had returned to Big Springs. A part of her wanted to rejoice, but another part of her was too filled with fear. Would he send her packing as soon as he awoke? That was a possibility. She'd known she couldn't live with Chester forever, but over the past four years, an alternative hadn't come about. Options for the daughter of the town's founding madam were few and far between.

Knowing there was no time for pondering right now, she filled a cup with coffee from the pot on the stove and carried it back into the parlor.

"He's been mumbling about a woman and a train," Chester said.

Probably remembering the last time he'd been in town, when he ran off.

Sophie bit her tongue to keep that thought to herself and knelt down. Welles was still shaking, his teeth chattering as she held the cup up to his lips. "Try to take a drink," she encouraged. "It'll warm you up."

She wasn't cold, but shivered as if she was as chilled as Welles when he opened his eyes. They were as blue as she remembered and staring straight at her.

"Soph—?"

"Drink," she said.

His hand wrapped around hers, and he tipped the cup, almost downing all the coffee in one gulp.

She pulled the cup away. "Not so fast. Go slow."

He nodded and pulled the cup closer again and drank the rest of the coffee. Chester was right beside her and switched cups, the empty one for a full one. Sophie helped Welles drink this one, too, much slower.

With a heavy sigh, he leaned his head back against the wall. "Th—thanks."

"What are you doing out in this weather?" Chester asked.

"Train. Stuck. Snow. People. Die."

He was still shivering, his teeth still chattering, and talking seemed to exhaust him, but he planted both hands on the floor, as if to get up.

"Sit still," Chester said at the same time she spoke.

"You can't get up yet." Sophie tucked the quilt around him tighter. "You're still shivering."

"Have to," Welles mumbled. "Train full. Die."

Sophie shivered at the thought. He was right. Anyone stuck out in this weather could freeze to death.

"I'll go get the sheriff," Chester said.

"No." Sophie stood. "You get some more coffee in him. I'll go get the sheriff."

Both men protested, Chester much louder than Welles, but she wasn't listening to either one of them. Even if Chester would have been able to walk across the room without the aid of his cane, he was too old to be out in a blizzard, and Welles was too cold. In the kitchen, she piled on the clothes. The heavy coat she wore doing chores—which had been Welles's when he'd lived here—mittens, a scarf and her tall boots. They were men's, but far more practical for working in the stables than any of the women's styles.

As she walked through the parlor, she told Welles, who was trying to get up but his legs and feet weren't cooperating, "You need to get out of those wet clothes." She then told Chester, "Make him eat some soup. It's still on the stove."

The wind tried to steal her breath before she'd even shut the door behind her. She pulled the scarf up over her face, leaving only her eyes exposed, and made her way down the porch steps. There was no way to know if the sheriff was in his office, and even if he was, he'd need help. Blizzard or not, there was one place men were sure to be.

The Whistle Stop.

It was closer to the livery than the sheriff's office, but she hadn't stepped foot inside the building for four years. Ever since the fate-filled events that had changed her life forever.

Despite what her mother's occupation had been, not a day went by when Sophie didn't miss her. Lola George had been an amazing woman. With quick wit, an infectious laugh and the ability to outsmart the wiliest fox, Lola had made her own way in life. It had been a way that many hadn't approved of, but Sophie had never wanted for anything.

Except for her own life.

That want had started shortly after they'd moved to Big Springs. Up in Wyoming few had taken much notice of the little girl living quietly, yet securely, in the back room of the house on the end of the street. There she'd even had a few friends who didn't care if she was "that girl."

But here, where there had been a few more "respectable" families who had made a point of singling her out, she'd started wishing things were different. That Lola wasn't her mother. By then she'd been twelve, and old enough to understand what took place in the rooms on the second floor while she slept in her comfortably furnished and securely locked back room on the first floor.

The guilt of that, of wishing Lola hadn't been her mother, once again stirred inside Sophie as she trudged through the blinding and freezing snow. Older now, at the ripe old age of nineteen, she understood Lola had simply been making a living for the two of them in the only way she knew how. Furthermore, Sophie had to admit, her life would be very different right now if she hadn't been so stubborn. When she'd turned fifteen and voiced her loathing of her life, Mother had arranged to send her east, to boarding school, to a place where people didn't know who she was, or who Lola was, and wouldn't hold that against her. But she'd refused to go.

Sophie's blind footsteps encountered something so solid she almost fell. Would have if the pole holding up the wooden awning that stretched over the boardwalk hadn't been right there for her to grasp ahold of. The Whistle Stop was the fourth building down. Using the pole, she stepped up onto the boardwalk and then shuffled left, up against the building.

It was like a refuge. Though it was still snowing and blowing, between the building and the awning she was protected a great deal from the elements and could actually see through the blinding whiteout. She was also able to walk faster, which she did, and arrived at the heavy outside doors that covered the swinging batwing doors that were used in the warmer months.

Her hands shook as she reached for the doorknob. The shaking wasn't completely because of the cold, nor was it because of the saloon. It was because the reason she hadn't wanted to leave Big Springs so long ago was the exact reason she was tramping through a blizzard and about to enter the saloon.

Welles Carmichael.

Chapter Two

Welles wasn't certain if it was the coffee, the heat from the parlor stove or the shock of seeing Sophie that warmed him, but he was doing considerably better than he'd been when he'd first opened his eyes and thought he was seeing things.

He'd gotten to his feet a short time ago and walked around the house he'd grown up in, getting himself more coffee and getting the blood flowing throughout his system now that it had thawed out.

"How long has she been living here?" he asked, staring at the bowl of soup Gramps had set down on the table.

Sitting down at the table, Gramps smiled. "Pert-near five years. Sit down and eat. She gets persnickety when it comes to not eating food while it's hot."

Welles glanced at the table that showed his arrival had interrupted their meal. "Why?"

"I suspect 'cause she doesn't like eating cold food," Gramps said while chewing the bite of bread he'd taken. "Don't bother me none. It still tastes good. Yours is hot. I scooped it out of the pot on the stove."

Welles glanced through the parlor toward the door Sophie had left through a short time ago. He hadn't been in any condition to go out there then, but he might be now. She wasn't a lot bigger than she'd been back when she'd bugged him to let her feed and water the horses. Turning back to the table, he picked up the bowl of soup. Drinking it would be faster, and should chase away the last of his chill so he could head back out. "I mean why has Sophie been living here for four years?"

With a shrug of his shoulders that weren't nearly as broad and muscular as they used to be, Gramps said, "Didn't have nowhere to go after her ma died."

"Her ma?" Taken aback, Welles nearly spilled the soup. "Lola George is dead?"

"Yep. She tried stopping some fella from shooting up the saloon and got shot."

"When?"

"Pert-near five years ago," Gramps said. "Want some bread?"

Welles shook his head and lifted the bowl to his lips. Lola George had run an enterprising business. Although some folks had looked down on the saloon owner, others had appreciated her business, and no one ever said no to the generous donations she'd made to every worthwhile cause in Big Springs.

He finished the soup, which had been so tasty he felt a bit guilty about drinking it down so quickly rather than using a spoon. "Why didn't Sophie have anywhere to go? Lola had to have plenty of money when she died. Money Sophie could have used..." He let his voice trail off, not sure what a young girl would have done, rather than move in with an old man. He was also looking for his boots.

"Lola did," Gramps said, "but James Hooper, you remember him, he was the bartender, he knew the combination to the safe and cleaned it out while everyone was at the funeral."

That was too close for comfort. So close it made Welles's spine stiffen. He hadn't stolen, but Colleen had. After she'd admitted whom she had stolen from, they'd parted ways, but the money was long gone. "Did they catch him?" Welles asked, spying his boots near the stove.

"No." Once again Gramps shrugged his shrinking shoulders. "Eventually, word of him reached town. His corpse, that is. In a mortuary out in California."

Not as concerned about James Hooper as he was Sophie, Welles asked, "What about the building? Did Sophie sell that?"

"Couldn't. Little gal didn't have any way to make the payments. She was just a girl. Bank took it and sold it to Hector Franklin. He calls it the Whistle Stop now."

A good splattering of anger hit Welles. At both Sophie's misfortunes and the sorry state of his boots. They were soaked clear through. He sat down in the rocking chair to pull them on anyway. "Wasn't anyone willing to help her make the payments?"

"No use," Gramps said from the dining room. "There wasn't anything she could have done with the building."

Welles was growing more frustrated by the minute. From several things. The way the town had treated Sophie, the way his boots appeared to have shrunk and thinking about Sophie trudging through the blizzard. "There had to have been something."

Gramps walked into the parlor. "You're not going anywhere."

The boot finally slipped on. Cold and wet, it made his foot hurt worse. Still, he grabbed the other one. He didn't have a choice. "It's bad out there. I should never have let Sophie go alone."

"She's made of tough stuff," Gramps said. "Has had to be. You can't go back out there. Less than ten minutes ago you were froze stiff."

"Sophie will be, too, if I don't get out there." Welles cursed as the other boot finally slipped on. He'd never known feet could hurt so bad. Glancing at the quilt that was leaving a puddle on the floor, he asked, "Do you have a coat I can borrow?"

Gramps mumbled something about bullheaded people before saying, "Yes. I have boots, too. Take those good-for-nothing ones off. I got some dry socks, too." Never one to mince words, Gramps added, "Come into the bedroom. Can't have you stripping naked in the parlor."

Welles still had some common sense and quickly pulled
the boots off, as well as the wet socks. Dry clothes would
take him a lot farther in the storm than wet ones. Leaving
his things by the woodstove, he quickly crossed the parlor
to the bedroom Gramps had entered. The floor was cold,
but he reminded himself to be thankful that Gramps still
used the downstairs room. While he'd lived here, he'd had
the entire upstairs to himself. Three bedrooms. Not that
he'd used the other two overly much. Mainly only when it
had been too long between washing the sheets on his bed.
He'd soon discovered the downside to that. He'd ended up
washing three sets of sheets instead of one.

Gramps was tossing clothes onto the bed, including a
set of long johns that were sure to be too short, but warm
nonetheless.

Welles started taking off his once new suit while his
grandfather continued pulling things out of his dresser
drawers. He held the shivers at bay while draping his wet
things over the chair and then putting on the ones on the
bed. They were too short, but dry, which instantly made
him warmer.

His mind was still on Sophie. "Why'd she move in with
you?"

"Seemed the logical choice," Gramps answered. "She
was already working at the livery."

"Why?"

"Because I needed the help."

Having sat down to put on the socks, Welles glanced
up. He couldn't say there was anger in his grandfather's
eyes, but there was disappointment. A splattering of sadness washed over Welles. "Gramps, I—"

"Said it all in your letters." His grandfather walked out
of the room.

Welles tugged on the other sock and grabbed both boots
off the floor while following his grandfather back into the
parlor. His letters hadn't said anything. They'd held money

and short notes stating he hoped all was going well. Which, evidently, they hadn't been. "What happened to your leg?" He'd noticed the limp Gramps walked with and the use of the cane, but had held back asking.

"Fell out of the loft. Old bones don't heal as well as young ones."

"Why didn't you tell me?"

"Didn't know where you were." Gramps shrugged. "Nothing you could have done anyway."

Welles was about to say he could have come home, would have, when a knock sounded and the front door opened at the same time.

A man, tall and snow-covered, walked in and shut the door with a heavy thud.

Instantly concerned, Welles asked, "Where's Sophie?"

"You must be Welles," the man said, turning back around. "I've heard about you. I'm Wade Kaplan, but most folks just call me Sheriff. Sophie's hitching up a team to the sleigh. Tell me where the train is."

"Welles hadn't even let Chester know he was coming home?" Jud Paxton asked while helping her put the harnesses on the team of big buckskin horses.

"No." Sophie's nerves were still strung too tight for conversation, and even if they weren't, she didn't have any answers. Not as to why Welles decided to show up in the middle of a blizzard. That was what Jud wanted to know. He and Welles had been friends. Welles had been friends with everyone, nice to everyone. Which is exactly why she shouldn't hold much credence in the fact he'd been nice to her when she used to sneak out of the saloon and spend her afternoons with the horses at the livery. She'd been just a kid looking for a place to belong, and he'd taken pity on her.

"Ready?" she asked.

Jud nodded. "I'll get the door so you can lead them out."

Hoping Sawyer Williams and J. T. Jones had been able to find the sleigh and dig it out, Sophie hunched her chin into her scarf as she led the horses into the blustery wind.

She wasn't sure what she recognized first, Chester's coat, or the fact that Chester wasn't wearing it. "You can't go back out in this."

"I have to," Welles shouted over the whistling wind while grabbing the reins in her hand. "There are people who are counting on me coming back."

"The sheriff has volunteers to help him," she said, not releasing the reins.

"And I appreciate each one of them," Welles said. "You get inside. You have to be frozen by now."

"Not as frozen as you," she retorted.

"We're all going to be frozen by the time you two stop arguing," Jud said, tugging the reins hard. "Good seeing you, Welles."

"Jud? Is that you?" Welles asked.

"Yup, under all these clothes is the one and only Jud Paxton."

They were yelling to be heard, but she could still hear the smiles in their voices, the happiness at seeing each other. Not paying close enough attention, Sophie had to jump back as the two started leading the horses forward. Glad she'd kept her footing, she started following alongside the team.

"Get in the house, Sophie," Welles shouted.

"I'll make sure the team is hitched," she replied.

"I know how to hitch horses to a sleigh," Welles said. "And so does Jud. Go on! Get in the house!"

There was nothing for her to dispute. The sleigh had been dug out, he and Jud were already hitching the horses to it and J.T. had already shut the livery stable door. For some reason she felt as if she needed to have the last word. "Don't work those horses too hard in this cold!"

"We won't!" Welles shouted above the wind that seemed

as if it was blowing even harder now than before. "Get inside!"

"I'm going," she muttered. There was nothing for her to do out here. With Welles here, there wouldn't be anything for her to do at the livery, period. Fighting the still-accumulating snow with every step as much as she was fighting to keep her mind from going on its own journey, she made it to the house, and was on the porch when the jingle of harnesses filtered through the wind. Her first instinct was to turn around, to watch the sleigh full of men leave, but she wouldn't be able to see anything, so she stomped as much snow off her boots as possible and then reached for the doorknob.

"Get in here, girl," Chester said, pulling the door open as she turned the knob. "You have to be as frozen as Welles was."

She gave her boots one last stomp and then stepped inside the house. "I wasn't outside that long."

"It doesn't take long," Chester insisted. "I shouldn't have let you go out there."

Removing her scarf, she tossed it over the back of a nearby chair. "You should have told Welles that. He's the one who shouldn't be out there again." Her mittens landed on the chair next. She didn't want to be this worried about Welles, but couldn't help it, either. "There's no way he could have warmed up that quickly. He'll get cold twice as fast this time."

"I told him that, but he insisted there are people waiting on him," Chester said.

"Jud, J.T. and Sawyer volunteered to go with Sheriff Kaplan. They didn't need Welles." She draped her coat over the back of the chair and then pushed aside her mittens to sit down and take off her boots. "All they have to do is follow the train tracks."

"Welles told Kaplan there are half a dozen people on the train," Chester said. "Not counting the train workers."

"That's what Frank guessed."

"You went to the depot?"

She stood to gather up her wet clothes. "No, Frank was at the saloon."

"The saloon?"

Carrying everything into the kitchen, she said, "Yes. It was closer than the sheriff's office. Several men had gathered there to wait out the storm. Even Jud."

"Jud?" Chester, close on her heels, sounded stunned.

"Yes, Jud. No one was looking to get a gun repaired today."

"Does Suzanne know?"

To the surprise of many, Jud and Suzanne had been married three years ago, and she'd turned Jud, who many thought was on his way to becoming a gunslinger, if he hadn't already been one, into a respectable citizen. "Frank said he'd stop by and tell her." Telling Chester everything would slow down his questions, so she continued, "Frank had arrived at the saloon right before I did, looking for the sheriff. He'd tried to send a wire to Kansas, to find out if the train had left on time or was held up by a storm there." Frank Green had been the depot agent since the first train had rolled into the Big Springs depot over a dozen years before. "The lines must have blown down because he couldn't get through, and when the train was well over two hours late, he figured something had happened."

"Welles said a tree fell over the tracks, and even if they could have gotten it moved, the train wouldn't have been able to take off again because they were down in the gulley, had just crossed the Snake River Bridge."

Sophie nodded, even though she didn't know the gulley or the bridge. She'd never been that far west of town. "Frank said he'd let Wes Merlin know to expect guests at the hotel, too." With her wet garments hanging to dry, Sophie went to the stove to add a log to the fire. "And that he'd get word to Doc Russell in case anyone needs him."

"That woman and baby might. Especially the baby," Chester said.

Something flickered inside Sophie. Ignoring it, she crossed the room to clear the lunch dishes off the table. "What woman and baby?"

"The one Welles was mumbling about when he first got here." Chester frowned. "I sure hope he didn't go and have a baby with that woman he ran off with. I was hoping he was done with her."

The dishes rattled in Sophie's hands. She set them down and balled her hands into fists to stop the trembling. Although Chester spoke of Welles often, that was the first time he'd mentioned Colleen. Mentioned knowing that Welles had indeed run off with her rather than going to buy horses. Unable to think of a reply, unable to think about the possibility of Welles still being with Colleen, Sophie spun around and headed for the stairs leading to the second floor.

"Where you going?"

Swallowing against the burning in her throat, she said, "To change."

There was no reason for her to care if Welles had married Colleen or not. The fact he was back was enough to change her life. Make her an orphan again. It wasn't as if Chester had adopted her, but after living with him for over four years, she'd come to look at him as family. The one thing she'd always wanted. Now she'd lose the only one she had all over again.

In her room she closed the door and leaned back against it. After several deep breaths, she admitted there was more to it than that.

The hope of someday marrying Welles, of having a family with him, had been her dream as a little girl. One she'd never been able to let go of completely. The first time she'd seen him working with one of the horses in the livery corral, she'd fallen in love. With him and horses.

She'd told herself that had changed when she'd heard about him running off with Colleen and stealing all of Chester's money. Now she had to prove it. And make sure it didn't happen again. The stealing and loving.

Chapter Three

This trip to and from the train went a lot faster than his first one. The hay on the sleigh made it more comfortable and warmer, too. He and Jud used some of the time traveling to the train to brush the snow off the hay and stir the dry stalks to the top. They'd also spent time catching up. Jud was married. Welles couldn't completely wrap his thoughts around that, partially because his mind was on Sophie, as it had been since he'd discovered her in the house. He couldn't help but wonder why she wasn't married. She was so pretty with those unique light blue eyes. He'd never seen another pair like them, and admitted they were even more striking than he remembered. She'd grown up, too.

He couldn't get his mind around the fact she lived with Gramps, either. Or that the town had forsaken Sophie the way they had. If not for Lola, and her generous donations, the school building, which also doubled as the church, would never have been built. Had everyone forgotten that? Other questions filled his mind all the way to the train and again on the way back.

The passengers and train workers had been glad to see them, and he was glad they were all still fine, and now bundled beneath the blankets he'd taken from his grandfather's house. The blizzard hadn't let up, and Welles was concerned about the horses. They were working up a sweat pulling the heavy load through the snow that was up to their knees. The pair of buckskins were a good-looking team of workhorses, not saddle ones, and he wondered where his grandfather had acquired them. Another question.

"Not much farther now!" the sheriff shouted.

"Go straight to the hotel," Welles shouted in return. "Get these folks inside." The mother had her baby tucked beneath the covers with her, but he was still worried about the little guy. Before the storm had hit, the baby had been giggling and cooing at anyone who'd looked his way. They, that mother and baby, were the reason he'd walked through the blizzard to get help. The other four passengers were men, and could have survived being out in the cold. For a time. The way this storm was still raging, they'd all be lucky to make it back to town.

Any amount of sun that had been filtering through the clouds and snow faded fast, and by the time they rolled into town, the darkness made seeing even more difficult. As the horses drew up next to the hotel, Welles jumped over the side of the wagon and reached up to take the swaddled baby while Jud helped the woman down.

"Thank you," she said breathlessly. "Thank you for coming back for us."

Welles handed her the baby. "Get inside the hotel. The doc should be there. Have him check you for frostbite."

"I will. Thank you again," she said, already hurrying toward the door being held open.

"I'll help you get the horses to the stable," Jud said.

The wind still had them all shouting at each other. "No. You get home to your wife. I'll see you when this storm blows over!" Welles climbed into the driver's seat and released the brake, giving the horses the freedom to move forward on their own. They'd find the stables by intuition faster than he would in this darkness.

His intuition was good, too, and about the same moment he had the urge to pull back on the reins, a door opened and the inside of the livery appeared. So did Sophie.

"Pull all the way in," she shouted. "There's room for the sleigh."

There was room; the barn was big, and neat and clean.

That wasn't what he was concerned about. "What are you doing out here?" His shout echoed off the walls and high ceiling because he let it out about the same time she shut the door. Setting the brake, he jumped down. "And what are you wearing?"

"Your old clothes," she said while looking into the sleigh bed.

They were his clothes, and he was jealous of them. With her cheeks all rosy red, her long hair sticking out from beneath the brim of the hat, and those britches hugging her hips and legs, she was more becoming than any woman he'd ever seen.

"Where are the passengers?"

Stepping over to unhitch the harness yoke, he answered, "At the hotel."

A frown formed and made tiny wrinkles between her dark brows. "All of them? Eve—even the woman and baby?"

"Yes, the doctor is there to check everyone for frostbite."

"Oh."

She set into unharnessing the team, and his intuition kicked in again, sensing something he could only describe as sadness or disappointment coming from her. Assuming it could only be because of the passengers, he said, "There wasn't room for all of them at the house. They'll be more comfortable at the hotel."

Her gaze met his briefly as she lugged the heavy collar off one horse. He couldn't decipher if there was doubt in her eyes or confusion. She'd turned away too fast. He couldn't figure why she'd want a house full of strangers, either. That wasn't the Sophie he knew. She hadn't liked strangers. Leastwise not all of the ones that kept the bat doors of the saloon swinging while she'd lived there.

That had been five years ago, and people change. He had during that time.

He pulled the collar off the other horse, recalling how vigilant Lola George had been about those strangers getting anywhere near her daughter. Sophie's bedroom had been on the far side of the room behind the bar, and both doors had been guarded. The one leading into the back room always had someone stationed near it, and the one leading into Sophie's room had an iron door with a lock that rivaled the ones at the jail.

He knew for certain how strong that door had been because he'd helped the blacksmith, Bronco Larson, install it shortly after Lola and Sophie had moved to town. That summer was when Sophie started hanging around the livery. School wasn't in session and she'd been bored staying in that little room all day. Lola had asked Gramps if it was all right, and Gramps had asked him.

It wasn't as if he'd been able to say no. He'd felt sorry for Sophie. Though her room held the finest furniture of any room in town, and she'd had dresses and toys that made the other girls jealous, she'd had a lonely little life.

Knowing that, and being able to relate since he'd lived alone with Gramps since his parents had died when he'd only been three, he'd given her a few small jobs, brushing the horses or filling their grain bins, all of which she completed perfectly. She'd been good company, too, full of the latest gossip that a child her age shouldn't have known. He'd enjoyed her daily visits. Until that final summer—somewhere throughout the winter she'd gone from a girl to a young woman—and he realized he was looking forward to her visits more than he should. He was five years older than she was. She'd only been fourteen, he nineteen, and liking her too much had started to worry him.

Which was part of the reason he'd listened to Colleen and went south instead of north. He was supposed to have gone to buy horses; instead he'd ended up at the gaming tables in New Orleans.

Switching his train of thought while leading one of the big horses into their stall, he said, "These are some fine horses."

"Yes, they are," she replied, leading the other one into its stall. "I named them Ben and Bob. B and B for short. I hope you don't mind."

Both big horses, B and B were in between them, making it impossible for him to see her. "Why would I mind?"

She walked around the back end of the horses. The wrinkles between her brows were back, as was her doubtful and confused look. "They're your horses." She grabbed two old saddle blankets and tossed one his way while walking back to the other horse. "They're the first horses you had delivered after you left. Don't you remember?"

While using the blanket to dry off the horse, he contemplated his answer. After arriving in New Orleans, which is where he'd discovered Colleen had stolen a goodly sum of money before leaving Big Springs and that the money she'd stolen had been his grandfather's, finding a way to pay his grandfather back became his mission.

He'd done that at the gaming tables. Lady luck seemed to become his best friend. That was where these horses had come from, and several others. Some men didn't know when to stop, and wouldn't until they'd lost everything they owned.

"I'd acquired these two unseen," he finally said.

Her silence had to be accompanied by another one of those wrinkled brow looks.

He was right. It was there as she poked her head around the horse he was still drying.

"Unseen?" She shook her head. "No one buys a horse unseen, especially you."

She would know that about him. It was the other things about him he hadn't wanted her to know. Then and now. He hadn't wanted anyone to know. But Lola had. Colleen had told him so. Shrugging his shoulders, he went back to drying off the horse. "I trusted him."

Sophie hadn't been able to believe most everything he'd said since the moment he jumped out of the sleigh, and this one wasn't believable, either. He was a stickler when it came to horses, those he bought, sold and rented out. Then again, maybe she'd never have known him as well as she'd imagined, because five years ago she'd never have believed he'd run off with a dance-hall girl and his grandfather's money. But he had. Run off with Colleen and every last dime Chester had at the time.

She'd been devastated by that. By his absence. He'd been the only thing she'd liked about this town, and it didn't get any better after he left. In fact, it became worse. If it wasn't for Chester, she had no idea what she would have done.

"I was sorry to hear about your mother."

Sophie had to draw in a breath before she could answer. Few people made any form of reference to the death of her mother. Not then or now. She figured they thought reminding her of who her mother had been would sully them, and she had come to accept that. "Thank you."

"I wish I would have known sooner."

Hanging the wet saddle blanket she'd used to dry off Bob over the rail, she asked, "Why?"

"Because I could have…"

His silence said he was trying to come up with an answer, but there wasn't one. She knew that. "There wasn't anything anyone could have done."

"I could have sent you some money or something," he said.

She withheld a sigh. "For what?"

"Whatever you needed it for. To move somewhere else. Or, well, I don't know, just whatever."

The butterflies taking flight in her stomach said he'd stepped up beside her, and all the swallowing in the world wouldn't settle those fluttering wings inside her. Closing her eyes didn't help, either. That might have made breathing more difficult than those silly butterflies.

She opened her eyes and twisted in the opposite direction, walking toward the grain bin to give B and B each a can full.

He followed. "I'll feed them. You go inside."

Anger rose up inside her. She'd been feeding the horses since he'd left, and liked it. The horses didn't mind who her mother had been. "Why are you here?" She filled both cans at the same time and moved toward the horses. "After five years, why do you just show up? In the middle of a snowstorm?"

He took one of the cans. "I didn't plan to arrive in the middle of snowstorm. I just wanted to see Gramps. It's been five years."

She knew exactly how long it had been, and knew history wouldn't repeat itself. Not for her or Chester because she wouldn't let it.

They both emptied their cans into the feed troughs.

"Put out that lantern. I'll get the other one," he said while taking the empty can from her.

Sophie took down the lantern hanging on the post, extinguished it and hung it back up, keeping one eye on Welles the entire time. She should be glad he was home. For Chester's sake. He wanted Welles here. Talked about it all the time. Despite his orneriness at times, she had come to care about Chester almost as if he was her grandfather, and knew he wasn't getting any younger. Which meant she had to be on guard for both of them. Chester and herself. If the rumors she heard were true, Welles couldn't be trusted. No gambler could be. Shortly after she'd been born, her father had decided he'd rather gamble away his money than take care of his wife and child, and had left. Never to be seen again.

"Ready?"

"Yes." She pulled on her mittens while walking around the sleigh. He grabbed a traveling bag out of the bed, blew out the last lantern and met her at the door.

The big door snagged on the snow as they pushed, but

it opened wide enough for them both to squeeze out. The snow was still falling, the wind still blowing, leaving drifts for them to trudge through.

She tucked her chin into her coat collar as they moved forward. Speaking was impossible. Not that she had anything to say. There were a dozen questions swarming her mind, but she wasn't certain she wanted to know the answers to most of them.

He hooked his arm through hers and said something, but the wind made it impossible to hear as he pulled her forward at a quicker pace. The darkness and blowing snow made it impossible to see. Although she'd made the trek from the livery to the house and back again a million times over, the blizzard made the familiar pathway confusing. By the time they reached the steps to the house, Sophie was so turned around, she was certain she'd never have made the short distance by herself.

Chester pulled the door open as soon as they stepped onto the porch.

"I was starting to worry about you two," he said.

"So was I," Welles said. "I would never have thought I'd get lost between the house and the stable."

"You didn't get lost," Sophie said while pulling off her mittens. "You brought us right to the door."

"The front door." He pulled off his hat and gloves. "I was aiming for the back one."

His grin, which was as mischievous as she remembered, made her heart flutter. He used to do that all the time. Make her heart flutter. Back then he'd made her smile, too, especially on days when she'd thought there was nothing to smile about.

"Best get those wet coats off before you start dripping on the floor," Chester said. "I have a pot of coffee on the stove."

"You always have a pot of coffee on the stove," Welles said. Then glancing at her, he asked, "That hasn't changed, has it?"

Sophie bit her lips together as she shook her head. The glimmer in Welles's eyes had her remembering happy days. Happy times. Something she hadn't allowed herself to do in a long time.

Welles never took his eyes off her as he removed his coat. "Some things never change."

The air stuck in her lungs as her heart skipped a beat. He looked older, more mature than before, and if anything, that increased his handsomeness. His eyes were as dark brown as Chester's coffee, and thickly lashed, and like always, had a slight squint as if they were hiding a deep, dark secret that he'd never reveal. "No, some things don't."

"I'll take your coat to the kitchen," he said.

Regaining an iota of her senses, she shook her head at the hand he held out. "That's all right. I got it." Gathering all of her wet things, she carried them into the kitchen and hung them near the stove, leaving hooks open for him to do the same. Then she sat in the chair, removed the heavy boots she used for barn work and replaced them with the shoes she wore around the house.

She should go change her clothes, too, but needed to check the pot roast she'd put in the oven. Thinking there would be others for supper, she'd made plenty. Far more than the three of them would eat.

"Sit down, Welles," Chester said. "Tell me about all the places you've been."

Welles sat, and if she'd been thinking about changing out of his old clothes and into one of her dresses, she wasn't now. She wouldn't miss hearing what he had to say for all the clothes in the world.

Chapter Four

Lying in the bed that was familiar in some ways, foreign in others, a good portion of guilt sat heavy and thick inside Welles. Gramps had been fishing for more information, had even laid out opportunities for him to lay claim that Colleen had been the one to steal the money, not him. He hadn't been able to take those opportunities for a couple reasons. Good reasons. The main one had been standing at the stove, all ears.

Colleen had told him that Lola had figured out he was more interested in Sophie, the young girl that she'd been back then, than a man his age should have been. He'd tried not to be, and had thought he'd made sure to never let on just how interested he'd been. Colleen said she'd never told anyone about Lola's concerns. As far as he knew, she hadn't. Not even after they'd left town, and he had to honor that. She'd kept his secret, so he'd keep hers. He'd paid back every penny she'd taken tenfold, and would continue to. That would have to be enough. Letting people, including Gramps and Sophie, believe he'd been the one to steal the money was the price he had to pay.

No matter how much it bothered him to have anyone believing he was a thief.

Much like his arrival, his departure hadn't worked out how it was supposed to. Sophie had been growing up, and not only had she still been too young for him, he'd known if Lola ever sensed his growing attraction, she'd have put a stop to Sophie visiting the livery. That would have crushed Sophie. She'd loved the horses, everything about them, and taking care of them had been her only fun. Knowing that, he'd suggested that he should take a trip up to Wyoming to buy horses. The livery business had been good, but they'd been doing more than renting out horses and buggies. They'd been selling them, and folks for miles around had come to depend on him and Gramps to have quality animals.

Gramps had readily agreed, and had given him a good amount of money to buy a dozen mounts. A nineteen-year-old with more money than sense proved to be just what it was. A disaster about to happen.

That was what had happened. A disaster. He'd gone to the saloon the night before, and did more boasting than he should have, and the next morning, feeling more than a bit under the weather, he'd saddled up and headed out of town. In less than three miles of traveling, he'd come across Colleen. She'd had one of the horses from the livery. One, due to his fog-filled head, he hadn't even noticed had been missing.

She'd told him about Lola, and how she was looking into sending Sophie east, to a boarding school, mainly to get her away from him. There had been more to it than that, but needless to say, they'd headed south, he and Colleen. He'd known it had been wrong, that he should have at least told Gramps, but his mind had been on Sophie, and he hoped, if he was gone, Lola wouldn't send her away.

Shortly after they hit New Orleans, he'd discovered Colleen had stolen more than a horse from Gramps. While boasting about his upcoming journey in the saloon, Colleen had questioned him on how he could have enough money to buy a dozen horses. His boasting had grown then, and in his state of mind that evening, he'd thought his secret would be safe with her. His secret about how Gramps kept a fair sum of money hidden in the hayloft.

Yes, he'd been an idiot, and had been paying for it ever since. On more than one account. It had taken a while to convince himself he liked the life of a gambler, and even longer to accept it was his only choice.

The wind was still making the windows rattle, and it had taken half the night, but the chill that walking to town yesterday had set in his bones was gone. He'd never been that cold, for that long, and never wanted to be again. However, there was work to be done, and he best get to it. As he tossed aside the covers, he grinned. He'd missed the sense of satisfaction that comes from taking care of something, someone, other than one's self, and was looking forward to heading out to the barn, saying good morning to the stock.

Layering on the clothes Gramps had loaned him yesterday and a few of his own, Welles made his way downstairs and out the back door. He couldn't remember the last time he'd risen before the sun—there had been plenty of times in the past five years when he'd been climbing into bed rather than out of it as the sun rose—but it felt good. Even the icy-cold air felt good.

Snow was no longer falling, but the wind was still blowing. He had to plow through waist-deep drifts on his way to the barn, but the good-morning nickers from the horses when he arrived in the barn was worth every step.

Call him crazy, but even the smell made him smile. While feeding, watering, checking over and cleaning up after all dozen horses in the barn, Welles started wondering why he hadn't returned sooner until the door opened and she walked in.

"What are you doing?"

The accusation in her voice and eyes was as strong as it had been last night when she'd asked why he'd shown up in the middle of a snowstorm, and much like last night, her nearness stirred things inside him that had no business being stirred.

"The morning chores," he answered.

"I do the morning chores." She looked around while gnawing on her bottom lip.

"They're all done."

She took a final glance around before asking, "How long

have you been out here?" He shrugged and held up the shovel in his hand. "Awhile. I was just heading out to start shoveling a pathway to the house."

The pinch of her lips said she wasn't impressed. "The horses will need to be let out into the corral. They'll get stiff standing in the stalls too long."

"I know, but they'll be fine for a few more hours." He carried the shovel to the door. "After I shovel a path to the house, I'll inspect the corral for ice. Don't want one of them slipping and breaking a leg."

"There shouldn't be any ice in the corral."

He stopped in front of her. "There could be. If the ground was warm enough, the snow could have melted before it started to stick, and then froze. That's why I'm shoveling a path to the house first, to see what the ground is like."

She was smart, and saw the logic in his answer, but she wasn't any more impressed; with him, that is. After a final glance around, she must have been satisfied to some degree, because she walked toward the door. He got there first and pushed it open for her, which didn't impress her, either.

"Breakfast will be ready shortly," she said without looking toward him.

"Thanks." He took a moment to glance at the sky, which had turned gray and ominous enough to be brewing up another bout of snow, before he scooped up a shovel full of snow and tossed it aside. "I'll be in as soon as I shovel a pathway."

She stood there for a moment, then started walking toward the house. "There's coffee ready now if you want some."

"I'll wait, but thanks."

He tried not to watch her walk away. Not only did he fail at that, he once again felt a bout of jealousy over his old clothes. The britches, the coat, the boots. Even the hat. None of them had looked that good on him. Not that he'd expected them to. He hadn't expected to be this drawn to her all over again. He had thought a lot about her over the years, hoping Lola hadn't sent her back east like she had wanted. He'd wondered about that, too, if she had gone and stayed back east, and right now he wondered about what Lola would think about how her daughter was dressed. How she was working in the livery and living with Gramps. That wasn't the life Lola had said Sophie would have. She'd wanted the best for her daughter. A life that was as opposite as the one she'd had as possible. A life he couldn't give her. He hadn't even been here when Gramps needed him, let alone a wife and family.

Those thoughts hung with him while he shoveled, and were still there when he entered the house that smelled of coffee and bacon. Sophie was now wearing a dress, and apron, and had her hair tied at the nape of her neck with a single blue ribbon. The locks formed long chestnut curlicues as they fell down her back.

"Take your coat off, boy, and come sit down so we eat while it's hot," Gramps said from his chair at the table. "That meal last night should have told you what a good cook Sophie-girl is."

"It did," Welles answered while taking off his coat. "The food smells as delicious this morning as last night's tasted."

"Well, quit lollygagging around and get over here," Gramps said as Sophie set a platter of pancakes on the table. "Everything's ready to eat and I'm hungry. Haven't eaten since yesterday."

Gramps made it sound like yesterday had been twenty-four hours ago rather than eight, but there was nothing unusual about that.

Welles arrived at the table in time to pull Sophie's chair out. She frowned, but didn't say anything as she sat and watched him walk around the table to sit across from her. Gramps was already filling his plate, handing over a platter of perfectly fried eggs.

Little was said while they ate, which was also not uncommon for Gramps. His meals had always been top priority. He had never been overly fussy about what he ate, as long as he ate, and ate his fill. Preferably without distraction.

Welles, on the other hand, preferred a bit of conversation. "This is delicious, Sophie," he said, nodding when she looked up. The curve of her lips was the closest to a smile he'd seen since arriving. "Thank you. And you've done a great job with the livery. Everything is in tip-top shape. Those are some good-looking and well-cared-for horses out there."

"Did you expect anything different?" Gramps asked before saying, "Pass me some more flapjacks, will you, girl?"

Her hint of a smile fell as she picked up the platter and handed it toward Gramps.

Holding down a flash of irritation, Welles said, "No, I didn't expect any different. I was merely complimenting Sophie on the meal and her skills at taking care of the animals."

"She's a natural," Gramps said. "Like you were."

This time it was a hint of guilt he squashed before Welles said, "I'm happy she's been here to help you." After swallowing the last bite of food on his plate, he added, "And will continue to be."

"Where are you going?" Gramps asked.

"To shovel the corral. The horses need to stretch their legs."

"I don't mean right now. Aren't you here to stay?"

Sophie's lungs started to burn, but she didn't dare let her breath out until she heard Welles's answer. She wasn't sure what she wanted that answer to be. If he said he wasn't staying, she wouldn't need to leave, but Chester would be disappointed. He wanted Welles here. Had for years. And Welles should be here, taking care of Chester, not her.

Welles was already at the door and shrugging into his

coat when he said, "It'll be a day or two before we'll be able to break the train loose from the tracks."

As the hair at the base of her neck quivered, Sophie shifted slightly to look at Chester, whose gray brows were knitted together. A moment later the door shut.

"Well, that answers it, doesn't it?" Chester said.

While she questioned what she'd missed, Chester asked, "You see that woman on the train? The one with the baby?"

"No. Why?"

"Just wondering." Chester grabbed his coffee cup with one hand and his cane with the other. "I have a bridle to finish for Sheriff Kaplan."

Sophie's insides were doing all sorts of things as she watched him walk into the front room, where he'd moved his leather working tools and table to when the weather started turning too cool for him to work on the front porch. Colleen. If that was who the woman from the train was, it would explain why Welles hadn't brought her to the house, knowing Chester may not be overly friendly to her.

The entire time she cleaned the kitchen, Sophie's mind twisted and turned. Although Colleen had left town the same time as Welles had, no one had thought the two had left together, except somehow, her mother had known, and told Chester. In all the years since, he'd never made mention of that to anyone, including her, and she never told anyone, either, hoping it hadn't been true. But it was.

Her curiosity, and concern, grew as she finished the morning chores, to the point she had to know. After bundling up to ward off as much of the wind as possible, she walked into the front room. "I'm going to the mercantile for a few things. Do you need anything?"

"How's the coffee supply?"

That was the only thing he ever asked about. "I'll pick some up."

"Hurry back. I don't like how that sky looks."

Sophie nodded and hurried out the door, instantly wishing she'd put on the heavy coat she used for chores rather than the woman's coat she wore for shopping trips. It had been her mother's and a lovely shade of blue. However, made more for its stylish appeal, the blue coat wasn't overly warm, especially as today's wind was as bitter as it had been during yesterday's blizzard.

After purchasing a few items, which took longer than it should have because news travels fast and Mrs. Hodgkin wanted to know if Welles had truly been the one who had walked to town and saved all those on the train, Sophie walked next door to the hotel.

Wes Merlin was as tall as most doorways and didn't have a single hair on his head, but he was always smiling, including when Sophie walked into the hotel.

"Good morning, Sophie," he greeted from behind his tall front desk. "What are you doing out and about so early this morning?"

"Good morning, Mr. Merlin," she replied, closing the heavy door. "I had some shopping to do and thought I'd stop to check on the passengers. See if they need anything."

"They're all doing fine," he said, "thanks to Welles."

"That's good to hear," she said, wondering how to bring up the subject of the woman and baby.

Gesturing toward the arched doorway that led to the dining room, Wes said, "Most are having their breakfast. All except the woman. She was down for water earlier and accepted a cup of tea, but didn't eat anything, even though I assured her it was on the house. I'll ask Martha to go see to her after she's done cooking breakfast for the others."

Although Martha was Wes's sister, she wasn't nearly as friendly or kind as he was. She might be to others, but Sophie had never seen it. "Would you mind if I went and checked on the woman?"

Wes's smile grew. "Would you? She hardly ate anything last night. She's in room six."

"Thank you," Sophie said, moving toward the stairway.

She was nervous, perhaps more nervous than she'd been in a long time. Or ever. Would Colleen recognize her? Remember her? Be irritated that she was living at Chester's? There was a chance it wasn't Colleen, but in some ways that was even more nerve-racking. Whoever this woman was, Welles had walked over three miles in a blinding blizzard to help her.

By the time she arrived at the door, Sophie's stomach was churning at the idea of meeting the woman Welles must be in love with. There was no reason the idea should bother her as much as it did, but it did.

Drawing a deep breath, she knocked on the door and prepared herself by holding her breath and tightening every muscle. When a petite blonde woman with cautious blue eyes answered the door, Sophie didn't know if she should be relieved, or worried.

Chapter Five

The snow was piling up again. He was either getting used to it, or spending a few hours with Jud and Suzanne had brightened his day so much the weather no longer bothered Welles. He tromped through the snow, thinking more about getting back to the house and enjoying lunch with Sophie and Gramps than the snow or the wind. He wasn't even wondering what Sophie may have made for lunch.

Unlike Gramps, he'd never worried overly much about eating, but had to admit, the meal last night and this morning had been tasty. He'd eaten in some of the finest restaurants in some of the largest cities west of the Mississippi these past few years, but there was something about a home-cooked meal and sitting around the table with family that a restaurant, no matter how fancy or expensive, couldn't compare with.

He hadn't realized how much he'd missed that until visiting with Jud and Suzanne. She'd invited him to stay for lunch at their place, and the house had smelled wonderful from the bread she'd pulled out of the oven while they'd been visiting, but he'd declined. Not only would Gramps expect him home, that was also where he wanted to eat.

Visiting with Jud and watching the couple interact, laughing and teasing each other, and talking about the baby that would arrive within a couple of months, had him wondering if there were other things he was missing. Things he'd never had, or could remember having.

It had been just him and Gramps. Both his parents had died when he'd been so young he hardly remembered them, but after seeing how happy Jud was—the last person he'd have expected to be married, especially to Suzanne, a preacher's daughter—Welles was thinking about his future. He'd always known there was more to life than the gambling he'd taken up the past few years. An occupation that had treated him very well, and he'd come to the conclusion he couldn't think about what *more* meant. Or was. He'd made his choice.

That might change someday, but not here. Not as long as Sophie was here.

As he stepped onto the front porch, and stomped the snow off his boots, he told himself Gramps would understand why he couldn't stay—once he got around to telling the old man.

The smell when he opened the front door made him grin. Fresh baked bread. He'd been hoping for that.

"Was wondering if you'd make it home in time for lunch," Gramps said, pushing his chair away from his makeshift worktable in the parlor. The same table that used to be in the barn, where Gramps had spent hours upon hours tooling leather into bridles and halters. "Sophie likes to eat while it's hot."

"I know," Welles said, taking off his coat. "You told me that, and that's why I'm here before noon."

"Where were you?" Gramps asked.

"I went over to see Jud's shop and visited with him and Suzanne."

"She settled that hooligan down, made him accept his responsibilities and become a respectable man," Gramps said. "You should take note of that."

An eerie little quiver tickled his spine as he wondered exactly what his grandfather was suggesting.

"Well, come on, let's eat." Gramps started walking toward the kitchen. "My stomach's been growling since she pulled that bread out of the oven."

Welles fell in step beside his grandfather, noting how

much shorter and slower the man's footsteps were now. He remembered how, for years, he'd had to run to keep up with Gramps.

Another memory struck him. The one day he hadn't had to run to keep up. It had been a rainy day, and he'd been cold, inside and out, as the preacher had said the final words over the graves of his mother and father. Gramps had taken his hand, and slowly they'd walked out of the cemetery.

Don't you worry none, Welles. You'll always have me, Gramps had said. *We'll always have each other.*

A hint of shame, at how he'd been the one to break that promise, washed over Welles as they entered the kitchen. While Gramps walked on, straight to the table, Welles stopped to stare at the woman setting a kettle in the center of the table. He wasn't as shocked as he was confused.

Glancing from the woman to Sophie, his confusion increased.

"There was no reason for Annie and Isaac to stay at the hotel when we have plenty of room," Sophie said.

"I hope you don't mind," Annie said.

Welles didn't mind; he just didn't see why. "No," he said. "Not at all. As Sophie said, there's plenty of room."

Sophie's gentle smile was for Annie, who smiled in return before she bowed her head.

"Thank you," Annie whispered.

"Let's eat while it's hot," Sophie said while walking toward the stove and pulling her apron off.

Welles walked around the table and pulled the chair out for Annie. Once she was seated, he moved over to pull one out for Sophie and waited while she hung the apron on a hook and walked back to the table.

As she was sitting, he whispered, "Where's her baby?"

"Isaac," Sophie said, as if making a point of saying the name, "is napping."

Relief washed over him. For a moment he'd wondered if

the baby had taken ill from the cold. Understanding that was still a possibility, he asked, "He's doing all right?"

"Yes," Sophie answered. "He's fine."

"Good to hear," he said, moving to his own chair.

The stew was delicious and plentiful, and he smiled his thanks at Sophie. There was no use trying to start up a conversation. Gramps would stifle it until he'd eaten his fill.

Gramps soon dished up a second helping of stew, and passed the ladle to Welles. While he added another portion to his plate, a faint crying sound filtered the room.

Annie instantly jumped to her feet. "Excuse me."

Welles waited until she'd disappeared at the top of the stairs before asking Sophie, "She wasn't comfortable at the hotel?"

Anger snapped in her eyes as her lips puckered. "No. It's full of men, other than Martha Merlin, and we all know how friendly she is."

Welles nodded as he stuck his fork in a potato slice. "I didn't think of that."

Sophie set her fork down with a clatter. "Why would you want to expose your son to that?"

Gramps spit out his mouthful of food while Welles tried hard not to choke on his. His eyes were watering by the time a solid chunk of a potato went down.

"She told you that's my son?"

"She didn't need to. I knew the moment I saw him."

"You knew—"

"Why didn't you tell us?" Gramps asked.

Stunned they'd even think the baby was his, Welles shook his head. "There's nothing to tell."

"He has your eyes," Sophie said.

"No, he doesn't." Anger rose at the idea they both thought so little of him. "I have my eyes."

She pushed her chair away from the table. "Oh, for heaven's sake. There's no need to lie."

He jumped to his feet and grabbed her arm as she stood.

It bothered him deeply that she thought he'd lied about something like that. "I'm not. That's not my baby." His spine quivered at the coldness in Sophie's eyes. "I'd never seen them before they boarded the train in Kansas."

Her glare said she still didn't believe him.

Could he blame her? He had lied to her before. When he left town and said he'd be back. Huffing out a breath, he said, "I don't know why she'd say that, but it's not true."

"Did she tell you that, Sophie-girl?" Gramps asked.

Sophie took a deep breath and pulled her arm out of his hold before she said, "No, she didn't."

Welles was so relieved he wanted to sink back down in his chair, but didn't because he wanted to know more. "Then why would you assume it?"

Huffing the air out of her lungs, she said, "Because there is no other reason for you to be here. You haven't bothered to come home in five years."

Irritated now because he couldn't tell her the truth, not the whole truth, he said, "I haven't traveled past here."

Gramps, who had started eating again, set his fork down on his plate. "How long do you intend to stay, now that you've traveled past?"

Welles questioned if now was the time, but ultimately knew it didn't matter. He'd have to let them know sooner or later. "I'll be heading to Denver as soon as the train is free. To a Christmas Day poker game. I've already paid the buy-in."

"So, that's not a lie," Sophie said, looking as disgusted as she had earlier. "You have become a gambler."

"I've never claimed it was a rumor," he answered. "It's how I've paid for the horses I've had delivered here over the past five years." He'd never had this gut-churning need to justify his behaviors. Not in years, and didn't appreciate it happening now. Gambling had been the way he'd paid Gramps back for the money Colleen had stolen, and more. Enough money to have dozens upon dozens of horses shipped home.

Sophie's glare told him exactly what she thought of that, and him.

The real reason he'd continued to gamble, long after he'd earned back Gramps's money, would no longer stay buried. He'd done it, become a full-time gambler, because of her. She hated gamblers, and that made him feel safe. That when he finally came home, she'd see that he wasn't the type of man she needed, realize she needed someone stable, responsible, and that would once and for all set him free. If she hated him, then he could let go of any last hope of them ever being together and, in time, stop caring for her. Stop loving her.

Fully annoyed at himself, at her, at life, he said, "That's what I do. I gamble." Pointing toward the stairway, he added, "Not marry women and have babies. Only a foolish man does that." Spinning around, he walked out of the room.

"Where you going?" Gramps asked.

"Out."

Sophie tried hard to keep her emotions under control. What was usually a simple feat took great effort, but she managed to hold her tongue and the tears that burned the backs of her eyes. Keeping her attention on the tasks at hand, she began clearing the table, wishing the entire time that Welles had been married to Annie, and that Isaac was his son. That would have been easier than knowing he was a gambler.

"I was hoping he'd get that all out of his system before coming home, Sophie-girl," Chester said.

"It makes no difference to me," she said, carrying dishes to the sink.

"Yes, it does."

The legs of his chair scraped the floor, but she didn't turn around or respond.

"But either way, this here is your home. Nothing and no-body will change that."

Sophie stacked the dishes on the counter, giving her something to do as Chester walked out of the room. The front door hadn't opened yet, so Welles hadn't left, and not wanting to hear what might be said between the two of them, she crossed the room and hurried up the stairs.

The closing of the front door echoed up the stairway as she reached the top, and needing to focus on something else, she knocked on the door of the room she'd given to Annie.

"It's me, Sophie."

"Come in."

Annie sat in a chair beside the bed, nursing Isaac beneath a blanket she'd draped over her shoulder.

"I was just wondering if I should keep some stew warm for you," Sophie said, closing the door behind her. Now that Welles was gone, Chester would have more to say, and she was in no hurry to hear it.

"Oh, no, thank you. I had plenty before Isaac awoke, but I'll be down shortly to clean the kitchen."

"That's not necessary. You're a guest," Sophie said.

"But it is," Annie replied, rubbing Isaac's bottom through the blanket. "It's the least I can do." A shameful expression covered her face as she added, "It's the only way I can repay your kindness."

Sophie sat down on the bed. At the hotel, Annie had agreed to come stay at the house because she didn't have the money to pay for a hotel room. Sophie hadn't questioned why, but now asked, "Where's Isaac's father?"

A serene smile filled Annie's face. "In Denver. We'd tried homesteading a piece of land in Kansas, but too many things went wrong. Daniel saw advertisements in a Denver newspaper and wrote to one of them. They offered him a job, but he had to arrive immediately. I couldn't go with him because I was too far along with Isaac, so I stayed with the neighbors until Daniel sent the money for the train fare so we could to join him. I'd packed plenty of food for my-self, but had to leave it on the train." She shook her head. "I know he'll be worried when we don't arrive as sched-uled, but I don't even have the money to send him a wire."

"Don't worry. Frank Green, he's the depot agent, will wire the other depots of the train mishap," Sophie said. "How long have you been separated?"

"Three months, but it feels like years." Annie removed the blanket enough to hoist Isaac onto her shoulder and began patting his back. "I can't wait for Daniel to see Isaac. He was so certain I would have a boy."

"May I?" Sophie asked, holding out her hands.

Annie's face brightened. "He might spit up."

"I won't mind," Sophie said.

An odd sensation spread through her body as she took the infant and propped him against her shoulder as Annie had been doing. He smelled so sweet and special, and as he nestled his head against her neck, Sophie closed her eyes, totally consumed by the tiny little life she held. How won-derful it must be to have a child. Someone to love fully and completely. That was what she'd dreamed of, and all she truly wanted, but it seemed to be more elusive than ever.

"When I opened the door this morning, I knew you were the miracle I'd prayed for," Annie said. "The men at the hotel were saying it could be three days or more before the train could leave for Denver. There's just no way I could stay there that long, not without any money."

"I'm not a miracle," Sophie said, "and don't worry about money. You can stay with us as long as you need."

"Mr. Carmichael had introduced himself to me on the train, but I certainly don't know him well enough to impose upon his family. Are you his sister?"

"No, and you aren't imposing."

"And I don't want to be." Annie stood up and laid the folded baby blanket on the bed. "I'll work for our keep. Just tell me what you need done, and I'll do it."

Chapter Six

The afternoon had gone by quickly, in some ways. In others, it had dragged into one of the longest Sophie had ever known. She'd found a basket for Isaac to lie in while she and Annie cleaned the kitchen and then washed his soiled diapers, visited with Chester and prepared the evening meal. In that entire time, Welles had not returned.

Not to the house. The snow that had continued to fall all day covered any tracks, making it impossible to know if he was in the barn or not. She didn't want to encounter him, but the horses needed their evening feeding. Leaving Annie to keep an eye on supper, Sophie changed into her work clothes, bundled up and headed out to the barn.

The pathway Welles had shoveled this morning was completely filled in, which said he most likely hadn't been back, and once again that filled her with mixed emotions. She'd imagined him coming home for years. Truth was, her imagination had gotten away from her over the years. She'd imagined Welles coming home to stay. As a respected man who would see how well she'd taken care of Chester and the livery and would want to marry her.

That couldn't even be considered a pipe dream. It was nothing more than a silly girl's daydreaming getting way out of hand. Just like it had years ago, when she used to dream of Welles marrying her. Before he'd run off with a saloon girl and became a gambler.

Memories of her mother's words echoed as she trudged the last few steps to the livery door. *Never trust a gambler.*

*They'll trick the love out of your heart as quickly as they
do money out of another man's pockets.*

The lit lanterns had Sophie considering closing the door
before she'd opened it all the way, but Welles had already
seen her, and she him.

"I've already fed them," he said.

She stepped inside and closed the door. He stood on the
other side of the sleigh, so she walked toward the horses
on this side first.

"While you're checking, you should remember I'm the
one who taught you how to feed."

She didn't acknowledge she'd heard him in any way.

"So now you know the truth," he said. "I'm a gambler."

Sophie drew a breath to hold her composure as she
walked around Ben to check his grain trough.

"You've known gamblers your entire life. Why should
one more matter?"

Something inside her snapped. Spinning around, she
marched back to the sleigh. "It's you it should matter to."

He shrugged. "Why? Gambling's been good to me.
Gramps would never have the amount of money he has in
the bank if not for my gambling. Me, either."

"And that's all that matters? Money?" She grasped the
edge of the sleigh with both hands. "I thought you were
smarter than that. Haven't you heard a fool and his money
are soon parted?"

"But I'm no fool," he said.

This would be so much easier if she hadn't fallen in love
with him all those years ago. Life would have been so much
easier. Realizing that was exactly what had happened and
that she'd have to stop daydreaming about a life with him,
the anger seeped out of her. "Perhaps not." She released the
hold she had on the sleigh. "But I am."

He shot around the rig, blocking her pathway to the door.
"No, you're not. Why would you say that?"

She shook her head, feeling little more than pity for herself. "Because it's true. I've stayed around this town, thinking, waiting—" She bit her lips together before the entire truth escaped.

"Waiting for what?"

She had to face the truth before she could figure out what to do about it. "For you to return."

"Why?"

Not able to face him, she glanced around, looking for something to catch and hold her gaze.

"So you wouldn't have to take care of Chester," he said quietly. "Wouldn't have to take care of the livery. So you could start living your own life. I'm sorry, Sophie. I never expected you to cover for me."

If that was what he thought, what he believed, then so be it. It was better than him knowing the truth. He'd taken a step back, and she used the space as an escape route.

Welles kept his hands at his sides. It would be easy to grab her arm, to stop her from slipping out the door, but it wouldn't change a thing. He was a fool. Why hadn't he taken that into consideration? Just this morning both Jud and Suzanne had said how several men had attempted to court Sophie, but how Gramps had kept every one of them at bay as strongly as Lola had kept everyone away from Sophie. Back then, before he'd left, there wasn't a man for miles around who didn't know exactly what would happen to them if they crossed the barrier Lola had put up around her daughter.

Including him, which was exactly why he'd left before that had happened.

He should never have come home, either. Sending livestock and money had been a good plan. One he should have stuck to. The game in Denver had been an excuse. He'd paid his buy-in as soon as he'd heard about it because it would give him a reason to travel through Big Springs.

Yes, he'd missed Gramps, but more so, it had gotten to

the point where he'd needed to know what had become of
Sophie. All sorts of scenarios had played out in his mind
over the years. That she'd gone east, or that she'd married
a local man, even had a couple of children by now, or that
she'd joined her mother's business. That one had never taken
root because he'd known her, and Lola, too well to believe it.

Never once, in any of his letters home, had he asked
Gramps about her. Partially because he didn't want to be
interested, or to let anyone know he was, but mainly because he thought not knowing was best. That with enough
time, he'd learn to forget he'd ever known her.

That may have been the biggest of all the lies he'd told
himself.

That had also been the reason he'd never stayed in one
place long enough for a letter from Gramps to reach him.
He'd traveled from the Mexican border to the Canadian
one, but had never stepped foot in Colorado since leaving.
Thought that would make him immune.

Spinning around, he took in another long look of the
livery. He'd wanted her to hate him, so why did it hurt? He
was such a fool, and didn't blame her for hating him. He
was the reason she couldn't get on with her life. She was
too busy taking care of Gramps and the livery. Although
he'd been hiding it for years, he knew what that felt like.
Not having a home of his own, or a family to return to each
night, wasn't as grandiose, as wonderful, as he kept trying
to make himself believe.

Gramps was right. Just like Jud, it was time for him to
become a respectable man. Accept his responsibilities. The
first of those needed to be to release Sophie from her responsibilities here. And from his heart.

Welles blew out the lanterns and stood in the dark silence for several minutes, wondering if he'd be better off
to just leave.

He might be, but that wouldn't solve anything for anyone. Pushing the dead air out of his lungs, he left the livery.

The house was warm and the smell of food inviting, yet the icy glares he received from Gramps and Sophie let him know just how welcomed he was.

Annie grinned as she hurried toward the table.

When he realized the basket she lifted off the chair he'd sat in for lunch held the baby, he said, "Leave him there. There's another chair in the parlor. I'll get it so you can sit beside him."

The meal proceeded as usual, to Chester's preferences, little conversation other than asking for dishes to be passed back and forth. Except for the baby in the basket. He made all sorts of cute little sounds. They made Welles smile, or maybe it was how Sophie kept glancing into the basket that was situated between her and Annie and smiling.

Either way, Welles couldn't keep his eyes from roaming to her and that basket. She'd enjoy having children, and considering the years she'd spent with Chester, she'd certainly know how to take care of them. Gramps was loving and kind, when he wanted to be, but most of the time he was on the ornery side, and selfish, which would explain why he'd kept every suitor Sophie may have had at bay.

She didn't deserve that, and she shouldn't be the one taking care of Gramps. He should be, whether the task was pleasurable or not.

When the meal ended, Welles carried the chair back into the parlor and set it next to the table covered with leather and tools. He waited there, and for Chester to set his cup of coffee on the table, sit down and hook his cane on the edge of the table.

Welles then crossed the room, added a log to the parlor stove, and then carried the rocking chair from there to the table.

Gramps looked at him expectantly.

The women were chatting in the kitchen, and knowing how small the house was, Welles kept his voice low as he sat down in the rocker. "We need to talk."

"'Bout time," Gramps said. "Every time I asked a question, you took off."

Welles gave a nod, accepting he had, yet said, "A talk about Sophie."

"What about her?"

"Why have you kept her here?"

"I already told you she didn't have anywhere else to go."

"Four years ago," Welles pointed out. "Most women her age are married, with a baby or two."

Gramps sat back in his chair and scratched his chin. "Is that what you want? Her to be married with babies?"

"It's not about what I want. It's about what she wants."

"Has she told you that's what she wants?"

"No, bu—"

"Me, either."

Welles stopped a frustrated sigh from escaping. "Have you asked her?"

Gramps reached for his coffee cup and took a drink before saying, "No need to. She lets me know when she wants something. Or just goes and buys it herself."

The moment of silence coming from the other room had Welles leaning closer. "Well, she can't go buy a husband, now, can she?"

"Ain't no man around here worthy of being her husband."

"From what I've been told, you've stopped any man from courting her before getting the chance to learn if they're worthy or not."

"Who told you that?"

"It doesn't matter who. The fact is it's true, isn't it?"

"If Sophie had wanted one of those men to court her, she'd have told me."

"And you'd still have stopped it."

Welles may not have seen the glare Gramps leveled on him in years, but he knew it well. Steam might spout out of the old man's ears at any moment, and a tongue-lashing was about to erupt.

"That's not fair to her," Welles said before Gramps had a chance to speak.

To his surprise, Gramps didn't erupt. Instead, he took another drink of coffee, set his cup back down and then leaned back in his chair before he said, "You've been gone a long time, and have no idea what that gal has been through. You don't know what she wants, either. How could you, when you don't even know what you want yourself? You've been chasing it for five years, and from the way it sounds, aren't done doing that."

Welles accepted that, but felt the need to justify it, as well. "I am done. I'll be back as soon as the game in Denver is over. Back for good."

Gramps shook his head. "If you were done, you wouldn't need to go to Denver."

"I've already paid the buy-in," Welles argued. "It was a thousand dollars. It would be foolish to lose that amount of money for no reason."

"Is it in your pocket?" Gramps asked while unhooking his cane from the table.

"Is what?"

Gramps stood and picked up his coffee cup. "The thousand dollars?"

"No. I said—"

"Then you've already lost it."

"No, I haven't. I have a chance to win ten times that amount. A hundred times that amount." Even as he said the words, Welles fully understood what Gramps was saying. He'd been taking a chance by staying away and not coming home. It had all been a gamble. And he'd lost.

"Doc said there was a chance I'd walk without a limp." Gramps leveled a solid stare on him before turning about. As he started walking toward the kitchen, he added, "When are you going to learn that sometimes we have to play the hand we've been dealt?"

Chapter Seven

"That sun is getting downright hot," Jud said, scooping up another shovel full of snow and flinging it off to the side.

"Freezing one day, sweating the next," Sawyer said, shoveling on the other side of the tracks. "Wouldn't surprise me to see it thundering and lightning tonight."

Laughing, others agreed as their shovels kept moving snow. Despite the backbreaking work of digging out the train, something they'd already been doing for hours, the entire group of men was in good humor. Welles had no doubt they'd remain that way all day. Working, laughing and joking around with each other. That was how it had always been.

The heat of the sun promised to hang around, and was needed to help melt away the ice that had built up under the snow. If they were lucky, by this afternoon the horses would be able to pull the train far enough backward that, with a hot fire roaring in her belly, the engine would have enough steam to get uphill and then onward into Big Springs.

By tomorrow, it would be rolling onto Denver. None too soon. He'd be on it, and as soon as he won a solid stake, he'd be rolling back into Big Springs. To stay. He understood what Gramps said, and he was playing the hand he'd been dealt. The chance of winning big was there, and he'd take it, get it and then bring that money back here, settle down and take over running the livery. Let Sophie marry some fella of her choosing while he took care of the old codger and the horses, and the house and everything else she'd been taking care of the past four years.

He'd do all that, and love it. Tossing another shovel full of snow aside, he let out a sigh. About as much as he was enjoying moving a mountain of snow. It wouldn't all be bad. Gramps was easy enough to get along with as long as a person knew what to expect, and he was actually looking forward to working with the horses again, being a part of the community. Having the money from winning in Denver, along with what he already had, would assure they would have all they'd need. And he'd pay Sophie for all she'd done while he'd been gone. She could use it to start her new life.

He wouldn't enjoy her getting married, but would get used to it.

It would have to be the right man. That was for sure. He'd make sure of that.

"Hey, Welles," J.T. shouted. "Isn't that one of Chester's rigs?"

They'd ridden out to the train in the livery's sleigh, but the direction J.T. pointed said he was referring to a different one. Welles walked across the tracks to see around the train. Sure enough, two of the horses out of the livery were pulling a sleigh. It was much smaller than the wagon one they'd used, and was carrying only two people.

Recognizing the driver, he set aside his shovel and walked forward. As the rig slid up next to the train, he asked, "What are you doing out here?"

Sophie didn't answer, but Suzanne did.

"We figured you men could use a hot meal," Suzanne said.

"We certainly can," Jud said, arriving at her side and helping her down.

"We packed it in straw and wrapped it in blankets to keep everything warm," Suzanne said after kissing Jud's cheek. "We'll carry it inside the passenger car and yell when it's time to eat."

Welles reached up to help Sophie down, and though she

let him, he got the feeling she'd have much preferred to climb down herself.

"We'll pry open the door for you," he said, gesturing toward the passenger car. "But it's cold in there."

Sophie turned about and started unfolding blankets draped over their cargo. "We expected it would be. As Suzanne said, we'll let you know when it's time to eat."

Welles walked over to the train and, with Jud's help, got the frozen metal door to open.

"Lord, but I love that woman," Jud said, looking at Suzanne. "Ain't she something?"

"She is," Welles agreed before he slapped Jud's back. "Come on, let's get back to work before we get yelled at for standing around."

Jud laughed. "Sophie isn't much for idleness."

"No, she's not," Welles answered. Jud had seen the glare Sophie was casting his way as much as he had. "And we best not be late when she calls that the food is ready, either."

"I guarantee we won't be," J.T. said, stepping up beside them. "I've been trying to get a chance to share a meal with Sophie for over two years."

Welles elbowed J.T. out of the way and walked toward his shovel. Although J.T. was a good friend, he would never be the kind of husband Sophie deserved. Matter of fact, none of those out here shoveling snow would be. They were good men in their own right, just not suitable for Sophie. She needed a dependable, reliable man, with enough money to pamper her with all the finer things in life.

It didn't take Sophie and Suzanne long to have everything ready, and even less time for every one of the six men with him to barrel inside the train. Welles walked into the car last, and went through the food line last. There was still plenty and it was steaming.

"Straw and blankets?" he asked.

Sophie shrugged. "And a tub of hot coals."

She was trying hard not to smile, but he let his roam free,

and nodded at her ingenuity as he sat down to eat. Even the coffee was hot, and the bread warm, which everyone enjoyed as much as the stew. They also enjoyed the fact Sophie had brought it to them, and weren't shy about letting her know that.

Her cheeks were pink, but that could have been from traveling out to the train, because she wasn't acting as if their attention affected her in any way.

It affected him. Stronger than it should have. Or maybe not. After all she'd done for Gramps, he owed her plenty, including protection from unwanted advances.

None of the men were acting that persistently, but he still kept his eyes on them. Every single one.

"Why are you staring at them that way?"

Pretending he had no idea what she was talking about, he asked, "Who, and what way?"

"Everyone," Sophie answered. "And like they are about to start dealing off the bottom of the deck."

"How would—"

"You know where I grew up," she interrupted.

"Lola never let you near the gambling tables."

"One doesn't need to be near them to know things." She lifted the lid off the kettle. "Want more?"

"No, thank you, though." He gestured around the room with a nod. "You decide to do this all on your own?"

She frowned slightly while asking, "Why? You think I'm not capable of kindness?"

"No, I know you're capable." He nodded toward the others once again. "This was just unexpected. It surprised me. You surprised me."

"Well," she said, putting the lid back on the kettle. "When I started making lunch, I asked Chester what time you'd be back, since you left without saying a word. Chester said he doubted you'd be back before supper, so I walked over to Suzanne's house to see if Jud had taken a lunch, knowing you hadn't."

Welles didn't want to put much into her being worried whether he'd taken a lunch or not, but couldn't help it. Trying not to let it show, he took a sip of his coffee. "And?"

"When Suzanne said Jud hadn't, I said that I was going to make a pot of stew and bring it out here."

"So you did," he supplied when she paused.

"I did." She nodded in the direction of the other woman walking toward them. "And Suzanne brought along cookies that she'd spent the morning baking and decorating."

"That I did," Suzanne said, lifting a plate out of a crate and removing the cloth covering it. "Would you like one?"

The plate was full of gingerbread cookies in the shape of little people and decorated with white frosting.

"They're good, Welles," Jud said. "She makes them every year and hangs them on our Christmas tree."

Suzanne grinned as she gently bumped against Jud's shoulder. "The tree my darling husband cuts down for me every year."

"That's right." Jud took a cookie. "I do, and will again as soon as this train's broken free."

"You best," Suzanne said before she carried the tray toward the other men.

Welles had known Jud for years, and had never seen a shine in his eyes like he saw right now. Truth was, he'd never seen the man so happy. Like he genuinely loved his life.

"Go ahead and eat it," Jud said, gesturing toward the cookie Welles held. "They melt in your mouth."

Welles took a bite and chewed. The cookie was tasty, but it wasn't melting in his mouth. In fact, it was the hardest cookie he'd ever eaten. Luckily, Jud had turned about and followed Suzanne. Welles picked up his cup of coffee, needing the liquid to soften the cookie enough to swallow.

Sophie was watching him and grinning. Not her lips, but her eyes, which reminded him of years ago. How cute she'd been. She still was cute, but also pretty. Very pretty. Her hair was hanging loose and the light blue scarf she'd had wrapped around her head was now coiled around her neck. Instead of his old coat, she was wearing a long, fitted one that buttoned down the front and highlighted the fact as to how much she'd grown up since he'd left.

Grown up into a beautiful woman. One he could fall head over heels in love with, if things were different. He'd left all those years ago because he knew the risks of letting what he'd felt for her grow, and had become a gambler, knowing that she'd never be able to return his love, for her sake. She deserved the life Lola had wanted for her. Married to a respectable, successful man, who would take her places. Travel the world. Lola had told him all that herself. That those were the things Sophie wanted. The things she dreamed of. The things she deserved.

His throat went dry. He took a drink of coffee while setting the half-eaten cookie atop his empty plate. "I'm not much of a cookie eater."

She stacked another plate atop his, covering up the half-eaten cookie. "Will you have the train broken free today?"

"Yes. It'll roll into Big Springs before nightfall."

"And then onto Denver."

He took a final swig of coffee, emptying the cup. "Yes."

"And you'll be on it."

"Have to, but I'll be back."

She nodded but didn't look up from the crate she was repacking. "Chester said as much."

"Won't take more than a few days. Then I'll be back for good."

"I won't wager on that."

She hadn't looked up, but more than her cold shoulder bothered him. "You don't believe me?"

"Why should I? Five years ago you said you'd be back in a couple of months."

He had said that. Then. "This is different."

With a slight shake of her head, she spun around, walked

toward where the others were now eating their cookies and began gathering empty plates.

Welles considered following, but only for a second. The faster he got this train broken loose, the faster she could get on to living the life she'd dreamed of. "Let's get back at it," he said, heading toward the doorway, knowing the others would follow.

The rest of the men did follow, except for Jud; he helped Sophie and Suzanne load up the sleigh and saw them off before he picked up his shovel again.

It may have been the food, or the visit, or the sun shining bright and warm, but the morale amongst the men was even higher as they dug. Within a couple of hours, the engineer and the fire tender had steam hissing out of the smokestack while Welles led the big horses to the end of the train and hitched them to the caboose.

The horses easily pulled the train backward, and there was still plenty of sunlight when, a short time later, the train started chugging toward town, leaving only him and Jud behind.

"Think we got time to check out that strand of trees along the creek?" Jud asked while they hitched the team back to the sleigh.

"Sure," Welles agreed. "Need some wood?"

"Need a Christmas tree," Jud answered. "That's how I got Suzanne to fall in love with me."

Skeptical, because he'd become that way, or maybe always had been and just realized it more lately, Welles asked, "A Christmas tree?"

"Yep." Jud checked the harness as he walked toward the sleigh. "Up until I cut down that first tree, she didn't have the time of day for me. Some might say she despised me."

"Half the town despised you at one time," Welles said as he climbed into the driver's seat. "You were wilder than half the outlaws in Kansas."

Jud laughed as he sat down. "I can't deny that, but I'd always had my eye on Suzanne, and that day, when I saw her leaving town with an ax, was the luckiest day of my life."

"Because she didn't use it on you?"

They both laughed.

"She was going out to cut down a tree, a Christmas tree. Walked all the way out to that land that Lola used to own, and when the time came, I appeared out of nowhere and offered to chop down the tree she'd picked out."

"You followed her."

"Of course I did. Hard saying what might have happened to her out there all alone." Jud's grin covered his entire face. "And then I carried that tree home for her. By the time we arrived at her house, I was invited to stay for dinner, which I accepted, and helped her family decorate the tree." Letting out a satisfied sigh, he added, "And the rest is history."

Welles steered the team down along the creek bed, wondering when the last time there had been a Christmas tree in his house. Had to have been years, and years. In fact, he couldn't remember the last time. Unless that had changed since Sophie came to live with Gramps.

Chapter Eight

Sophie forced herself not to walk to the window again. She wouldn't be able to see anything anyway. It was dark out. It hadn't been when the train whistle had blown hours ago, or when Welles had arrived. He hadn't bothered to stop and say he was home. She should be thankful he'd taken care of Bob and Ben before he left again. He'd taken care of the sleigh, too, parked it next to the barn and covered it with a tarp.

"Would you like me to set the table?"

Lifting the plates down out of the cupboard, Sophie shook her head. "You've been working all day."

"Mending a few clothes?" Annie chuckled. "That was nothing."

Much like cooking had been when she'd first come to live with Chester, sewing was completely foreign to her. Things like cooking and sewing hadn't been a part of her life up until then. She'd mastered cooking, but not sewing. Which didn't seem to bother Chester, so she'd never forced herself to do any more than absolutely necessary. "It was more than a few. Nearly everything Chester owns had a hole or two in them." Sophie insisted. "I've tried, but sewing, even so much as a button back on, is beyond me."

"Well, I didn't mind in the least." Annie reached up and took down four cups. "And I don't mind setting the table, either."

Annie chatted on and though Sophie nodded, or verbally agreed, she truly had no idea what the other woman said. Her mind was on Welles. Where he was. What he was doing. The very things she'd been thinking about since he'd arrived two days ago. She didn't want to be thinking about him so much. And had tried not to, but it was impossible. As impossible as it had been five years ago.

There were so many reasons why she couldn't love him, and none as to why she could, or should.

He was a gambler. He'd left Chester—an old man—on his own. He'd stolen Chester's money. He'd run away with a saloon girl. He was leaving again. To attend a poker game. She couldn't trust him. Would never be able to trust him, or believe him, so why? Why did she care so much about him?

"Are you all right?"

Sophie shook her head and then nodded. "Yes, I'm fine. Why?"

"The potatoes were boiling over." Annie put the lid on the pot that was now at the back of the stove. "You've been out of sorts since you got back from taking lunch to the train. Did you catch a chill? Feel a fever coming on?"

"No. I was just lost in thought, I guess."

Annie's cheeks pinkened as she said, "That happens to me. Especially when I'm thinking of being reunited with Daniel."

"That will happen soon," Sophie said.

"By Christmas, thanks to all of you," Annie said. "I feel as if I'm in a house full of angels. Welles for walking through that terrible blizzard, coming back for us and digging out the train today. You for bringing us here. Chester for letting us stay. I truly don't know what I'd have done without all of you."

Annie's teary eyes and heartfelt declaration was so touching, Sophie gave the other woman a hug. "We've enjoyed having you here. You and Isaac, but you would have been fine without us."

"No, we wouldn't have," Annie said, wiping at her eyes. "During the time we waited on that train, I knew if Welles didn't make it to town, none of us would make it. What he did was the most unselfish act of kindness I've ever seen, and I'll never forget it. Forever be grateful to him."

Even if Sophie had a response, the opening of the back door would have interrupted it.

"Good evening, ladies," Welles said as he took off his hat with one hand and shut the door with the other.

Sophie drew a deep breath to keep his smile from overly affecting her. It didn't help much; neither did busying herself at the stove. Annie was full of questions about the train, and Welles had the answers she wanted to hear. The train would depart for Denver by tomorrow.

Chester entered the room, and soon they were all seated at the table, with Isaac in his basket on the chair between her and Annie. Sophie would miss the baby when they left. He was full of giggles and cooing sounds that filled her with the most wonderful sense of happiness. He also had her thinking about her future. What she wanted, and what she'd never have if she didn't do something about it. That meant realizing there was no place for Welles in her future. She'd already known that, but actually accepting it was harder than she'd imagined.

It shouldn't be. And might not be, if he hadn't kept looking her way with a grin that said he was hiding something. That look was nothing new. His eyes had always had a glimmer that said they were hiding a secret.

By the time the meal was over, she was telling herself she was glad he was leaving in the morning, and hoped he never came back.

Making herself believe that wasn't as easy.

She and Annie were just finishing the dishes when Welles returned to the kitchen. "Good, you're done. Come into the front room."

Sophie wanted to ask why, but was also trying to make herself believe she'd be better off not talking to him.

The furniture had been rearranged in the parlor, leaving

a large empty space in front of the window. Frowning, Sophie glanced at Chester, who merely shrugged.

"Will you hold the door open for me?" Welles asked, looking at her.

Cautious, because she had never liked surprises, for they rarely were the good kind, she walked to the door and held on to it as Welles walked onto the porch. A moment later, when the top end of a pine tree entered the opening, the air stuck in her throat. A wave of memories, all wonderful, washed over as Welles carried the tree into the house.

As she closed the door, she took a moment and closed her eyes, letting the memories fully engulf her. Oh, how she'd missed having a Christmas tree. No matter how unconventional her growing up years may have been, she'd always had a Christmas tree. Most years it had been set up in her bedroom, which had made it all the more special, as had the way she and her mother would spend one entire evening decorating it.

The box of ornaments they'd used were under the bed in her room, and each year she'd considered asking Chester about getting a tree, or even acquiring one herself, but had refrained. For as kind and generous as he could be at times, Chester was not the sentimental kind, and she'd surmised he wouldn't have appreciated the fuss and hassle of a Christmas tree.

Her belief was confirmed as Chester said, "What are you hauling that in here for?"

"Because tomorrow is Christmas Eve," Welles answered, standing the tree upright and twisting it until the cross boards nailed to the bottom of its trunk sat even. "Every house needs a Christmas tree on Christmas Eve."

"Says who?" Chester demanded.

He was looking at her, and a bit of the happiness inside Sophie began to seep away.

"Me," Welles answered. He was looking at her, too.

"What do you think, Sophie, right here, in front of the window?"

"And who's going to haul that thing out of here after Christmas?" Chester asked. "You'll be long gone."

It might be a small step, but if she wanted things to change, she had to take steps in that direction. Her desire for a tree this year had increased tenfold this morning when Suzanne showed her the cookies she'd made to hang on their tree. "I will," Sophie said. "And yes, right there is perfect."

"It is perfect." Annie stepped closer to the tree as she whispered to the baby in her arms, "Look, Isaac, it's your first Christmas tree."

Annie's joy was so apparent, her wonderment so sincere, even Chester bowed his head with a touch of chagrin pinkening his weathered cheeks.

With her eyes sparkling, Annie asked, "Can we pop some popcorn and string it? And we could make paper decorations, or tie ribbons on the branches."

Annie's enthusiasm was like a summer breeze filling the room with warmth and happiness. Giving free rein for her own joy to grow, Sophie nodded. "Yes, yes, we can do all those things. And more. I'll be right back."

Her excitement continued to grow as she hurried from the room and ran up the stairs. It had been years since she'd pulled out the box of ornaments, and the prospect of doing so had her heart welling with joy. It would be like having a piece of her mother back, a way to fill the void that had been inside her since her mother had died. She had mourned her mother's death, but because of the circumstances, because of who her mother had been, had never truly allowed herself to cherish the wonderful memories she did have of her childhood.

The crate wasn't heavy, but it was large, and the contents fragile, so she forced herself to take a deep breath while pulling it out from under the bed and again as she hoisted it into her arms.

Neither deep breath slowed the excitement that contin-ued to build, but did give her the clarity to make the trip down the stairs with more caution than she'd used going up.

Welles was in the kitchen, opening and closing cupboard doors. "Do we have any popcorn?" he asked.

Gesturing with her chin, she replied, "In the cupboard next to the door. There's a glass jar of it behind the corn-meal."

"I'll get it," Annie said, having laid Isaac in the basket sitting upon the table.

"I'll carry that for you," Welles said, approaching the stairs.

"That's all right. I have it," Sophie said, stepping off the staircase.

"What's in there?" Annie asked.

"Ornaments." The smile on her face grew with memo-ries. "Beautiful ones."

Annie, now clutching the jar of popcorn to her chest, gasped. "Real ones? Store bought?"

"Yes," Sophie answered, holding on to the box a bit tighter as she walked across the kitchen. For the first time in years, it felt like Christmas inside her, and the anticipa-tion of opening the box, of experiencing the memories, was joyfully overwhelming.

Chester must have realized he'd met his match in this instance, because he was using his leather snippers to trim off a few wayward branches.

Acknowledging his participation as she set the box on the sofa, Sophie said, "Thank you. It truly is a perfect tree now."

The old man grumbled, but the grin he tried to hide in-creased Sophie's delight.

"I've seen ornaments in stores," Annie said, still clutch-ing the popcorn jar. "But never knew anyone who owned any."

"Now you do," Welles said, setting the basket holding Isaac on Chester's worktable.

Sophie squeezed her hands together in order to ease their trembling before opening the box. As the others gathered around, she sincerely hoped all of the ornaments had survived being stored for so long.

"Oh, this is so exciting," Annie whispered.

"Come on, Sophie-girl," Chester said. "Don't keep us waiting."

Although Welles didn't say anything, it was his gaze she met as Sophie glanced up. The smile on his face, the shine in his eyes, nearly took her breath away.

"Open it," he said quietly, nodding toward the box.

She carefully untucked the edges of the canvas, and her hands trembled as she pulled it off the crate and set it aside. The straw had settled, but appeared undisturbed. As she brushed aside the top layer of straw, her own gasp couldn't be contained. Lifting out the creamy-white porcelain angel with spun-glass wings, she had to blink aside the moisture that formed in her eyes.

"We always hung this one on the very top, and packed it away last, so it could guard all the others."

She hadn't realized she'd said that aloud until Annie spoke.

"It's beautiful," the other woman whispered. "And so delicate."

"Did you hang it first?" Welles asked.

Sophie shook her head. "We hung it on last, when the rest of the tree was completely decorated."

"Here," he said, holding out a hand. "I'll set it aside while you pull out the others."

Ready to see more, she handed him the angel, and reached into the straw to lift out the pink bell. There was an identical red one, and she picked that one up, as well. Handing the pink one to Annie, Sophie said, "Here, you hang this one." Gently shaking the red one, she added, "But ring it first. That's what my mother and I always did. It was our way of ringing in Christmas."

Annie shook the bell but said, "You hang yours first. It's your tree, and your ornaments."

Sophie's throat was swelling from memories. She and Mother had always hung the bells simultaneously. Speaking around the lump, she said, "No, you go ahead. It's Isaac's first Christmas tree. Hang the bell for him."

"Why don't you hang them at the same time?" Welles asked.

"Oh, yes," Annie replied. "Let's ring them first, and then hang them at the same time."

Welles held his silence while watching Sophie. He'd thought the tree would make her happy, but hadn't expected to see such a change in her. It was as if someone had lit a candle inside her, and it burned so bright, light filled the entire house.

"All right," she agreed with Annie's suggestion.

They both stepped forward, ringing the tiny bells before hooking them on suitable branches that took them each a moment to find.

To his surprise, as both women laughed at their own branch-searching antics, Chester clapped his hands.

"Well done. They look perfect," Gramps said. "What else you got in that crate?"

"The perfect one for you to hang up," Sophie said, stepping closer to the box. "Just let me find it." After setting several colorful glass balls aside, she pulled a miniature horseshoe out of the straw. "Here, Chester, this one is for you."

Gramps laughed and cheerfully took the ornament and hung it on the tree.

"I have one for you, too, Welles."

His heart slowed to dull and heavy beats as she held up a single playing card. The ace of spades. A hole had been punched in the top and a red ribbon laced through it.

"Hang it on the tree," she said, handing it to him.

He almost flinched as his fingers touched the card. They felt singed.

"Oh, look at this one," Annie said.

Welles didn't look; his eyes were on the card. He was a gambler, had been for years, but he'd never felt ashamed of it until this moment.

"Hang it on the tree, Annie," Sophie said. "Chester, here's another one for you to hang."

"They are all so beautiful," Annie said. "Where did you get them all?"

"Around the world," Sophie said. "Mother would order a new one each year, and we'd talk about where it came from and how we'd visit there someday."

As the ornament-hanging continued, Welles tucked the card into his pocket, and watched the others digging in the crate and pulling out baubles like they were hidden treasures. He hadn't seen Gramps so cheerful in a long time, but more than that, he'd never, ever, seen Sophie so delighted. So happy as she shared that box of ornaments.

That did something to him. Something odd and unique. In all his years of gambling, of winning pots of money, he'd never experienced the well of warmth that seemed to pour out of the center of his chest as Sophie's delighted laughter tinkled the air.

He didn't even know what she was laughing about, but she was. Her eyes were sparkling, her cheeks shining, and she had a hand pressed to her heart. Gramps might have said or done something funny, or Annie, or even little Isaac. Welles had no idea, but at that moment, knew he was looking at something he'd love to see again. And again.

Sophie happy.

Sophie laughing.

"Looks like that's all of them, Sophie-girl," Gramps said, pawing his big hands around in the straw.

"Do we hang the angel now?" Annie asked.

Welles had forgotten about the angel, and as he turned

to retrieve it off the table, Sophie stopped him by laying a hand on his arm.

"Not yet," she said. "We have to pop and string the popcorn. The angel is the very last thing that goes on."

"I'll go put a kettle on the stove and get some thread and needles," Annie said.

"Four needles," Sophie said. "Everyone has to help."

She made a point of looking at him and Gramps, a look that said there would be no arguments, as she picked the jar of popcorn off the table.

Gramps let out a long but satisfying sigh as he said, "That was a mighty fine thing you did here tonight, Welles. Bringing home this here tree. A mighty fine thing."

Welles nodded, but his eyes were on Sophie, who was still smiling brightly.

"Yes, it was," she said while turning toward the kitchen. "It truly was."

"Hold up there, Sophie," Gramps said. "There's something else in this crate."

Frowning slightly, she set the popcorn down.

"It's not an ornament, though," Gramps said.

Sophie's gasp and the way she put a hand over her mouth had Welles turning toward Gramps.

"What is it?" he asked.

"I don't know." Gramps lifted a small package out of the crate. "It looks like a present."

Glancing back toward Sophie, Welles moved, stepping up beside her and taking a hold of her arm.

"What is it?" Annie asked, entering the room. "What's happened? What's wrong?"

"Nothing's wrong." Sophie sniffled and wiped at her eyes. "I'd forgotten about this part."

"What part?" Welles asked, increasing the hold he had on her arm as he felt her shake slightly.

She was smiling, even as unshed tears glistened in her eyes. "Each year, when we packed away the ornaments,

Mother always hid a present for me in the bottom of the crate. I'd forgotten all about that." With a hand pressed to her chest again, she shook her head. "I shouldn't have. It was always one of my favorite parts. An early Christmas present."

"You got to open it right away?" Welles asked.

Once again she shook her head. "No, not until after we hung the angel."

Welles didn't need to imagine how much that little present meant to her at this moment. The look on her face said it all. It even made him choke up. Clearing his throat, he draped an arm around Sophie's shoulders. "We better get that popcorn popped, then." As he used the arm to turn her about, he said, "Put the present under the tree, Gramps."

When the first batch of popcorn was done, he and Gramps were given instructions on how to string it together while Sophie popped a second batch and Annie saw to Isaac, but it wasn't long before they were all four poking needles through the soft kernels.

Gramps was telling stories of his childhood, and eating more popcorn than he was stringing, but no one minded. Especially Welles. The tiny needle felt far too small for his hands, and maneuvering into a fluffy kernel in such a way the end wouldn't break off was nearly impossible, but he kept on trying. It was almost as if they were all racing, seeing who could get the most popcorn strung, but inside, he sensed the others were just as keen as he was to get the tree done so Sophie could open her gift.

It struck him then that she might want to do that in private. Sitting on the floor next to the sofa that she and Annie sat upon, he touched her knee with one hand.

"If you don't want to open your gift in front of us, you don't have to," he said quiet enough for only her to hear.

She shook her head, still smiling as bright as earlier. "No, I have to open it as soon as the tree is done. That's what Mother would want." She let out a little giggle. "Some years she was more excited than I was for me to open it because she'd forgotten what she'd wrapped."

"Oh, Sophie, you have such special memories," Annie said. "I hope I can do the same for Isaac."

"You will." Sophie's expression grew serious as she turned his way. "Thank you, Welles." She pinched her lips together for a moment. "You've allowed me to remember things that I should never have forgotten. Wonderful, wonderful things."

"Your mother was a great lady," he said.

"And a wonderful mother," she said. "I should never have forgotten that."

About to get choked up again, he scrambled to his feet and held up his long string of popcorn. "Well, I think we have enough popcorn, don't you?" He was about to let go of one end when she jumped up and grabbed his hand.

"Don't let go. It'll fall off."

His heart had landed in his throat with enough force to make his eyes bug out. He hoped they weren't, because looking into hers, directly, deeply, was the most fascinating thing. The warmth from her hand was spreading up his arm, across his chest and downward, stealing his breath.

She let go, and blinked before looking aside and saying, "We have to tie the ends together."

Fighting the desire to pull her forward, wrap his arms around her and kiss her, left him incapable of moving for a moment. Until an ounce of common sense kicked in. He looked aside, too. "You're right. I have to get rid of the needle first."

His heart was still pounding, his thoughts jumbled, but he managed to get the needle off the thread. He stood back while she and Annie tied the strings together and then wound the one long continuous strand around the tree.

"It looks so beautiful," Annie said as they stepped back to appreciate their handiwork. "Perfect, just perfect."

"Almost." Without turning around, Sophie asked, "Welles, will you get the angel?"

He walked over to Chester's table. Isaac was in the basket, sleeping soundly, and that, too, seeing the baby resting so peacefully, so contently, touched him in a way he'd never been touched before. Not wanting to contemplate the whys and hows of the things affecting him tonight, he grabbed the angel, walked to the tree and handed it to Sophie.

"I can't reach," she said. "You'll have to do it."

Tonight was already making him wonder about things, so he said, "I'll get you a chair."

"No, you do it."

The shimmer in her eyes almost undid him.

"Just wrap the wire under its wings around the top branch," she said.

Stretching on his toes, he did as instructed, and was instantly awed by how the light caught in the spun-glass wings. Almost as if a real angel had entered the room, set upon granting all sorts of Christmas wishes.

Chapter Nine

Sophie sat on her bed, looking down at the open locket in her lap. The picture of Mother was beautiful, exactly as she remembered, and the perfect gift. The locket had been in the ornament box for four years, since their last Christmas together, yet looking at the picture inside the locket made it feel as if it had been yesterday.

You can do anything, go anywhere, be anything you want to be, Sophie, her mother had said shortly before that fateful day. *Don't ever let anyone tell you differently. All you have to do is believe it.* Mother had laughed and hugged her before adding, *And be willing to work for it. It's not just going to fall in your lap.*

"Oh, Mother, that's what I've been doing, isn't it? Waiting for it to fall in my lap. Waiting for Welles to return and fall in love with me." Sophie drew a deep breath and glanced out the window, at the moon shining brightly. "He returned, but he hasn't fallen in love with me, nor is he the kind of man I should marry."

Sighing, she continued, "He's a gambler, is leaving again tomorrow for a poker game on Christmas Day, and let it be known he's not interested in marrying anyone. But his return gave me something I've been missing."

She lifted the locket and pressed her lips to the picture. "Thank you. Thank you for so many things that I took for granted. For the advice that I never heeded, for the love you gave so unconditionally." Reaching over to set the locket on the table next to the bed, her hand stalled. Wrapping her fingers around the locket, she climbed out of bed. "And for making me realize that the past is in the past. It's all right to remember it, embrace it, but I shouldn't let it stop me from living."

There was one spot for this locket tonight.

She slipped a shawl over her shoulders, quietly opened the door and then crept down the hall and stairway on her tiptoes so the boards wouldn't creak.

As she rounded the doorway from the kitchen to the parlor, she had to stop and stare in awe. The moonlight, reflecting off the snow outside, shone through the window and caught on the glass ornaments, making the entire tree glisten and sparkle. It was beyond stunning, beyond beautiful.

"Sneaked down for another peek?"

She couldn't stop the smile that sprang onto her lips at the sound of his voice. Welles may not be in love with her, but somehow, right now, that was all right. Maybe the day would come when she wouldn't love him, either. That thought made her sad. She'd loved him for so long, not loving would be as wrong as not loving Chester. Which would never happen.

"I want to hang the locket on the tree," she whispered. "It seems the fitting place."

"It does." He stepped around her. "Need help?"

He had on clothes, but his shirt was unbuttoned, as if thrown on quickly, and there were no socks on his feet.

"Yes, if you don't mind. Right up there by the angel."

He hooked a hand around her elbow. "That's what I was thinking."

They walked toward the tree, but he stopped a few feet away. "You stay here, and let me know when the light catches on it."

"All right."

He took the locket she held out and carried it to the tree, where he hooked it on one branch, then another, and another, waiting each time for her to shake her head. When he hooked it on yet another, the moonlight caught it, and the entire locket appeared to light up.

"Right there," she said. "Right there."

He stepped back and stood next to her, examining the tree for a moment before saying, "Perfect."

"It truly is. Thank you again."

"So, are you still dreaming about visiting all the places those ornaments came from?"

That had been another memory she'd completely forgotten about. "No, that was more of Mother's dream than mine. She wanted to see the world. I think that's why she ordered these ornaments from all over, satisfying that need in some way." She couldn't remember which ornament had come from where, not even years ago, but Mother had, and talked about how beautiful each place must be.

"You haven't had a tree since your mother died?"

"No, it wasn't something Chester was interested in."

He glanced around as if he wanted to say something, but wasn't sure he should.

"What is it?" she asked.

"Why have you let Chester rule your life?"

She wasn't angered, just confused. "What are you talking about? Chester hasn't ruled my life."

"J.T. said he's been trying to eat a meal with you for two years."

She huffed out an exasperated sigh. "Because before then, he'd made it a habit of stopping by right at suppertime. He wasn't the only one, either. I told Chester he should start charging them for meals like Martha does at the hotel. So he put a stop to it." Defending Chester at times had become habit, and she did so again. "That wasn't controlling my life. That was controlling the moochers from eating our food."

He was silent for a moment, then asked, "Have you been happy here?"

She contemplated that before answering, "Yes, I have. Even if I'd had somewhere else to go, this is still where I wanted to live." Stepping forward, she walked to the tree and touched the little red bell. "I have land, you know."

"I do. Jud told me you still own that quarter section outside of town."

"It was paid for, so the bank didn't take it, and Chester pays me a wage, so I've kept the taxes paid."

Welles stepped up beside her. "Will you move out there?"

She shrugged. "I don't know. Not as long as Chester needs me."

"What about you? What about what you need?"

The impulse to say she had everything she needed here arose, but seeped away slowly. That was a lie. "Maybe when you return for good, and I can trust that you'll take care of your grandfather, I'll move out there."

"By yourself?"

The idea wasn't appealing, but it was an option.

He turned away from the tree the same time she did, and they both stopped, facing each other and waiting for the other to move. He didn't. Neither did she, but knew she should. The thoughts that bounced into her head weren't unfamiliar. They'd been there this evening, when he'd stood up holding his string of popcorn. It was harder to quell them this time, especially the one about kissing him. And the one about feeling his arms around her, holding her tight, hugging her.

She closed her eyes, trying to block his image, hoping that would help. Instead, what she was thinking about happened.

How, she wasn't overly sure, but Welles's arms were around her, and his lips touching her. Slowly at first, and so soft she leaned forward, making sure it wasn't her imagination.

The pressure of his kiss increased, and her hands, all on their own, wrapped around him, under his shirt where the warmth of his body sent a wave of heat rushing into hers. An urgency filled her, and she stretched onto her toes, wanting things she'd never dared to think about wanting.

The intensity of his lips increased, as did the strength of his arms holding her, pressing them together, their thighs, their hips, her breasts against his chest. It was all so wonderful. So amazing.

Welles broke the kiss so fast she almost stumbled as he let her loose and stepped back. She caught herself, but nearly stumbled again when she saw the look on his face. He looked almost scared, fearful. She glanced around and upon seeing nothing, looked back at him.

The regret that was now in his eyes, she recognized it well. And it hurt. Spinning around, she walked as far as the doorway, and then ran across the kitchen and up the stairs.

What had been a nearly perfect evening turned into a sleepless and fretful night.

Although she had no desire to see anyone, Sophie climbed out of bed when the sun started turning the sky pink and put on her chore clothes. She was a fool, that was what she was. She'd known Welles didn't love her. Never would. She should never have wished otherwise.

Burying her feelings for him wouldn't be as easy now, not after kissing him. Even hurt and frustrated, the memory of how amazing kissing him had been remained front and foremost in her mind.

The smell of coffee met her as soon as she pulled her bedroom door open, and Chester sat at the table in the kitchen.

"Welles has already gone out to feed," he said. "Guess he wanted to get an early start with leaving today and all."

"I suppose so," she said.

"Got any ham leftover from last night?"

"Yes, would you like pancakes with it?" She was trying so hard to sound normal, it hurt.

"That would be good."

She nodded, and though there was no need to be reminded of anything, she walked into the parlor. The sight of her shawl draped over the edge of the sofa made her throat burn, and her eyes. When she glanced toward the tree, the ornament that was hanging on a low branch had her pinching her lips together to keep the tears at bay. He hadn't hung that card up yesterday, had put it in his pocket instead. It was there now.

"It didn't fall over," Chester said loudly from the kitchen. "I already checked."

If she didn't like things, she had to change them. Even if those things were inside her. "You're right." Drawing in a breath of fortitude, she spun around to walk toward the kitchen. "It didn't."

Welles hung out in the barn as long as possible. He had to go inside the house eventually. Not only to say goodbye, but to pack, get ready to leave. He should never have kissed Sophie last night. It had confirmed the one thing he hadn't wanted confirmed. He was in love with her and probably always would be.

The shout that made its way through the open door confirmed something else. He couldn't hide out here any longer.

He walked to the door and stepped out into the bright sunshine. "I'm coming."

"Well, hurry up," Gramps shouted from the back porch. "The rest of us are starving in here."

Did he really want to return to this? To getting up early to feed the stock and listening to Gramps complain about eating, and most everything else? Late nights of gambling did have a certain appeal.

Something else that had more of an appeal entered his mind. He'd changed himself on purpose, became a gambler. If he'd done it once, he could do it again. "Go ahead and eat," he shouted. "I'm going to go check on what time the train's leaving and will get something at the hotel."

"It won't be as good as Sophie's," Gramps shouted.

Nothing will ever be as good as Sophie.

Chapter Ten

"I knew this was a house full of angels," Annie said. "That locket hanging there proves it. She's here, watching over you. I can feel it."

Sophie smiled at Annie. "Me, too." Even though she and Isaac had only been there a short time, she was going to miss them. "Pick an ornament to take with you, for you to remember Isaac's first Christmas tree."

"Oh, no, I couldn't."

"I insist," Sophie said. "Any one you want."

"I—"

"If you don't, I'll pick one for you."

"But you've already done so much for us."

Sophie stepped up to the tree and chose a blue bulb that had an angelic face painted on it, knowing Annie had admired it greatly last night. "How about this one?"

"Oh, I love that one."

"Then it's yours," Sophie said, tucking the ornament in the basket beside the sleeping baby. She then picked up the basket. "I'll carry him to the station for you." If she was smart, she'd say goodbye now, not take the chance of watching Welles climb aboard the train, but Annie had too much to carry herself. Besides the basket Isaac had grown used to sleeping in, there was another basket packed with enough food to get them to Denver and then some, as well as Annie's traveling bag that Welles had delivered to the house yesterday.

Annie had already said goodbye to Chester, who was sitting at the table brooding because Welles hadn't come back to say farewell. As Sophie opened the door, the train whistle blew and again when they walked along the road that was dotted with puddles from the melting snow.

"Be careful," Sophie warned. "It might be slippery."

"I can't believe how much snow has already melted."

"It's melting fast today," Sophie answered as they walked. "It's melted a good amount just since I walked to the depot this morning." She had to bite on her bottom lip before adding, "To find out what time the train was departing."

Welles hadn't been at the depot then, but he was sure to be now. He wouldn't miss the train, that was for sure.

The whistle blew again as they stepped on the platform, where Frank met them and took the food basket and traveling bag from Annie. "Saw you coming," he said. "Hurry aboard. The train's ready to pull out."

Sophie lifted a corner of the blanket covering Isaac and kissed his little forehead before handing the basket to Annie. "Write when you find the time."

"I will," Annie said, leaning over to give a quick hug. "I promise. And thank you again for everything."

Annie hurried aboard, and Frank, who had already carried her other things into the passenger car, closed the door and then stepped away while waving toward the front of the train, signaling for it to pull away.

The windows were fogged over, so seeing inside was impossible, but Sophie watched it leave anyway, blinking at the stinging of her eyes and wondering if Welles would return this time.

The wood beneath her feet rumbled as the train gained speed and the caboose rolled past.

What she saw then kept her feet glued to the platform. The hissing and rattling of the train was too loud to speak over. Not that it mattered. No words formed as she watched Welles step across the tracks and then onto the platform.

Questioning if she was seeing things, she shook her head,

slowly because she didn't want to take her eyes off him. Didn't want to be imagining things.

He shrugged as he walked closer.

A wave of trembles spread over her. After pinching her lips to stop them from quivering, she said, "You missed your train."

"No, I didn't. That wasn't my train."

She couldn't hope. Wouldn't hope. Not even while the shine in his eyes made her want to. "There's not another one until next week."

"That won't be my train, either." He took her hand, squeezed it and then used his hold to encourage her to step off the platform beside him.

"What about your poker game? Your thousand-dollar buy-in?"

"I played my last hand last night."

He could have left last night, after hanging her mother's locket on the tree, and there might have been a game at the saloon. But deep inside, she sensed that hadn't happened.

They'd crossed the street, and he paused only long enough at the livery to open the barn door and pull her inside.

Closing the door, he leaned against it as he took her other hand. Holding both of her hands firmly, he stared at her for so long, so deeply, she began to tremble again. From head to toe.

His thumbs rubbed the backs of her hands. "When I left here five years ago, it was supposed to be to buy horses, but horses had very little to do with why I left."

"I know. Colleen—"

"I ran into her a few miles out of town, but she wasn't the reason I left, either." He tugged her a bit closer. "You are the reason I left, Sophie. You were, are, so beautiful, so sweet and kind, and lovable. And that's what had happened. I'd fallen in love with you."

Her heart, which was already racing, threatened to leap right out of her chest.

"But you were young, too young, and I was the reason Lola was talking about sending you away. I didn't want to see that happen to you. I knew leaving would crush you. So I decided I was the one who needed to leave. When I ran into Colleen, she made me realize a couple of months wouldn't be long enough. You'd still be young and I'd still be in love with you."

He let out a heavy sigh. "Once we reached New Orleans, and I found out Colleen had emptied Chester's money box, I focused on winning enough money to pay him back. That continued to be my focus. Winning money to send here, buying horses to send here. I thought all that, the time, the focus, would make me forget all about you."

There were so many things she wanted to say, to admit, but couldn't. She was too afraid. Afraid her hopes were letting her hear what she wanted to hear, not what he was truly saying.

"When I heard about the Christmas Day game in Denver, I knew the train would take me through here. I figured the hour layover would give me time to check on Gramps, find out what happened to you and head back out again." He shook his head. "That didn't happen, and I can't blame it on the snowstorm. The moment I saw you, I knew I'd never forgotten anything about you. I tried to deny it the past couple of days." He shook his head. "And then I kissed you."

Her insides were trembling so hard, speaking was nearly impossible. All she could ask was, "And?"

"My bluff was called." He squeezed her fingers. "I've been in love with you since you were young, and so was I. It's not something I'll ever outgrow, ever get over. I'm home to stay, Sophie, and I hope that you're interested in letting me show you how much I love you."

Sophie closed her eyes, taking a moment to relish in the joy erupting inside her.

"I know it's a gamble. I know I've disappointed you, but I think, I hope, that you already love me, just a little."

"A little?" The amount of love inside her right now could fill the barn, the world. "I've loved you for so long, I don't know how to not love you." She took a step closer so her lips wouldn't have far to go to meet his. "And I never want to stop."

The touch of his lips against hers opened everything she'd buried deep inside. A love so immense, there was no controlling her response. Her arms wrapped around his neck and returned his kisses with a frenzy that could have shocked her. If she'd have let it. But she was done with that. Done with holding anything back. She knew what she wanted, and it was time to take it.

"I'll never gamble again," he said between kisses. "I promise." After a few more kisses, he said, "I'll be the most reliable, most respectable, man you've ever met." After one more kiss, he pulled his lips completely off hers, and held her face with both hands. "And I'll take you wherever you want to go. Anywhere in the world. Everywhere your ornaments came from."

"I love you, Welles, just as you are, and there's nowhere I want to go." The happiness inside her was so great, so massive, her eyes stung with tears of joy. "Everything I want is right here."

"Marry me?"

She gave herself enough time to say, "Yes," before kissing him again. His lips, his neck, his chin.

His kisses ran along the side of her face, her forehead. "I'll build you a house on your land, if you want, or buy some other land."

"Someday, maybe," she said while placing more kisses along his jaw. "Chester needs us here right now."

Welles pulled too far away for her to keep kissing and grasped her upper arms. "You don't mind that? Taking care of Gramps for at least a few more years?"

"If I minded taking care of Chester, I'd have left years ago." She ran a hand up his chest until it was right over his heart. "He'll be very glad you're home to stay. Almost as glad as I am."

"Should we go tell him?"

Slipping both hands around his neck, she pulled his face forward. "In a few minutes."

As his lips met hers, he said, "Or an hour."

* * * * *

*If you enjoyed this story you won't want to miss these
other great full-length reads
by Lauri Robinson:*

Winning the Mail-Order Bride
Married to Claim the Rancher's Heir
In the Sheriff's Protection
Diary of a War Bride

CHRISTMAS
WITH THE OUTLAW

Kathryn Albright

Dear Reader,

Thank you for journeying with me one more time to Oak Grove so that Abigail could have her own happy-ever-after. I've grown to love this imaginary town and the people that make it so fun. Here's to communities and the souls within them who share in each other's joy and grief, and who look out for their neighbors. May your Christmas be bright!

Kathryn

Dedication

I'd like to dedicate this Christmas story to my wonderful readers. It is a joy to write stories for you.

Chapter One

Oak Grove, Kansas—1879

Abigail White bent over the counter, reading the next edition of the *Oak Grove Gazette* with a critical eye. If this proof was perfect, she and her brother could go ahead and print the rest for circulation tomorrow.

The bells above the door jingled, disturbing her concentration as her brother entered the office, bringing with him a brace of cold November air.

"Morning." He strode past her and the printing press and down the narrow hallway to his small office in the back.

She followed. They had to discuss the upcoming advertisements for the special Christmas edition of the newspaper. She had tried yesterday during Thanksgiving dinner, but he had put her off, saying he wouldn't talk business on a holiday in his new home. She'd been shocked. In all the years they had lived together he had never minded talking business. Now, with a wife and daughter, he was putting up walls and keeping her more and more at a distance.

"We need to talk, Teddy."

He shrugged from his overcoat and hung it on the wall peg, and then hooked his bowler hat over his coat. His shirt was more rumpled than usual. "Sorry I'm late. Dorie had a fussy night. I think she was overly tired from yesterday's excitement."

"You don't think it was the apple pie I made, do you? I found it a bit tart." She'd had an upset stomach herself, but she certainly wasn't going to admit that to Teddy. He had growled at her enough over the years about her lack of skill in the kitchen.

When he didn't immediately answer, she prompted him. "Teddy?"

"Maybe. It might have been the pie. She had a spoonful of stuffing too. Anyway, she's sleeping hard now and so is Hannah." He walked past her and into the kitchen, rubbing his hands together and blowing on them to warm them. He stopped at the stove. "No fire yet? No coffee?"

She shook her head. The paper was more important. She really wanted him to—

Teddy sighed. "It wouldn't hurt for you to try. Coffee is not that difficult." He crumpled a handful of old newspapers and stuffed them into the belly of the stove, followed by a scoopful of coal.

She'd simply been concentrating on a new article. "I've been busy."

"Pulling typeset?"

"That and other things." She pulled the pencil out from where it rested over her ear and slipped a small notepad from her apron pocket. She'd just had another thought about the Christmas edition. She jotted down a word to help her remember it. "Look… Teddy…"

"You could have visited more with Josiah."

She drew back. Josiah. Again. "I did! We talked about the Betterment Committee."

"That's not what I mean. You could have asked something personal, even just asked how he was."

She scowled. "I wasn't interested in how he was. Now that the Betterment Committee has supplied the twelve women and they are all happily married off, I don't see the need for the committee anymore. I wanted to find out what he was going to do with any unused funds."

He looked up from the coffeepot.

She wasn't ready for the compassion she saw in his gaze. "Stop it, Teddy. I know I've complained about the committee in the past. I'll admit, I was slightly bitter. None of those men ever took a second look at me."

He sat down at the small table, waiting on the coffee to boil, a routine that had played out often over the past eleven years. He'd been sixteen and she eleven when the cholera had swept through their neighborhood in Philadelphia. It took Father first. Their mother's dying instructions had been to take the family printing press and leave before they came down sick too. After several years in Missouri, they'd settled here.

"What about the men that are left?"

She shrugged. "Cowboys and farmers? What would we talk about? Crops and planting schedules? Cattle? I have nothing in common with them. And that includes Josiah Melbourne."

"You don't let anyone close enough to know you, Abby. You are all…"

She wouldn't let the fact that he had used her nickname lower her defenses. She crossed her arms over her middle. "What?"

Teddy sighed. "Sharp edges and prickles."

"Where is it written that I must marry anyway? I have my position here at the *Gazette*. I am fine." She disliked talking about this subject. It was so…*personal* and it never accomplished anything. Turning from him, she took two mugs down from the cupboard.

"I just hate to see you alone."

"Not everyone is destined to find their perfect match. You said yourself that no man wants a woman smarter than him."

He covered his mouth as he coughed. "Not quite. What I said was that it would take a man who is confident in his own abilities to be your complement."

"It's the same thing, just couched in more pleasant words. And there aren't any such eligible men in Oak Grove, so that's the end of it." His assessment stung in ways he'd never understand. Didn't he realize that she'd rather stay single than sit across the table and try to converse with a man she had nothing in common with? She wanted someone with whom she could discuss ideas and debate issues. It wasn't a matter of being prideful. It was a matter of being realistic.

"You should see this as fortunate," she continued. "I'm here to take care of the *Gazette* when you are busy and I don't mind playing the spinster aunt to Dorie. So please don't worry about me."

"You are being melodramatic. Twenty-two is not spinsterhood."

She didn't bother to reply. Instead, she plopped the newspaper proof down in front of him. "Can we please get to work? Patty Owens has asked to do an article."

He slipped his glasses from his vest pocket and curled the wires over his ears, then peered at the newspaper critically. "She's still in school," he said, as if that closed the matter.

"It's her last year. I told her we'd need a proposal and a sample of her writing."

"Hmm." He kept reading.

"I was her age when I started."

He looked up from the page. "I don't have time to work with her. I'll leave it for you to decide. Make it for the Christmas edition, since that is your responsibility."

It wasn't until much later, after Teddy had gone home and she'd locked the front and back doors to the *Gazette* office, that she took her candle and climbed the stairs to her room. The conversation with her brother had played in her mind all day. Did she push people away? Was she the one keeping her distance?

Teddy knew her better than anyone—knew the best and the worst of her and still he stood by her. If she were truthful with herself, some of their biggest arguments had been a test to see if he would leave her. She knew she was difficult at times. Yet he had always stayed. Even happily married, he included her in his life.

She set the candleholder on the table by her bed. The nights were so long and quiet now. She wrapped her shawl closer around her shoulders and sat down in the rocking chair by the window, staring down at the main street of town. Lamplight shone from the second-story window above the Taylors' barber shop. Next door to them the bank was dark. The entire street, down to the church and school at the end, was bathed in silvery-blue shadows from the half-moon. Beyond them, the dark meadow blurred into the night sky, where a myriad of stars twinkled.

Now that Thanksgiving had passed, everyone's thoughts would turn to Christmas—her first one completely on her own. With the weddings this year, it seemed that life here was all about settling down. A handful of town folk, she and the mayor included, were the odd ones out. Hence the awkward dinner at her brother's house.

She didn't have a close friend—never wanted or needed one as long as she had Teddy. Friendships could be…messy. It was better to keep a comfortable distance. As a reporter, it helped her to stay objective. That way she could present a story honestly. The trouble was, she had never felt so lonely as she did now with Christmas looming. This time between the two holidays was supposed to be filled with good cheer and friendship. How could that be if she had no one to share it with? She didn't even know how to go about making a friend or, with her sharp tongue, keeping one.

A dash of light trailed across the sky over the church steeple—there and gone the next second. A shooting star!

Memories flooded her of sitting on the steep back steps of their brownstone in Philadelphia, safe in the crook of Father's arm. Even though she knew it was only nostalgia urging her, she closed her eyes and concentrated on the streak of light that she had just seen. *I wish for one true friend this Christmas. Please!*

* * *

The town of Barton, Colorado, shrunk in the distance as Russell Carter leaned low over the withers of the horse he'd "borrowed" and rode stealthily down the narrow deer trail and farther into the thick pine forest. He kept to the trees and followed the rock-strewn river down the mountainside. If his luck held, he'd get to the station ahead of the sheriff and take the train east. If it didn't, he'd have to ride at night and rest during the day.

Every jarring step his mount took caused the pain in his side to flare. He held his arm tight against the gunshot wound and clamped his teeth together to keep from crying out. Since he'd used up a mountain's worth of luck by surviving this long, he figured he didn't have much left.

Wanted for murder... The sheriff's voice still rang in his ears.

It all happened so fast that it was jumbled in his head—which was pounding. He must have hit it hard when he fell. He crunched back down, resting his head on his mount's neck. He had to make it out of here. He just had to...

Chapter Two

"Miss White! Miss White!"

Abigail stopped in front of the mercantile and waited, shifting the packages in her arms.

Patty Owens hurried toward her, breathing hard from her rush down the boardwalk. Her face was so pink from exertion that half her freckles had disappeared. She waved two papers in her hand. "The samples of my writing you wanted."

Abigail was late for her appointment with Sheriff Baniff. She really didn't have time for conversation. "Deep breath, Patty." She suddenly realized that she'd been tapping her foot impatiently and stopped. She wasn't sure whether she should encourage the girl. Newspaper work required long hours, and the income from the *Gazette* wasn't enough to hire another person.

Abigail shifted the box she held and took the papers. "Are your parents agreeable with this?"

Patty blew out a breath. "Just this once, since Miss Burnett is grading it as a school project."

Abigail realized she was tapping her toe again. When had that started up? She stilled it. "All right. Have you figured out the focus for the article?"

Patty looked a bit surprised. "Well...Christmas of course."

As though this time of year there was nothing more important. "That's a broad subject."

"Well...I thought that I'd interview each of the children in class and find out what they want."

Abigail shook her head. "Too self-serving of the children. Christmas is about giving, remember? Stop by the *Gazette* when you come up with something a bit more focused." She gave Patty a stern look. "And that doesn't mean I'm saying yes."

Patty lowered her shoulders. "This is important to me, Miss White."

"I'm beginning to realize that." She was impressed with the girl's tenacity. "We'll talk again. For now, I have an appointment with Sheriff Baniff I must attend."

She watched until Patty disappeared into the mercantile. Likely, with Christmas just around the corner, the girl would get caught up in any number of activities and forget about the article. She hurried to the newspaper office, where she dropped off the packages and handed Teddy his mail, then she grabbed her notepad and marched across the street to the hotel.

The first floor of the hotel housed the main restaurant in town. Sheriff Baniff sat enjoying a cup of coffee at his regular table by the far window. Once, he had explained that he liked to be able to see out. Even though Oak Grove was fairly tame for a town, it could get rowdy in the spring and fall when ranchers drove their cattle to the stockyards on the east edge.

"Sorry I'm late, Sheriff."

He started to rise.

"No. Please," she said quickly. She unbuttoned her overcoat and left it on a nearby chair before sitting across from him.

Rollie Austin approached the table. "The usual, Miss White?"

"Yes. Thank you." She had tea during these sessions with the sheriff. It was much more refined than coffee.

Rollie disappeared into the kitchen.

Flipping open her notepad, she pulled the pencil from above her right ear. "Now. What news, Sheriff? Any more ideas about the fire in Mr. Owen's wheat field?"

"Vagrants. It looked to be initially contained."

Abigail jotted that note down. "Like a cook fire?"

"Yep. Whoever started it is long gone."

She tapped the end of her pencil on the table, mulling over the facts she knew about the fire. "What about a group of boys? Boys are fascinated by fire."

At that moment, Rollie came with her cup of tea. She held her tongue, conscious of the fact that it was Rollie's boy, Kade, along with several others near his age that, when together, had a mischievous bent. Then another thought came to her. She lowered her voice. "Do you suspect liquor was involved?"

"No evidence of it."

She stirred honey into her tea. "If you find out anything, please let me know. According to the paper from Dodge City, a number of ladies are pressuring the state legislature to declare a law prohibiting the sale of liquor in the entire state."

Sheriff Baniff huffed out a breath. "That won't make our saloon owners happy." He withdrew a folded piece of paper from his vest pocket. "I received this from the marshal in Barton, Colorado. There was a murder at the silver mine there two days ago. The murderer escaped. He is believed to have boarded the train and headed this way. I want you to get the article into the next edition."

"Forewarned is forearmed, I always say. Wouldn't that be frightening to have a murderer in our midst?" She unfolded the paper.

And forgot to breathe.

It couldn't be. Russell Carter! His hair was shorter now, and he wore a small mustache and goatee. She let out a slow breath.

The sheriff narrowed his gaze. "Are you all right, Miss White?"

Inside, she was shaking. She concentrated on breathing regularly while she folded the paper back up and tucked it inside her notepad. "Yes. Absolutely. I have a strong constitution."

"Then you'll take care of it?"

"Certainly. What…what did you say he is accused of? Murder? Are there any particulars that I can include in the article?"

"Something about a long-standing grievance. The foreman was pushing for better working conditions. He walked into the company office. There were words. And he was shot."

"And then Russ—the man pictured here—got away?"

"He was last seen at the train station."

"If he took the train, he could be anywhere by now. Denver, Chicago, San Francisco. It's been three days." She rose from her seat. She had to tell Teddy. Russ was his good friend.

"You're not going to finish your tea?"

"No. I believe I have enough information to get started. Thank you, Sheriff. I'll contact you if I have any more questions." She stuffed her pencil over her ear, gathered her coat and rushed out.

Oh, this was dreadful! She wasn't sure how she made it across the street and through the front door of the *Gazette* office. She threw her belongings onto the counter, not caring about the possibility that ink might get on her coat. "Teddy! Teddy!"

"Back here!" He was hunkered down behind the printer.

"You need to see this!" She glanced about the room to make sure no one else was there. "It's about Russell Carter!"

Teddy straightened up. "Russ? It's been a few years."

"Well, yes. I know. Four at least. He's gotten himself into trouble."

"What has he done now?"

She wasn't surprised at Teddy's attitude. Russ had instigated a fair amount of mischief and pulled her brother in with him in the past, but nothing like this! "I don't think his smile or his good looks will be enough to get him out of it. His face is on a wanted poster! The sheriff just asked me to write up an article for the paper."

He frowned. "Here, let me see that." He repositioned his round glasses on the bridge of his nose and spread the poster out on the counter.

She repeated the sheriff's words.

Slowly, Teddy folded the paper and met her gaze. "This is bad."

"What about the sheriff's request? Must we follow it?"

"I am surprised to hear you say that. I thought you never forgave Russ."

Her brother's words brought back memories she'd rather not dredge up. They'd been a threesome—her brother and Russ and Tim—and at seventeen, she had set her cap for Tim. Then Russ had fixated on heading West to mine in Colorado. He convinced Tim to go with him. Her dreams had been crushed.

"That's neither here nor there. Russ was your friend. This is a blow."

"I never thought he'd kill a man." Teddy sighed. "Makes me think there is more to the story."

"I should go ahead with the article?" The idea still bothered her. "I suppose there is no other way?"

"We can't manipulate the law for our own—or a friend's— gain."

"That was Russ's problem. He could smile his way out of any situation." The things he'd gotten away with had irked her to no end.

"Looks like things have caught up with him." Teddy turned back toward his office. "Hard to work after news like this. Think I'll call it a day."

She watched from the doorway as he hung up his apron and shrugged into his overcoat, a bit envious that he had a wife and daughter waiting at home for him. Once he was gone, she locked the door and pulled the dark green blind on the front window. When they'd first started in Oak Grove, they had burned the oil lamps late into the night, working hard to make their fledgling business successful. When Teddy married, he wanted more time with his family and so had curtailed that. Now, with the days growing shorter and colder, no one ever stopped in after dark.

After a bite of cheese, a sourdough roll and warmed-up coffee, she carried the coffeepot out the back door and tossed the leftover coffee and grounds onto her garden plot. Dusk had settled over the town. Lamplight flickered in the front window of the doctor's house. A shiver went through Abigail as she realized how chilled she'd become standing there. Quickly, she turned and hurried back inside.

She lit a candle from the dying embers in the stove, poured herself a glass of water from the pitcher and headed upstairs, taking the poster of Russell Carter with her.

Chapter Three

The next morning when she descended to the main floor of the shop, sunlight streamed in the front windows and pans rattled in the kitchen. A rich aroma wafted her way. Teddy had the coffee brewing.

"Good morning," she said, stepping into the kitchen. A pan sat on the stove, alongside the coffeepot. "You've made breakfast?"

He plunked a bowl of creamed wheat in front of her and handed her the crock of honey. "I have a meeting with the building committee this morning."

"Then why are you bothering with my breakfast?"

"You've lost weight. Hannah noticed it at church on Sunday. You're not eating since I moved out."

"I'm fine." She couldn't very well tell him that she didn't like to eat by herself.

"You get distracted and forget."

"Well, I've been caught up in a new book. I'm afraid the oil lamp was still burning when I awoke this morning."

Teddy shook his head. "You know that you can always join us for supper. Hannah has mentioned it several times."

"Don't be silly. You need your time with your family. Once a week on Sunday is quite enough. Besides I have every intention of becoming a better cook."

He raised his brows, but didn't reply, instead downing the last of his coffee. "I need to get to the meeting." The bells above the front door jangled as he left.

It was toasty warm in the kitchen. She ate, wondering

absently how her brother got the creamed wheat so perfectly smooth. Surely it couldn't be that difficult.

A muffled scrape...sounded down the hall.

She lowered her spoon. A mouse? This was certainly the season for them. They sought warmth and sustenance inside as much as any person would this time of year. Oh, how she detested rodents.

There it is again!

Situations like this, she wished Teddy still lived here. Slowly she stood and grasped the broom from the corner, prepared to sweep whatever she found out the back door. She only hoped it wasn't larger than a mouse. At that thought, she paused. Now that she considered it, it did sound larger than a mouse. Not a rat. Surely not a rat...

She scanned Teddy's office. Nothing amiss there. She tiptoed farther down the short hall toward the storage room. Her heart pounded. It was ridiculous to be so intense about such a small creature, but that didn't change the fact that she was. Gripping the broom in one hand and clasping the doorknob with the other, she took a deep breath and slowly opened the door.

A man! At the far wall, atop the piles of old newspapers, lay a man! He was curled up, facing away from her. His shoulder shifted ever so slightly with his ragged breathing. In... Out... In... Out...

"You, there!" she said, mustering her sternest voice. "Just what do you think you are doing?"

No response. Was he a vagrant? The quality of his overcoat certainly didn't look the part, although it was caked with mud. How in the world had he gained entrance? She'd locked the doors last night, hadn't she?

She jabbed the stiff bristles of her broom into his back. "You there! You have to leave. Speak to the preacher if you are in a bad fix. You can't stay here."

He began to move, slowly at first, and then he flopped

over to his back. A groan broke the dried seam of spittle on his lips.

Good heavens! It was *Russ*!

She dropped the broom and rushed to him. "Russ! What happened? What…?"

He was so pale! His lips were cracked and dry, his breathing shallow, his eyes closed. There was a scrape and bruise on his cheek. Blood stained his brocade vest. She drew back, fisting her hand. "Oh, Russ. You've been hurt."

His eyes fluttered open, unfocused. Although dull in the shadows of the storage room, she remembered in the sunlight they had dazzled her, shining crystal blue.

"I'm Abigail. Do you remember me?" she asked.

His brows furrowed, but then slowly he nodded—a subtle, barely there movement of his head.

"You're hurt. I'll go for the doctor." Her heart was pounding. *Lord, don't let him die!*

"No doctor. Water," he rasped out the words, then a cough racked his body. He grimaced with pain.

Water. Yes. That might help. She rushed to the kitchen, grateful that Teddy had already seen to filling the pitcher from the well that morning. She poured half a cup and carried it back to him. Squirming her hand under his neck, she supported his head and held the cup to his lips. He took a sip and then, exhausted from the effort, dropped his head back and closed his eyes.

She waited, hoping he would gather his strength and explain to her what had happened. She studied him further. His mustache could use trimming, along with his weeks' worth of whiskers. He was still one of the most handsome boys—she corrected herself—men, she knew. Yes, he was definitely a man now.

"Please let me fetch the doctor for you. You've been bleeding. I don't know anything about taking care of wounds or sickness."

"No. I just need to rest." A shiver coursed through him.

This storage area was the coldest room. The outside wall faced north and there was no stove or fireplace. It was a good place to store things, but not an injured man.

"I'll get a blanket." She hurried up the stairs to Teddy's old room and ripped the two from his bed. She grabbed the pillow too. When she returned, Russ hadn't moved.

A pile of newspapers made for a hard, uncomfortable bed, but she had no idea what else to do. She couldn't manage moving him. She did her best to straighten him out and then covered him, tucking in the edges of the woolen blankets around him, then she wedged the pillow under his head.

She held the cup of water to his lips once more. When he felt the pressure of the rim, he raised up slightly and drank, greedier this time. He opened his eyes. "Thanks, Angel," he croaked, and then dropped his head once more to the pillow.

Angel? Truly the man did not remember her. He could save his insincere endearments for another woman—one more gullible.

As she watched, his breathing evened out, so much so that she presumed he'd drifted off to sleep. His face lost some of its pastiness. His tousled, dark brown hair needed a wash. Actually, most of him did by the looks of his wrinkled clothing and muddy boots. And she worried about his wound. That needed attention.

Where was Teddy? This was his predicament. Not hers. Russ was *his* friend. She didn't want him here, dragging her or Teddy into whatever mess he'd made. *Murder.* It was still so hard to believe.

And he was hurt. She frowned at the thought. She couldn't let that sway her. Likely any injury was his own fault.

She stepped closer. "Russ? Russell?" When he didn't make any movement, she took hold of the blanket and drew it down slowly. "I'm just going to check that area where you were bleeding. I want to make sure it has stopped and see if I should bandage it." As she spoke, she unbuttoned his vest and then his shirt.

Black hair peppered his chest. On his right side, near his waist, blood oozed slowly from the center of a congealed glob. It was the size of her fist! She couldn't fix this. She raised her gaze and found him watching her, his eyes mere slits in his face. "You need a doctor. Please."

He shook his head. "No one can know I'm here."

Frustrated, she marched from the room. She might not have gotten on well with him, but she didn't want him dying! She counted to ten, then grabbed a clean towel from the kitchen cupboard, folded it and returned, pressing it against the wound.

Russ clenched his teeth and groaned.

She released the pressure slightly. "What caused this? A knife? A bullet? A stick?"

Bells jingled, announcing someone's entry into the office.

Great. Just great. Why didn't Teddy get back here and help?

"Miss White? Miss Abigail?"

Patty! That's all she needed. She pulled the covers up to his chin. "Be still. And be quiet."

Patty waited at the counter at the front of the shop. The girl shifted her weight from one foot to the other. "You have no idea how excited I am about working with you. What did you think about my writing? Will you take me on?"

Abigail didn't have time for this! She needed to get back to Russ. Then she spied the stubby end of a pencil poking through Patty's thick auburn hair, just over her ear. Something softened inside her. On a sigh, she withdrew the two folded papers from her apron pocket. "These are well written. You are aware that reporting won't be the same as a short piece of fiction or a persuasive argument."

"Oh, I understand that!"

"And what about a tighter focus for your idea?"

Patty grinned. "Since you thought that asking each child what they wanted for Christmas encouraged selfishness rather than the giving spirit of the holiday, I decided to make it about something bigger. Something that everybody would benefit from."

"Can you elaborate?"

"It would force the children to think of others. Not just themselves."

"An example, please?"

"Well…for instance, in the summertime there is no shade anywhere in town except for a few covered boardwalks. Wouldn't it be nice to ask for seedlings to plant about the town? Perhaps one by the school for shade when the children play out of doors and one by the church for our summer ice-cream social. Another example would be a few benches down by the river for people to sit on when they fish or take a Sunday stroll?"

Abigail remembered the park she'd played in when she was young. There had been a lake…with small boats for people to use. "It's a much better idea."

Patty beamed. "Then…I may begin interviewing the children?"

"Absolutely."

"Eee! I can't wait to tell Miss Burnett! I'm going to have my first published article!" Suddenly, Patty danced forward and hugged Abigail—a quick, excited squeeze. "I have to get home. Oh, thank you, Miss White! Thank you!" She rushed out the door.

Abigail stared after her, dazed by the girl's enthusiasm. And her hug. She wasn't used to being hugged.

"You promised to publish it without even setting eyes on it?" Teddy said from behind her.

She startled. She hadn't heard him come in the back way. "Her writing samples were good."

"It could be rubbish."

"I'll help her."

Her brother raised his brows. "I believe you are getting soft, Abigail White."

She suddenly remembered about Russ. Dropping the writing samples on the counter, she took Teddy's hand and dragged him toward the back room. "Come quick!"

He followed her to the storage room, stopping short when he saw that a man lay on top of the pile of newspapers.

"It's Russ."

He met her gaze, then looked back at his friend. "Is he conscious?"

"He's been injured. There is a wound on his right flank."

Teddy raised his brows. "You didn't get the doctor?"

"He bid me not to. Teddy…what are we going to do? What if the sheriff finds him?"

"Not a word of this to anyone until we can sort this out."

Between the two of them, somebody had to be the voice of reason. "But he is wanted by the law! If we keep quiet, we'll…we'll be implicated. We could lose everything we've worked so hard for! Keep in mind that it's not just us anymore. There's Hannah and Dorie to think of too."

Teddy lowered his shoulders with that weight.

"It's been four years since we last saw him. We don't know what he's been doing since he left Missouri. People do change and not always for the good."

"Not that much. Not on the inside."

She pressed her lips together. "It is dangerous for us to help him. Teddy, he is your friend. I realize that makes this difficult."

"I think you are as confused as I am over how to manage this."

She sighed. There were too many variables, too many what-ifs bumping around in her head. "We are taking such a risk. What if he dies? What then?"

"We can't let that happen."

Suddenly Russ flung his arm out, and his eyes opened to stare, glassy and unfocused, at the flickering light of the candle. Sweat coated his face. Alarmed, she shoved the candle plate at her brother and peeled back the cover to

Russ's waist. Fresh blood seeped through the clean towel over his wound.

He grasped her wrist. "The whole place is going to blow!" he said urgently, his eyes wild. "Get out of here! Run!"

He wasn't himself! The strength he still possessed in his grip surprised her. She was frightened. "Oh, Russ. I have to get the doctor. I must." She feared what might happen if she waited a second longer.

He didn't seem to comprehend her.

Teddy met her gaze, his own uneasy. "Go."

She flung her heavy shawl over her shoulders and hurried out the back door.

A thin layer of icy dew clung to the brittle shoots of dead grass and crunched under her shoes as she ran past her barren garden plot and the outhouse to the next street. Dr. Graham lived only a stone's throw away, the first house on the corner.

Sylvia, his wife, answered her knock. The scent of frying bacon wafted out to Abigail.

"What is it, Miss White?" The doctor asked, coming to the door a second behind his wife.

"A friend is feverish."

He threw on his coat and grabbed his black bag, which sat ready by the door, and followed her.

She led him into the storage room. In the time she'd been gone, Teddy had lit the lamp and hung it from the ceiling hook. "He was injured a few days ago and doesn't seem to be healing."

The doctor nodded briefly to her brother and then leaned over Russ to examine him. He drew down the covers and peeled away the dressing. "This needs attention. Bring a bowl of warm water and several clean cloths."

She hurried to the kitchen and filled a pan with water. As she waited for it to warm, Teddy and the doctor appeared at the doorway, supporting Russ between them. "We're moving him up to my old room. The lighting will be better there for the doc."

Upstairs? She nodded her agreement. Teddy's old feather tick would be much more comfortable than the pile of news-papers in the cold storage room. And she supposed if he cried out in the night, needing something, she would be nearby in her bedroom across the hallway. Still, it seemed a bit too familiar…

A few moments later, an anguished yell reverberated through the building. What in heaven's name were they doing to him? She poured warm water from the kettle into the basin, grabbed the towels and ran up the stairs. Russ lay on the bed, his face pasty white, and all of him as still as death. Was he even breathing?

The doctor leaned over him, a bloody tool in his hand. "The bullet is out."

The air rushed out of her. A gunshot wound! Perhaps when he killed the man, it was in self-defense and not mur-der at all! There were any number of possibilities. "Then he will recover?"

Doctor Graham wet a towel and cleaned Russ's side. "The next twenty-four hours will tell."

This was more than she had bargained for! She had never taken care of someone so horribly sick. What if she did something wrong? What if she made him worse?

The doctor bandaged the wound and then cleaned off his tool.

"What do I need to do? What about his fever?"

"I'll leave this with you." He handed her a small bottle of powder. "If his fever spikes, give him half a teaspoonful of this mixed in a glass of water. Otherwise, sponge him down every hour with tepid water until his fever breaks. If he chills, blanket him up good and warm."

The magnitude of her responsibility suddenly hit her. "I've never cared for someone this sick. Teddy and I have had a cold on occasion, but neither of us are prepared…"

"I'm afraid no one asks for situations like this. I'll send my wife to help if you would like."

"No!" she said quickly. The less people who knew of Russ's presence, the better. "I mean… I'll figure it out."

Doc Graham's eyes narrowed. "Your friend has a lot to answer for when he starts feeling better."

"But you will keep this to yourself? We have reason to believe he may be in danger."

"Which puts you in danger as well, not to mention the rest of us who live here."

She hadn't considered that. Up until now, she'd only thought it was the sheriff who would bring trouble.

Dr. Graham frowned. "Should the sheriff ask me directly, I'll be honest about all this. I owe that to the good folks of the town."

"I understand," she said. "Thank you."

He turned and headed down the stairs.

Teddy turned to her. "I'll see the doctor out and then get started on the paper. You better stay up here with Russ. If he wakes, you will need to quiet him."

"Very well. I just wish Russ were well enough to tell us what is going on. The not knowing is worse than anything."

Chapter Four

Russ woke to a brightness behind his eyelids and the harsh pain of trying to swallow. His throat felt like he'd downed a spoonful of hot gravel. Then he realized his side hurt as though an iron bar pinioned him. Beside him, Abby rose from her chair and walked to the window, where the rays from the sun slashed through the glass and across his pillow and face. She unhooked the sash, letting the heavy dark green curtains on each side of the window straighten, pitching the room into gray twilight.

He'd sensed her presence throughout the day. Little Abigail, all grown up. As he slipped in and out of sleep, he'd heard enough of her conversation with Ted to know that she wasn't happy he'd shown up. She had reason to feel that way, considering some of the things he'd done in her past.

Yet, even with her reservations toward him, she'd been surprisingly gentle when she slipped her cool hand under his neck, supporting his head gently as she offered him sips of water every hour. And once she'd added honey and thinned the bowl of creamed wheat with milk, he'd managed to get half of it down.

She sat back down and stared at a notebook in her hand.

"What's that you have, Abby?"

She startled slightly, but then stuffed the notebook into her apron pocket. "You're awake. Are you feeling better?"

"Some water?"

"Oh. Of course!" Quickly she poured half a glass and held it to his lips. Her hands were shaking slightly, and some water spilled down his cheek. She dabbed it away with a cloth, and when her gaze rose to meet his, her motion slowed and then stopped.

He'd forgotten how her brown eyes captured the light. Intelligence simmered there…and lots of questions.

He swallowed. It was easier after the cool water soothed his throat. "Thanks."

"Teddy and I are anxious to know what happened. I'll… I'll just get him."

Before he could stop her, she disappeared from the room. He didn't feel like talking. Not yet. His brain felt sluggish, his tongue thick and slow. But he owed them. He wouldn't be alive without their help.

A few minutes later, Teddy appeared at the door. "Good to see you among the living. What's going on, Russ? How did you get that wound you have there?"

He coughed, and white-hot pain ripped through his side. It felt like he'd been shot all over again.

Abby rushed out and then returned with a small, embroidered cushion, which she tucked against his side. "Hold this when you cough. It will help allay the pain."

How did she know? Anyway, he wished she would slow down. The room was starting to spin with her constant movement.

"Take your time," Abby said quickly. "Was it self-defense?"

Ted scowled at her. "Let him talk."

Same old Abby. She never could keep quiet when she wanted answers. At one time, her constant questions had annoyed him. Then he realized what she'd just said. What was she talking about? "Self-defense?"

"You're wanted in Colorado for murder. Is it true?"

Murder? What? "I didn't kill anyone." At least…he didn't remember killing anyone.

Bits and pieces of that evening started to come together. Johnson…shooting McCabe, then turning the gun on him.

The room wouldn't stop spinning. Had he hit his head some-where along the way to Oak Grove?

Downstairs, a door opened. "Mr. White? The paper rolls came in."

Abby glanced at her brother—fear lighting her eyes. "It's Jamie…"

Russ didn't want them in trouble because of him. He gripped his side and tried to sit up. "I should go…"

"Lie back, Russ." Ted pressed his shoulder, pushing him back down to the bed. "Jamie works for me. You are safe for now. No one knows you are here."

The room spun. He gave up struggling and collapsed back on the hard bed. Criminy, he was weak! "I…I didn't kill anyone."

Then the blanket was tucked around him again and sud-denly the room went dark. A shiver coursed through him.

Abigail slipped the pencil from above her ear and tried to concentrate on an article for the coming edition while keeping one ear attuned to Russ's breathing. Without her help, Teddy would never get the paper out by Saturday. She jotted down a teaser for the extra Christmas edition.

A low moan issued from Russ's parted lips.

She leaned over the bed and checked his forehead. Still warm, but not as hot as earlier. She checked the tempera-ture of the water and then wrung out the washcloth. As she leaned forward to wipe his face, she heard the door open downstairs. She stopped, the cloth hovering an inch from Russ's nose. What if Russ cried out? What if some-one heard?

A few seconds later, the front door of the shop opened and then closed again. Teddy called up the stairwell. "I've sent Jamie on home. Everything all right up there?"

She walked to the top of the stairs so that she could see Teddy. "He's resting easier," she said softly.

Her brother nodded and then turned back to his work.

She walked back into the spare bedroom. Russ hadn't stirred, but on the chance he was listening she said softly, "I'm going to sponge you down again."

She pulled the covers to his waist. His shirt remained unfastened and his suspenders looped on each side of his torso. She had steeled herself against the sight of him before, but now the dying rays of the setting sun sent long shadows across his face and his bare chest, revealing muscles and planes previously hidden. He truly was a handsome man. The sight started a flutter in her abdomen. Heat rushed up her face. Oh, my, but she had to quell that sensation or she'd never get done what needed to be done.

Gingerly, she dabbed the cloth on his forehead. When he didn't move or cry out, she pressed it to his cheek, holding it there for a moment. Dipping the cloth once more into the water, she wrung the excess out, and then pressed it to the other side of his face.

He had always been handsome. She'd forgotten how long his lashes were—dark brown and thick, they lay still against his flushed, angular cheeks. In the intervening years since she'd last seen him, he'd lost the softness she remembered. His jawline appeared stronger and squarer behind the stubby growth of dark beard.

Russ, what have you been up to for the past four years?

She finished bathing his face and neck. He seemed calmer, more relaxed. Still, his skin was hot. There was nothing for her to do but continue. She wrung out the cloth again and began on his chest where the scattering of springy dark hair cushioned her administrations. The butterflies in her stomach started up again in a frenzy.

She avoided the bandaged area on his right flank and finished the bathing to his waist. Then she set the washcloth and pan of water aside, buttoned up his shirt and covered him.

He'd always wanted to make something of himself. When he made up his mind to head West to find his fortune, he'd almost persuaded Teddy to go with him. But thankfully Teddy had learned what life would be like for a girl in a rough mining camp and he'd backed out. That's when Russ had focused his efforts on Tim. Tim had been Teddy's replacement.

"How is he doing?" her brother said from the doorway. She hadn't heard him climb the stairs.

"Has he woken at all?"

"No. But he seems to be breathing easier. The medicine Doc Graham gave him helped."

"Good." Teddy let out a sigh.

"We're not running the article about Russ, are we?"

"No."

"What will we tell the sheriff?"

"We'll figure out something."

She realized then, that he wore his overcoat. Alarm rippled through her. "You're not leaving, are you?"

"I have to get home."

"I know that. But…it isn't appropriate having Russ here with me overnight."

"Do you see an alternative? I think we should keep to our schedules to avoid suspicion."

She followed him as he headed back down the stairs. "I don't like this, Teddy." And ironically, it wasn't because they harbored a possible murderer. Truth be told, Russ stirred something in her. Seeing him again brought back feelings she'd determined to leave behind when she left Missouri. Feelings that made her…uncomfortable.

"It is only for a few days, until he's feeling better. I'm sure he will leave then."

Abigail pursed her lips. No help there. Her stomach had been in a perpetual knot since he'd arrived, yet if he left, would he be on the run forever?

She locked the door behind Teddy, then walked through to the front of the printing office and pulled the shades. She didn't want to care about his problems. It had hurt too much before when he ignored her and taunted her. Why, oh, why, of all places, had he chosen to come here?

Just what had she gotten herself into?

Chapter Five

She slept fitfully, worried that Russ might need attention during the night. She kept her bedroom door open, waking three times to listen to his breathing. Each time, she rose, checked his forehead for fever and, finding it warm, sponged him down.

Dreams chased her of the four of them—Teddy, Russ, Timothy and herself—when they'd lived in Missouri. Russ was good-looking at seventeen when she'd first met him. He had a winning smile that he used often and to its best advantage. Girls aplenty hung on his every word. Girls who looked past the fact that he made a pittance working at the grocery store owned by his family.

He had never given her more than a cursory glance. At twelve years of age, she was gawky and skinny, practically invisible. He'd considered her a nuisance more than anything. She'd had to harden herself against the myriad of tiny insults he unwittingly tossed her way whenever he came around to see Teddy. For the five years she'd known him in Kansas City his opinion hadn't changed.

Toward morning her dreams turned darker as the nightmare of the sheriff discovering Russ played out in them over and over in a myriad of ways.

When early morning light filtered into her room, she rose for the fourth time, dressed quickly in her serviceable dark green dress and, after peeking in on him, hurried downstairs to start a fire in the stove and warm more water. She unlocked the back door for Teddy and Jamie and then carried the basin of water and a new cloth and towels upstairs.

* * *

The first thing he noticed was that the intense pain that had dogged him with the simple act of breathing had diminished to a dull ache rather than a scorching fire. The second thing he noticed was that he lay on something soft—not the hard, unforgiving ground. And somewhere he heard humming…and felt safe.

How could that be?

Pale light pressed against his eyelids. He opened his eyes, squinting against the daylight that seeped around the edges of long dark curtains. A room. A bed. An empty chair. Then he heard a pot scraping on the iron plate of a stovetop and the sound of water being poured…

Which reminded him that he needed to relieve himself. The moment he curled to his left to get out of bed, pain shot up his abdomen and side. He fell to his knees on hard plank flooring and put a fist to the bandage—the pain sharp at first, and then dulling as he held pressure there. Slowly he peeled his fingers away, expecting to see them soaked with blood. They were clean! He dragged in a shaky breath and used the chamber pot from under the bed. Then he crawled back under the covers.

Light footsteps sounded. Someone climbing stairs.

"Russ? Russ? Is that you?"

The events of the past days came flooding back to him. Abby…

She stopped in the doorway. Her plain green dress showed off subtle curves and brought out the rich color of her eyes. She hadn't had any curves before. He remembered teasing her about it.

"Good. You're awake. I brought some tea with honey." She set the tray down and helped him lift his head. She paused, one brow arched. "I can see that tea doesn't thrill you. Teddy used to have brandy hidden away. I'll look for it later."

Gone was the high-pitched voice he remembered. It had

deepened to a rich tone that reminded him of smooth, honeyed whiskey. Her voice hadn't suited her before. It certainly did now.

He cleared his throat. "Where is Ted?"

"Married. Going on a year." She slid onto a chair beside the bed and helped him take another sip.

She seemed comfortable with him. As if to touch him was a normal occurrence. With that thought, memories of someone wiping a cool cloth over his face and chest came to him. *Her?* Wasn't she too young to be taking care of a grown man?

But wait… Years had passed since he'd last seen her, since he'd left Missouri. How many?

He glanced at her hands. No ring.

She'd always been so proper. Stiff and uncompromising—that was the Abby he knew. As if to make a misstep on the narrow road she'd set for herself would ruin everything. He was sure her extensive rule book didn't allow an unmarried woman to see a man with his shirt off. Yet…here she was. Little Abby…

He drained the cup on his next sip. It wasn't very big—a woman's dainty, painted teacup. He was glad that she held it. In his hand, it might shatter. Well…maybe not so much now considering how weak he felt. He lay back against the pillow as a wave of gratitude washed over him that she'd been here…that Teddy had been here. "So…I made it to Oak Grove."

"You wouldn't have made it an inch farther. What in the world happened, Russ?"

He was still trying to sort that part out. "A lot. I…uh… appreciate you taking me in." She hadn't wanted to. He remembered hearing that much during a lucid moment.

Startled, she met his gaze. "Russ… Of course, you are welcome. We've had our differences, but I would never want you…"

"Dead?" He gave a half laugh to cover his frustration.

His life had suddenly come undone. To hell with the tea-cup, his life was what was shattered, and he'd played a part in letting it happen. "We didn't get on all that well, you and me. Guess you're entitled to your own opinion."

They were harsh words, but honest.

She avoided his gaze. Where was her patent keen retort? Her silence now could only mean one of two things. Either he'd been so near expiring that he really had frightened her or, which was more likely, her opinion of him was still mired in the mud. Unspoken, but heavy in the room, was their last parting.

She set the teacup aside. "How is Tim?"

So it was still Tim. He blew out a breath, a sense of un-ease weighting his gut. "He's married now. Loves ranching. He and his wife are expecting their first baby."

She pulled back, her composure stiff. "Then he's content living in Colorado."

"Abby. He wasn't for you."

She pressed her lips together. "That really isn't any of your business. Then or now."

Why was she still angry with him after all this time? Didn't she realize that she had deserved someone who was more her match? Someone stronger, with more grit than Timothy. Someone a heck more like himself. "If he had re-ally wanted to stay, he would have."

"You're implying I should be grateful that you whisked him away?"

"Yeah. Maybe you should." Tim was too easily swayed. She would have been bored after a month of marriage. Russ figured he'd saved her from a pile of grief and he wasn't one bit sorry about it. "It proved his mettle."

A moment passed as she mulled over his words. "Teddy once said the same thing."

"There you go."

She met his gaze. "No one calls me Abby here. When

we moved here, I asked Teddy to introduce me as Abigail. It's more professional."

"Hmph. I like Abby." She'd always be Abby to him.

Amusement flashed in her eyes. "You would." Then her entire demeanor softened as she lowered her shoulders. "I suppose I like it too. And, Russ…I'm glad you felt you could come to Teddy…come to us for help. Friends are… so very important."

As long as they don't shoot you, he thought bitterly. How long had it been since then? "What day is it?"

"Early Wednesday. Morning has just broken. I found you yesterday in our storage room."

Four days then. McCabe was shot on Saturday. Word would be out about him.

She studied him, her dark brows knitting together. "The important thing now is that you are better. You are going to be all right." She stood. "I'll see to some breakfast for us."

He wasn't used to having anyone worry over him—not since his own mother. Yet he couldn't deny that it felt good to be among friends he could trust, friends who cared. "Sounds good. I'm starving."

A wry smile formed on her lips, revealing dimples on each cheek.

He remembered those dimples. At thirteen, they'd been inconsistent with the rest of her sharp-edged personality and she hadn't showed them much anyway. Now? Hmm…

"Starving it is? Then you must be feeling better. Perhaps you won't even mind my cooking."

How difficult could it be to whip together toast and eggs? "You've got to be teasing." And then it struck him. Abby? Teasing?

Her cheeks flamed pink. "No. Actually, I'm telling the truth." She scooted from the room.

Abigail hurried down the stairs. She'd never had a con-versation like that with Russ. Not ever. In the past he'd taunted her. It was a game he played very well and she'd been the one to lose. Every time. This…this had been different. He'd even owned up to his part in making her life miserable! Was it because he was sick now? Or had he changed?

She stopped at the bottom of the stairs. Or…had the years changed them both?

While she was frying two eggs, Teddy came in the back door, dropped his coat and hat on a chair and greeted her. He watched her for a moment. Did he notice her face? It still felt hot.

"Is that for Russ? He's awake?"

"Yes." She slid the eggs onto a plate and handed him the tray she had prepared. "Give him a chance to eat before you pester him with questions. Who knows how long it's been since he had a decent meal. Besides, I want to hear what he has to say. I'll be up as soon as I have a bite."

Fifteen minutes later, she entered the bedroom. From the sound of things, Teddy had been filling Russ in on his year of being married. The plate she'd sent up was empty.

"More?" she asked.

Russ shook his head. "But thanks. It was good." His gaze remained on her a trifle longer than necessary before he looked back to Teddy. "Guess you both are wondering why I'm here."

"We're interested in your version," Teddy said. "Sheriff Baniff already let us know his."

"I'd hoped word hadn't spread this far yet. Your sheriff is probably not like our marshal in Barton, but that doesn't mean he won't do his job by the book and send me back there."

"You don't trust the man there?" Abigail asked.

"He listens to the wrong people. And the wrong people— or person—has an iron grip on that town. All I could think about when I found out I was being arrested was to get away. I hopped the first train I could."

"Which happened to be heading this way," Teddy said.

"Tell us what happened. From your one letter, I thought you were set for life in the mining business."

Russ held his side, coughed and then winced. "That was what…three years ago? It was about the time Tim married and turned rancher. He sold his share of the mine to a man named Johnson and together Johnson and I started the Barton Silver Mining Company. A year later, Congress started buying and coining silver again. Things really took off then."

"I remember printing an article about that act," Teddy said.

"I went a little crazy at first. I'd never had a surplus of money before. I spent a lot of time in Denver enjoying… things. I rounded up investors so that I could get shelters built for the workers and their families and started up a company store. While I traveled, Johnson saw to the books and kept an eye on things at the mine.

"Then six months ago, I heard about grumbling among the workers. Johnson said he'd implemented a few changes. He told me not to worry and that it would take time for the men to adjust. But things went from good to bad, and then to worse. I met with the foreman, Ben McCabe. He complained about the prices at the company store and the fact that the equipment was falling apart. He was plenty agitated. He threatened to talk to the newspaper."

"Was it true?" Teddy asked.

"I told him I'd check on it when I got back from a trip I'd planned. That was a mistake. I shouldn't have put it off. He went to the newspaper about things. Adding fuel to the fire, by the time I returned to Barton an accident had occurred that injured two workers. McCabe was in the office arguing with Johnson about it. Johnson had no intention of listening or changing anything. He taunted McCabe and McCabe rushed him. Johnson drew his gun and shot."

Russ shook his head. "It was murder. McCabe wasn't armed. I said as much. Johnson turned to me and said he wasn't going to hang for it. Then he shot me."

"If what you say is true," Abigail asked, "how are you the one charged with murder?"

"When I came to, Johnson was gone, his gun was in my hand and I was bleeding all over the floor. I got to my feet and headed to the doctor's house. While the doc patched me up, I heard Johnson in the next room talking to the marshal. He mentioned my argument with McCabe and then he said I shot him. The marshal believed him. The minute the doc turned away, I took off and kept going until I ended up here."

Teddy ran a hand through his hair. "Well, this is a mess."

"It's my mess. I'll straighten it out. Just as soon as I'm strong enough. I should have seen it coming. I placed too much trust in Johnson."

Abigail had never known Russ to take the blame for anything. That alone made her trust his story. He wasn't just Teddy's friend. She wanted to help him. "I wish Mayor Melbourne could help you. He's our attorney here."

He met her gaze. "I thought you wanted me out of here as fast as possible."

"You heard me?" She'd thought he was too out of it for her words to register. "I was frightened. All we'd heard from the sheriff was that you killed someone."

"I don't want you in trouble on account of me. A few days. That's all I ask and I'll be gone."

"Where will you go?" she asked.

"To Denver on the back roads. There's a lawyer there I trust."

"Until then, you are welcome here." Teddy stood. "I better get busy on Saturday's paper."

Her brother left, and when she turned back to Russ, his eyes were drifting closed. Her brother believed him, and as suspicious as she had been at first, she believed him too. She took his tray and headed down the stairs.

Chapter Six

Thursday morning, Abby appeared with a basin of warm water, soap, and a washcloth and towel. "I thought you might give this a try yourself."

Her cheeks held an interesting pink glow as she backed away from him. *Abby? Embarrassed?* She had bathed him before when he was ill, but now that he was conscious, she wouldn't help? He found a certain humor in the whole thing.

He sat up, bracing himself against the stab of pain he knew would come. It was duller than yesterday. He wrestled with his shirt, wincing once as he tried to free his arm of the sleeve. The effort exhausted him. The humor he'd found only moments before evaporated. He hated feeling weak. "A little help here?"

She hesitated at first, but then stepped closer and helped him with his sleeve. When she had freed him of his shirt, he breathed a sigh of relief and flopped down again, closing his eyes.

"Can you manage now?"

He opened his eyes. She had inched toward the doorway. Her cheeks were now definitely red. The entire situation obviously flustered her.

"What if I said I couldn't?" The challenge slipped easily off his tongue.

She frowned. "I'd say you were lying to me."

She reached into the water, grabbed the washcloth and threw it at him. It landed on his chest with a big sopping wet slap.

"Oomph!" He jerked, doubling over and tightening his muscles as his wound rebelled in an explosion of red-hot pain. "Abby!" he gasped. "I was only teasing!"

"As was I!" She turned and tromped down the stairs.

He lay there, letting the pain subside, a bit stunned. What had just happened? Little Abby...still full of sass, but all grown up. A slow smile stretched his cracked lips.

He squeezed the excess water from the washcloth and started in washing himself. It wasn't the same as a good soak at a bathhouse, but he wasn't complaining. In the end, he smelled a lot better than he had before. The activity wore him out. After that, he dozed.

A few hours later, a man's voice put him on alert— vaguely familiar, but not Ted's. Abby entered the room and introduced the tall, dark-haired man beside her as Doctor Graham. He examined the wound and then redressed it, satisfied with the healing.

"Thank you, Doc. For everything."

Graham leveled a look at him. "Gunshot wounds raise a lot of questions. Since the Whites have vouched for your character, I'll keep quiet. However, if the sheriff asks about you, I won't lie."

"Sounds fair enough." Looked like he'd better get his strength back as fast as possible and get out of town before anyone else had a chance to discover his existence.

A little after the noon hour, Ted brought him a meal of meatballs and noodles in a creamy sauce. "From my wife for Abigail. I brought extra for you."

"I think marriage agrees with you, my friend. You've got that satisfied look about you."

Ted grinned. "Best choice I ever made. You might like it yourself."

"I'm doing just fine on my own."

"Yes. I can see that. Shot up. Living off an old friend."

He let the jibe roll off his shoulders.

Ted tossed two newspapers on the bed. "Thought you might want to catch up on things."

Looked like a Denver paper and an issue of the *Gazette*. "Thanks. Where's Abby?"

"She's chasing a story idea for our Christmas edition."

Hmm. It would have been fun to tease her again, maybe ask her to read to him. "Would you have pen and paper? I need to post a letter."

"Is that wise, my friend?"

"I'll hold on to it. Maybe post it the day I leave for Denver."

Ted looked at him meaningfully. "And post it from a different town?"

Right. Anything posted from here could put people here at risk. "All right."

Ted found some notepaper for him and then headed back down the stairs to work. Russ dug into the meal in front of him. He grabbed the Denver paper. Had news of his escape reached there? The paper's date was a week before the trouble at the mine, so it was little help. Since news had made it to Oak Grove, he would have to assume that it had reached Denver and he'd count on a harder time getting to the attorney without being recognized.

In the activity downstairs, he heard the squeak and groan of the printing press along with Ted occasionally giving direction to the boy, Jamie.

Russ read for a while, and then dozed. Then he woke and wrote a short letter to the foreman's widow telling her how sorry he was about her husband's death. He wrestled with whether to tell her the truth and to warn her about Johnson. After hearing Johnson's version of the incident, she probably wouldn't believe him anyway. In the end, he decided that the less she knew, the safer she would be. He put a few bills in the envelope, vowing to himself to send more money when he could. He tucked the letter in his vest pocket for safekeeping.

* * *

Abigail attached the large red bow to the *Gazette*'s front door and stood back. "How is that?"

"Better," Patty said. "Now it looks ready for Christmas."

Abigail blew on her hands and then stuffed them into her rabbit fur muff. "Let's go then. Lots to accomplish this afternoon."

Their first stop was in front of the mercantile, where they questioned neighbors who walked by about Christmas plans and hopes. Patty interviewed the children while Abigail listened and then suggested ways for her to phrase her questions for better results. The girl caught on quickly. With her outgoing personality, people eagerly responded.

"Our last stop of the day," Abigail said as they approached Mrs. Corwin's small house. Jamie's mother lived almost a mile from the town. A hound lay on the porch.

Mrs. Corwin came to the door. Her red hair held streaks of gray, and her face was lined from the sun. "Oh, it's you, Miss White…and Patty! Come in. Don't let that fool dog in with you."

Once inside, Abigail pulled out her notepad. "Reverend Flaherty mentioned that you've had items disappear lately. Can you elaborate?"

"Maybe you should ask Mrs. Eddy." She sent a sharp look through the window to her neighbor's house on the hill.

"That is our next stop."

They spoke for a few more minutes and then said their goodbyes and headed to the widow Eddy's. The dog took an immediate shine to Patty, limping along beside her.

Mrs. Eddy poured tea and set out a plate of cookies for them.

"These are scrumptious," Patty said. "Would you share this recipe in the Christmas edition of the *Gazette*?"

"Why, if you think people would enjoy it!"

"Perhaps you could bake some for the Christmas Party,"

Abigail suggested. "You are planning to come, aren't you? Jamie could drive you and his mother into town."

Mrs. Eddy's gracious attitude soured immediately. "We don't socialize. Not since she accused my goat of stealing her things!"

Before long, Abigail and Patty headed back to town.

"What a waste!" Patty said. "Three years and the feud is still going on. Those two could be keeping each other company, especially in the winter. Christmas is the perfect time of year to forgive old hurts."

Abigail remained silent. How could she respond when she'd held her grudge against Russ for five years? Had she been as unbending and unforgiving as the two women? The thought made her uncomfortable.

When they arrived at the fork in the road, Patty surprised her with a brief hug before departing toward home. She was the most demonstrative girl Abigail had ever known. But the hug felt nice, and not nearly as awkward as the first time she'd done it.

Chapter Seven

Dusk approached, and Russ heard the door bells jangle. Then Abby spoke to Ted, her voice muffled. Odd, how he anticipated seeing her, even more so after her display of spirit that morning. Now that he felt better, he realized there had been many times over the past few days that he'd woken and she was sitting by his bed, reading or writing. Guess he'd gotten used to having her around.

When she entered his room, she had a package tucked under one arm, which she held out to him.

"A present?" He worked his way into a sitting position. Then he tore off the tan paper wrapping, revealing a crisp new carefully folded shirt.

She slid into the bedside chair. "I knew I wouldn't be able to get all the blood and dirt out of your old shirt and I didn't want to take it to the laundry. Someone might question that bullet hole."

"Where did this come from?"

"The seamstress in town."

"Wasn't she curious why you'd want a man's shirt?"

"I told her it was for Teddy and that he'd been complaining that his old ones were too tight."

That surprised him. Lying wasn't in her rule book. It was one of the things he'd respected about her. "Thought you hated lies—even little white ones."

"I do. But Teddy *has* been complaining. He is gaining weight on Hannah's good cooking. However, he is in need of shirts with more room around the middle. I asked her to make this one larger at the shoulders. You'll have to try it on to see if she got it right."

"I'll pay you back. I promise."

Her deep brown eyes held his as she leaned forward. "I don't care about the money. Just clear your name, Russ. That's more important than anything else. You don't deserve to be on the run the rest of your life."

That wouldn't happen. He wouldn't run. He'd face his accuser, and he'd either get his life back or he'd hang. "I don't deserve to be at the end of a rope either."

"I would never want that."

Her words, her earnest tone, jolted him. "You believe me—that I'm innocent," he said in wonder. "Now there's a miracle."

She pulled back, breaking the intimate spell. "Well. You certainly could use one. And it is the season for miracles."

"I could use a few more headed my way."

"You've already had more than one."

"How do you figure?"

She ticked them off her fingers. "Your partner didn't kill you outright. And you escaped and made it all the way here where we could help you."

"You're right. Guess I should be more grateful." He'd been a fool to trust Johnson. The man had engineered his death and it could still happen if the law caught up to him. But he couldn't have a better friend than Ted. Even prickly Abby was pretty great to have on his side—more than great.

She glanced down at the newspaper in his lap. He'd folded it repeatedly, making it into the shape of a hat. "I see that you have been active. Did you actually *read* the paper?"

"Got a little bored. No one around to tease."

Finally, she smiled. "You deserved that wet washcloth this morning, but I didn't mean to cause you pain."

He was glad to have the incident cleared between them. "I'm tougher than I appear."

She picked up the newspaper hat. "So, which article was your favorite?"

"Hmm… Is this a test to see if I really did read the paper?"

Her smile widened. "Could be."

"Honesty. That's what I like best about you."

"Be careful. Not everyone does. I'm fairly outspoken when I believe something."

"Ah, the sharp tongue of a journalist. But as I remember, you always backed up your opinions with sound reasoning. At least…*most* of the time."

"Is that a compliment?"

She looked unsure, as if she couldn't quite believe him. Didn't the people here in town recognize her talent? Or was it him? Had he been the one to dismiss her in the past?

She blinked and looked away. "What matters is that you are mending."

He wasn't going to let her change the subject so easily. "My favorite was your opinion piece about the Betterment Committee and the remaining funds. You had good ideas for using the money. You're a good writer."

She colored slightly. "I write decently, but I'm no good at telling a story, or a joke for that matter."

He grinned. "That's my area."

"And you are very good at it. I used to envy the way you could get anyone to see things your way. You nearly had Teddy talked into Colorado. And then Tim succumbed. Plus, you could sweet-talk any woman between the ages of one and ninety that came within a twenty-foot radius. You can be very persuasive when you want something."

He reached for her hand, but then stopped before touching her. The one girl he had wanted to be persuasive with back then had been too young and he'd had nothing to offer her. He'd had to leave to seek his fortune. And now, unless he cleared his name, it wouldn't matter. He tightened his hand into a fist and lowered it to the mattress.

"Truly, Russ… I do hope your way with words helps you when your time comes to stand before a judge. I wouldn't want anything to happen to you."

She probably only meant her words in friendship. It couldn't be more than that, could it? "Tell me about your day," he urged, anxious to keep her there. "Mine was nothing to talk about."

She relaxed her shoulders, inclining her head. "I spent the day with a girl who wants to be a reporter. She is trying her hand at an article for our Christmas edition."

"A girl after your own heart?"

"Perhaps. We chased down a story between two women who used to be the best of friends but now can't find a nice thing to say about each other."

"So—a feud."

"Or simply gossip."

"How did it start?"

Her look was doubtful. "You really want to know?"

What he wanted was to keep her with him. The afternoon had gone on forever without her to talk with to pass the time. "Yeah."

He would have liked to say he hung on every word as she told him the story, but her honeyed voice bewitched him, lulling him with its soothing qualities. Her face lit up as she spoke of a dog and a goat and the week-to-week happenings between the two women.

"Then the goat is taking the laundry?" he asked when he suddenly realized she had stopped talking.

"Mrs. Eddy denies it."

"She would. Will you investigate further?"

She shrugged prettily.

"I thought reporters were always after the truth."

"I am! But it's hardly news—more along the line of gossip. It might make a fun human-interest story."

"Could be interesting…"

"Perhaps."

* * *

She hadn't intended to spend so much time with Russ. Her brother needed her in the office. Yet the afternoon had blended seamlessly into evening while Russ told tales of Colorado and the mining business and she spoke about living in Oak Grove. When Teddy appeared with a light evening meal of hot stew and bread and butter, she'd been surprised to realize the last rays of the sun were setting.

As she rose to light the lamp, the serious expression on her brother's face made her pause.

"The sheriff stopped in today while you were gone. He asked about the article."

"What did you tell him?"

"That you weren't feeling well."

"I hope he doesn't hear differently from any of the people I spoke with today."

"It will buy us a few days. But his visit impressed upon me more than ever that if Russ can't clear his name, you and I could end up in jail. We can't beg ignorance. Not since Sheriff Baniff has shown us the wanted poster." He dragged a hand through his hair. "I'm going to Barton."

"What? Teddy, that could be dangerous!"

"You don't need to go," Russ said. "I told you, this is my mess and I'll fix it."

"You are in no condition to fix anything," Teddy said. "And it's just a fact-finding mission. Now that you are on the mend, Abigail can handle things in the print shop for a few days. I'll tell my wife it's a business trip."

Her heart sank. Another lie. "When?"

"Tomorrow. The noon train will put me in Barton by suppertime."

When Teddy left for home, she sat down in the bedside chair. "I don't remember a time when Teddy has been away more than a day," she murmured.

Russ studied her. "He's smart. He'll be all right."

"I know. It's just…first he goes off and gets married…

and now he's leaving town on a trip that may prove dangerous."

"But he is coming back," he said slowly, studying her. "Give me your hand, Abby."

She crossed her arms over her middle. No man had ever taken her hand but for Teddy, and long ago, her father. "Why?"

He smiled. "So suspicious. You've already bathed me. Am I asking for so much?"

Something clutched in her belly. Bathing him to bring down his fever was one thing. This was different. He was asking her to let down her guard.

Yet hadn't his first thought been to seek them out when he was hurt? Trust like that was a gift. She valued it, even though Russ's trust came to her indirectly through her brother. She supposed that meant she cared something for Russ. Which meant she mustn't relax her caution. He was dangerous in manners of the heart.

He curled his fingers once, beckoning… "Abby… I'm not going to bite you."

She tightened her arms. "You forget. I've known you a good long time. I know how easily you charm girls." *And then leave them with a bruised or broken heart.* That would not be her.

The smile on his face dissolved. "I'm not that fool boy anymore."

"No, you're a man. Foolish?" She swallowed. "I haven't figured that part out yet. Either way, you are a poor risk."

Her words sounded harsh to her ears. How must they sound to him? She did feel the need to protect herself from him. She was suspicious. He'd never once turned his charm on her. Why now?

"We fought all the time, Russ. We don't get along and you don't need to assuage my worry. I'm fine."

His eyes narrowed as he contemplated what she said. "Do you want to know why we fought all the time back then?"

"I already know. I was a millstone and in the way. Because of me, Ted couldn't accompany you on half of your escapades."

He shook his head. "That wasn't it at all. You were young. Too young. And innocent. Not to mention, you were my best friend's sister. If that doesn't make for a dangerous combination, I don't know what does."

Ever so tentatively, she uncrossed her arms. "You can't possibly mean that you liked me. I'm not so gullible. You are trying to twist this."

"I'm not." His expression was dead serious.

"Back then you either ignored me or you constantly taunted me."

"Not constantly. Only when Tim came around."

She couldn't believe what she was hearing! "You were jealous?" Could it be true? She thought back over old hurts, old memories. Everything seemed to be changing and shifting. Had she really been so blind?

"I didn't handle it well, but I handled it the best I knew how."

She stared at him. Confounded. This was beyond anything her imagination could have dreamed up!

"I figured with all we have been through it was time to set things straight. We're friends, you and me. Now, will you come here?"

"Friends?" Slowly she took a step nearer the bed.

He reached up…and she slipped her hand into his. Immediately she felt enveloped by his warmth. She stared at their hands, intertwined, unable to look away, her entire arm tingling.

"That's better. Now, Abby. About Ted. I know you worry about him. I know, because you never seem to stop thinking, analyzing and worrying about everything, whether it is in your control or not. Your brother is one of the smartest men I know. He'll be careful."

She sank to the bedside chair, searching for the right

words to acknowledge him. Then she realized she didn't need to say anything at all. The quiet was fine. The warmth of his words and of his hand holding hers continued to glow inside her all the way down to her core. This was... very pleasant.

A moment later, he squeezed her hand and released it, and then turned back to his meal.

Chapter Eight

Russ stood at the side of his bed and forced himself to walk across the room one more time. The effort and pain winded him. Tomorrow, Saturday, would be a full week since the shooting. By now, he should have been well enough to leave, but it seemed traveling for three days with a bullet lodged inside hadn't been the smartest thing for his health. Thank God, when Abby had found him, she hadn't listened to him and instead went for the doctor. With her and Ted sticking their necks out for him, he was determined to make it up to them. To do that, he had to get his strength back.

After Ted had left for the train, it was quiet. Russ strained his ears to hear what Abby was doing downstairs. She must be bent over her desk in the front room, writing or editing articles. A while later, he heard pots and pans clattering in the kitchen and then, finally, her footsteps on the stairs.

"I wondered what was going on up here," Abby said from the doorway. Her dark, delicate brows rose. "Are you all right? You look pale."

"I'm fine. Just pushing myself to move. When Ted returns, I want to be strong enough to manage a horse."

He took in her dark burgundy dress and the way she had brushed her hair up into a fancy knot on top of her head and braided a red-and-gold ribbon in among the rich brown strands. She also smelled of cinnamon. He felt the unfamiliar tug of jealousy. "You're going out?"

"For a little while. I'm decorating the town hall along with some of the other women in town. Patty talked me into it. It's a chance to find out what traditions they observe for Christmas for a write-up in the special edition."

He tried to concentrate on what she was saying. He knew her job was important to her. He felt the same way about his situation at the mine, only he'd really messed that up somewhere along the way. Trouble was, he was irritated at his slow progress. He slipped back onto the bed, letting out a frustrated sigh as he draped his left arm over his forehead. He was bored. He was sick of the bed, sick of the room, and he didn't want her to leave.

"On my way back should I pick up a steak from the restaurant for you?" Her voice held a hint of amusement.

He moved his arm away from his face and looked at her. "Along with whatever you made downstairs?"

She grimaced slightly. "Despite the smell coming from the kitchen, I'm afraid that I am a much better reporter than I am a cook."

He groaned. "You burnt it?" He'd been looking forward to something sweet. At her dejected nod, he couldn't help chuckling. "Then a steak, medium rare, from the restaurant sounds good."

Her eyes sparkled.

He had noticed years ago that she was attractive, but now each day brought a new facet of her features, a new expression that enchanted him. She had a quiet beauty, one that intrigued him more every day. One that made it hard to take his gaze off her.

"Why are you staring?"

He didn't want to speak of the thoughts he'd just had. It was already obvious that she thought him a charmer and telling her he thought her pretty—even beautiful—would probably sound insincere and solidify that assumption. "You've changed, Abby."

She raised her brows.

"You used to be…difficult."

She smiled slightly. "I still am. I simply hide it better."

"I've decided that it's a sign of your intelligence. Makes me wonder, if you'd been in Barton, would you have noticed the situation with the workers long before things came to a head? McCabe felt squeezed between the men he supervised and Johnson. Things weren't right for a long time. I should have noticed it sooner and taken steps."

To his surprise, she stepped closer and took his hand in both of hers, much the same way he had done with her yesterday, only much more tentatively. "Don't get discouraged. Hopefully we will know more when Teddy returns."

As she started to release him, he caught her wrist. "I'm going to miss you while you are out. Hurry back."

Her mouth opened.

He'd flustered her. He didn't know if that was good or bad, whether his words were met with delight or dismay. Like she'd said, she was good at hiding her opinions now.

"I...I'll be back before you know it."

Reluctantly, he released her and watched the back of her burgundy skirt flare as she dashed from the room.

Her heart beat in double time as she rushed down the stairs and threw on her coat. Her fingers shook as she fastened the large buttons on it and tied the silk ribbon of her felt hat under her chin. What had just happened? He wasn't toying with her, was he?

Her desire had been to calm the frustration he was feeling. It wasn't hard to see he wanted out of the untenable situation in which he found himself. But if she were truthful with herself, there was more to the small action and it wasn't altruistic at all. She hadn't been able to stop thinking about him, going over every moment she'd ever known with him. When he had taken her hand yesterday evening, a barrier had fallen away. She thrummed inside with nervous energy, yearning for another touch, another glance, another word from him.

It was all so...exhilarating. And scary. And dangerous.

Yet he pushed himself to get stronger. He would leave and that would be the end of this. What had happened to guarding her heart? This was foolish and unwise. He might very well not see himself clear of the murder charge.

Oh, Teddy! Return with good news, she breathed into the crisp, cold air as she closed and locked the office. Russ had to clear his name. He just had to!

She met Patty at the town hall.

"It's narrowed down to a few larger items." Patty consulted her notes. "A playground with swings and see-saws. Benches along the river for fishing or just sitting. A community-wide snowman-building contest when we get a good snow. And a big Christmas tree for the town's Christmas Party—one that they can decorate."

Another long list peeked from behind the paper Patty held. "What is this?" Abigail asked.

"It's not exactly what you were looking for, but I had to write them down. Once the children got started, they kept talking and bringing up more ideas."

Abigail read over the list. Justin Carlson wanted a new coat and gloves for his father. Kristine Gibson was asking for help with the milking until her sister recovered from her accident. Even the schoolteacher had listed six basic primers for schoolchildren whose families could not afford to buy them.

"I see what you mean," Abigail said. "The Carlsons haven't recovered from the flooding last spring. It was particularly hard on them. Trouble is, Mr. Carlson is extremely proud. He won't appreciate something like this in the paper. What we need are a few secret angels."

Patty grinned suddenly. "Or elves."

Abigail mulled that over. "Write your article about the big items. We'll put that in the paper and at the party everyone can cast their vote on the one they most want. Then we can take it to the Betterment Committee. About these others… Let's put our heads together and figure something out."

When they finished decorating the hall, Abigail stopped by the restaurant for a steak supper—one with potatoes and green beans. She asked for generous portions. That way she could have a few bites herself. Otherwise, she would have to search for something edible in her own cupboard, which after her earlier cooking fiasco held little appeal.

In her kitchen as she divided the supper onto two plates, butterflies darted through her belly in anticipation of seeing Russ. Oh, this wasn't good. Friends. That's what they were. That's *all* they were. She must guard against feeling anything more. He wasn't staying. It was foolish to hope… And yet, she did. She desperately hoped his name would be cleared. And if it was, she hoped he would not forget her.

There. She'd admitted it to herself. She cared for him. Deeply. And she wanted him to see her not as Teddy's sister, but as herself. As a woman he might come to care for.

She picked up the tray and headed upstairs.

His eyes lit up the moment he saw her. *The way to a man's heart is through his stomach.* She would *not* let herself think that way.

He rubbed his hands together. "You remembered! You're amazing."

Those darn butterflies started flying about inside her twice as fast. He had probably used those words on other girls…other women…over the years. They weren't all that flowery or special. Telling herself did nothing to quell her delight at hearing them directed at her.

"Wait!" He maneuvered his legs over the side of the bed. "A steak dinner deserves a table."

It was then she realized that a second chair had been brought into the room.

He pulled out the bedside table and positioned the chairs. "All we need is a tablecloth."

That he tried to make it a bit special touched her. No one ever had…

While they ate, she told him about her day. "I didn't realize that Mr. Carlson was still having a hard time. I should have followed up on that months ago. There may be others still hurting from the floods. Or that the schoolchildren cared so much about a pine tree for Christmas. Where would we get a pine? There's not a one on the prairie."

"In Barton a man can't see more than fifty feet for all the pines blocking the view. Someday, I'd like to show it to you."

What would it be like to see the mountains and the trees instead of the endless rolling plains? More than that…to see them with him? He couldn't know the turmoil he'd started inside of her by his casual words. Had he really meant them?

"I'd like that too," she said hesitantly. "Perhaps when Dorie is older. Teddy and Hannah and I could take the train."

He forked the last green bean into his mouth. "Once all this is behind me, I'll make that happen."

His words were like a dousing of sleet. *Once this is behind me…* It was true. Planning was fruitless until he faced his accusers. And in doing that, there was no guarantee he would be exonerated. She might never see him again. "I can't stand thinking about you facing what is ahead on your own. Do you have friends there who you can count on?"

"The attorney in Denver will help. I'm not sure about anyone in Barton. Johnson has muddied up my reputation there." He studied her silently. "You're worried."

"Very much." She glanced away. "Wouldn't it be something if we could have a practice go at life? Then we would be prepared for the difficulties."

"Only if it meant you wouldn't be angry that I persuaded Timothy to go to Colorado."

That was what bothered him? Her? With all the other things he had on his mind that were so much more pressing?

She stood and stacked their empty plates back on the tray. "I'm not angry, Russ. I don't know why I held on to the anger for so long. My feelings for Tim were infatuation.

I see that now." There had been no rose-colored glasses to distort her view of Russ. She'd seen his worst and his best. And what she felt for Russ was already so much more than anything she'd ever felt for Timothy. Every moment she spent with him increased the fullness in her heart and made her aware of how special, how important he was to her.

"I never meant to hurt you." His voice—gentle and full of remorse—melted the last vestige of hurt inside.

"I'm glad you explained yourself. Let's put it behind us. It's over. No more regrets." Even though neither of them had said the words *I'm sorry*, Abigail felt immeasurably better. She reached for the tray, intending to carry it downstairs.

"When I left the mine, all I could think about was getting away from Barton. If the first train that arrived had been going to Denver I would have ended up there."

"I realize that."

He rose to his feet. "It's important that you understand. Seeing you again after all these years—it might have been chance…" He took her hand and seemed to search for the words he wanted to say.

Her arm tingled from his touch. "I do, Russ. But…it's difficult to concentrate on what you're saying when you touch me."

Amusement flashed on his face, but then he grew serious again, his startling blue eyes earnest. "I'm glad that train came here. Very glad."

Her heartbeat sped up. "I am too."

He drew closer. "I've missed you, Abby. I didn't know how much until I saw you again."

The deep timbre of his voice thrilled her. His words thrilled her. She swallowed. "I feel the same."

His gaze drifted to her lips.

A shiver of desire raced through her body. "Russ…" she whispered. "What…?"

He smiled. "Must you always analyze things? Come closer and I'll show you."

He wanted to kiss her! Her heart beat triple time. She couldn't have taken a deep breath if she had wanted to.

He brushed aside a wisp of her hair, his light touch sending tingles over her temple. "Your thoughts are still churning. I can see it on your face. You know me, Abby. I won't hurt you. I promise. Not ever again."

"You will leave."

His eyes clouded over. "Not because I want to."

She leaned closer.

He slipped his hand behind her neck and pulled her toward him, closing the last inch between them. His lips met hers, warm and gentle and firm. Her breathing stopped… and then started again. And she melted inside. Everywhere he touched, he caressed, causing tingles to spread through her. A whirlwind swirled inside her. This…this was right. This was wonderful!

Her first kiss…

His pulse kicked up as he breathed in the scent of cinnamon that was Abby. She relaxed, softening against him. Innocent. Honest in her feelings. She wasn't like the other women he'd known. She didn't flirt. She didn't tease. She was a breath of fresh air. And precious. Little Abby!

He dropped light kisses across her cheek and delighted when he heard her sigh. Then he came back to her lips, wanting more of her. There was no maybe about it. He was getting in over his head. She had intrigued him as a girl and now she bewitched him as a woman.

Reluctantly, he pulled away.

That stub of a pencil still balanced on her ear. Seeing it, seeing her, a tenderness came over him that he'd never known before. He cared for her. Really cared for her. And he didn't want to hurt her. He waited for her to speak.

Her cheeks were a bit flushed, her eyes overly bright. "Uh—"

Abby? At a loss for words? It was so unlike her that he grinned.

She swallowed. "Do you mind if we don't talk about this? I'm afraid it will ruin things. And it was rather...special."

He grew serious. It was special, whatever this was between them, and he wanted more of it. She was the type of woman who would expect a future. His was murky at best. He had no idea what his held, but he knew in this moment that he wanted it to hold her. "I don't mind at all."

"I'll just take your tray down," she said, her face, her eyes, still dazed.

"Any dessert?"

She smiled softly. "You just had it." Then she disappeared around the corner.

Chapter Nine

Russ finished his fifth walk around his bed, even going so far as the small hallway. He tested himself on a few of the stairs, finding it difficult, but not impossible. His strength was finally returning.

Abby watched from where she sat working on the article about him. He would be gone before it appeared in the *Gazette*. She had moved the chair near the window to take advantage of the sunlight flooding in through a thin parting of the curtains. The softness of her cheek, the line of her nose, were outlined in light. As requested, he hadn't brought up the kiss, but he knew she thought about it. He could tell by the way her gaze lingered on him and the sudden flush that came to her cheeks when it did.

He thought about it too. The urge to ask her to wait for him badgered him. He realized the need to be practical. So he said nothing.

The train whistle blew. One o'clock.

"That should be Teddy arriving," she said. "I suspect he'll stop by his house to make sure Hannah and Dorie are doing well before coming here."

Half an hour later, Ted entered the *Gazette*'s office and joined them upstairs.

"You were right to get out of Barton," he said immediately. "Men are looking for you who are only interested in the bounty."

"How did you hear that?"

"I stopped in to see Tim. He said there are a good many

workers who don't believe you shot McCabe. However, being a stranger, none of them would open up to me."

"They can't afford to lose their jobs. Johnson has got them all in his grip," Russ said bitterly. "Did you talk to him? Johnson?"

Ted nodded. "I posed as a supplier from Denver, someone interested in providing dynamite for the mine who you'd invited down to see the operation. The minute I started asking questions about you, your partner clammed up. Within three hours, he had someone following me. Don't worry—" he motioned for Russ to relax "—no one followed me back here, but it confirms that he is hiding something."

Russ dragged a hand through his hair. "I'd hoped you'd find something that could help. Thank you for trying, buddy." He had overstayed his welcome and the time had come to get to Denver and do what he could to clear his name. No use prolonging things.

He glanced at Abby as he pulled a few bills from his vest pocket. "There is enough here to pay the doctor."

Abby's gaze searched his. "Russ…"

"I'll leave in the morning."

Ted took the money and tucked it into his coat. "I keep a mount at the livery. A bay gelding."

"You'll get him back. I promise."

Abby put her work aside. "Ted! No! He's not ready!"

"It's not our decision." He met Russ's gaze. "I'll make sure the horse is fed and watered well tonight, and then bring him around to the back before daylight."

"I'll be ready."

Abby sat like stone as her brother walked out of the room. A moment later, the bells over the *Gazette*'s front door jingled as Ted left.

"It's time," Russ said. "Abby… I can't live a life on the run. I won't. I need to get to Denver and see the attorney and somehow get myself clear of this mess."

"But you're not strong enough. Please…please listen to reason. You know I'm right."

He did know she was right, but it didn't change the fact that he had to leave. He hadn't slept last night thinking about it…thinking about her. "I've put you and Ted at risk for far too long."

"What if your wound starts bleeding again? What if you grow faint?"

"I'll take it slow. I'll be careful." He didn't want her worrying about him.

"Is there nothing I can say to make you stay?" Her eyes brimmed with tears.

This wasn't like her. "Where is your practical side?"

She sniffled, looking down at her hands in her lap. "It left the moment you kissed me."

His chest tightened. "Oh, Abby. You knew this day would come. I've been honest with you all along."

He walked to her and pulled her to her feet. She came to him, circling her arms around his waist. She tucked her head against his chest.

A tenderness swept through him as he hugged her and felt her entire body shudder with a breath. He'd never felt such a strong connection with a woman before—one that spanned years. The memories of her were precious.

"If it helps to know… I don't want to leave either. Kissing you didn't appease my desire, it made it grow. I want more. Of you. Of us. But until I straighten out this mess I am mired in, I won't make promises that I might not be able to keep."

Her head nodded against his chest. She said something, the words muffled into his shirt so that he couldn't understand her. Then she drew back and looked up at him. "You'll let me know what happens? I don't want to read about it in a paper. You'll write?"

He hugged her against him again, squeezing lightly. "Oh, Abby. I'll write. Or send a telegram." He lifted her chin, staring into her big, pretty eyes.

He'd known Abby wasn't someone to dally with all along and still he'd dared himself with that first kiss. If he kissed her now as he wanted to, it would change things between them forever. Knowing that didn't change his course as he lowered his head and gently pressed his lips to hers. He cared for her. He loved her. But what lay ahead prevented him from saying the words. Into the kiss, he put every tender hope, every desire, every care he held for her.

When Teddy returned with the news that he'd seen to his horse and left payment at Dr. Graham's with the man's wife, Russ was up walking the length of the room. Her heart ached with each step he took and each time he tightened his jaw to steel himself against the pain. He wasn't healed enough. He wasn't ready!

"You'll need a few supplies—water, blanket, food," Teddy said and looked at her. He expected her to put the necessary items together.

She didn't want to do anything that would hurry Russ's leaving, but he would go whether he had supplies or not. She gathered up the articles she had been crafting. "I'll get everything together now."

"Hannah is making a welcome-back meal for me." Teddy directed his words to her. "You are invited to supper. I'll bring a plate back for Russ later, but I want you to plan on staying at our place tonight."

She stiffened. If that happened she wouldn't be able to see Russ off. He'd slip away before the sun came up. "I don't see—"

"No arguments."

She closed her mouth into a tight seam. The look that passed between her brother and Russ spoke volumes. She didn't know whether Teddy could tell the change in the feelings between Russ and her, but now that Russ was better, her brother wanted to keep things on the up-and-up.

She descended the stairs, tossing her notebook and the articles to scatter on the counter.

In the storage room, she plucked a satchel from its hook on the wall, then gathered the items Russ would need in the kitchen—apples, cheese, bread.

"Miss White?" Doc Graham cracked open the back door slightly and called.

She dropped the satchel and welcomed him in.

"I heard that Ted came by my house. Thought I'd take one more look at how your friend is getting along."

"He's upstairs. Teddy is with him."

He headed up to the second floor and Abby turned back to her task. Once everything was packed she hung the bag back in the storage room, ready for the morning.

The bells jangled at the front door. "Miss White! Are you feeling better?"

Sheriff Baniff!

Stunned, she rushed toward him. She needed to get him out of here as quickly as possible! "Yes. Much. As a matter of fact, I finished that article you asked for."

"I'll take a look at it."

She hurried to the other side of the counter and presented him with her write-up. Dr. Graham could be heard at the top of the stairs talking to Ted. A moment later he appeared at the bottom.

"Afternoon, Doc," Sheriff Baniff said.

"Sheriff," Doc Graham said with a nod. He darted a glance at Abby.

"Somebody ailing?" Baniff asked.

She should say something—perhaps that Teddy had caught her cold—but the words wouldn't come.

"Thought you said you were better, Miss White."

"I am. There's nothing going on." Only her heart. Hammering in her chest.

His eyes narrowed suspiciously.

"It's just Te—" Her face flushed, giving everything away.

Baniff turned toward the stairs. "Mind if I take a look at this 'nothing'?" He headed up.

When the sheriff was out of earshot, Doc Graham turned to her. "Hope your friend is not in too much trouble. Seems like a decent fellow."

They both waited there…waiting for the inevitable. A moment later she heard the men descending the stairs. When they came into view the sheriff had Russ in iron handcuffs.

Baniff stopped in front of her and the doctor. "Anyone else know about Russ Carter other than the three of you?"

She shook her head. "No one else. And Doctor Graham only knew he was injured. He doesn't know about the rest."

Baniff's jaw tightened, his gaze sharp.

"Please, Sheriff." She had to make him understand. "Russ is a good man. He couldn't have done what they accuse him of."

"You know that's for the courts to decide." He looked at each of them in turn. "You all have some explaining to do. Don't set a foot outside this office. I'll be back once I get Carter locked up and my deputy up to speed." He paused and gave a chin nod toward the article on the counter. "Guess I won't need that now."

Russ's gaze met hers. "Guess I should have left a day earlier." He gave a half-hearted smile. "Thanks for stitching me up, Doc."

The sheriff tugged Russ's arm, urging him toward the door. Russ set his jaw as the motion pulled at his injured side.

"Sheriff Baniff," Abby said. "None of this is right. He's not dangerous. He doesn't belong locked up in jail."

"He'll take off if I don't confine him."

She glanced at Russ. *Would he?*

He nodded.

Oh, Russ! "Well, he's innocent until proven guilty. Remember that. And he's been injured. Please treat him with care."

The sheriff tipped his hat to her. "Think I got it, Miss White." He headed out the door with Russ.

Abby followed them to the boardwalk with Teddy and Doc Graham. The jail wasn't far, just down the street, but Russ hadn't walked that far since his injury. As he stepped off the boardwalk down to the dirt, one knee buckled and he clutched his side. She started toward him.

Teddy took her arm. "Wait, Abby."

Sheriff Baniff tightened his grip on Russ and waited for him to catch his balance.

"The sheriff is a good man," Doc Graham said. "He's just doing his job. He'll sort through all this and do the right thing."

"He just has to," she said. "I cannot consider the consequences otherwise."

They walked back inside the printing office. Teddy offered the doctor a cup of coffee and got one for himself while they waited for the sheriff to return. Abby sat on a tall stool at the counter. She wasn't angry with the doctor. He had been a big help to Russ. But she was fiercely angry at all who had conspired to hurt Russ—Johnson most of all.

When Sheriff Baniff returned, he took each of them separately aside into Teddy's office to hear their own version of the story. The interrogation took twenty minutes apiece. They must have matched up, because when he finished with the doctor, he had no further questions for them. "I'll just check the upstairs once more, if you don't mind."

Abby followed him up. She picked up Russ's hat and vest from the foot of the bed. "I think this is all there is. Will you take these to him?" She held them out, and as she did, she noticed a paper tucked in the inside vest pocket. She withdrew it. An envelope. It was addressed to a Mrs. McCabe in Barton, Colorado.

"I'll take that along with his things," the sheriff said.

Downstairs, while the rest of them looked on, he opened the envelope. Two hundred dollars in large bills had been stuffed inside, along with a note. The sheriff read it first. "Condolences," he said. "But he doesn't mention his innocence. I find that incriminating."

"He didn't do it," she said. It didn't matter how many times she had to say it, she would forever if it would only help Russ. "You need to ask him why."

"I intend to." He stuffed the letter and money back into the vest. "You are all free to get on with your business tonight. I'll telegraph the marshal in Barton that I'll be bringing Carter on the Kansas Pacific tomorrow."

Chapter Ten

Russ lay on the cot, staring at the ceiling, his hands clasped behind his head. The fire in the stove had died down in the early hours of morning. He would have been an hour on the road to Denver if he hadn't been discovered. As it was, he was stuck here in the cold jail cell while the morning light slowly turned the gray outline of the buildings outside his window to muted colors.

Deputy Chadwick walked over to the small cast-iron stove and threw in a scoop of coal. He looked as tired as Russ felt. They'd both been up most of the night. What would Russ encounter in Barton? Would anyone believe his story after the lies Johnson had spread?

Sheriff Baniff entered the one-room building carrying a covered plate. "Anything new to report?"

"No, sir," Chadwick said. "Quiet all night."

Russ eased his legs over the side of the cot and sat up.

Baniff grabbed the cell keys from their hook on the wall. He unlocked the cell door and handed the plate to Russ, then relocked the door. "You're good to head home then, Deputy. Thanks for your help."

Chadwick slipped on his wide-brimmed hat and headed out the door.

Russ ate the breakfast of eggs and toast and bacon and was slipping the plate through the bars of the cell to the sheriff when Abby walked into the sheriff's office.

She looked like she hadn't slept well either. Her hair had been hastily swept up on top of her head. She'd even forgotten her bonnet. She strode straight to the cell door and grasped the bars. "I'm so sorry this happened! I couldn't think what to say!"

He hadn't expected her to take the blame on her own shoulders. He didn't want her holding on to any guilt because of him. "I'm the one who landed unannounced on your doorstep. The responsibility is mine, starting all the way back in Barton. Like I said, I should have spoken more with the workers. I should have watched Johnson closer."

"You couldn't have known he would betray you and then turn the town against you. Teddy said those men want to hang you. You need someone there to make sure you get a fair trial. I want to go with you, Russ."

They wouldn't listen to her. Not for a minute. But he loved that she was willing. "You think they would care what you said? You are a stranger to them."

She shook her head, her eyes tearing up. "Probably not."

"Oh, Abby. Don't cry." Her tears tore him up inside.

She stamped her foot. "There has to be a way to help," she said, her voice filled with frustration.

He slipped his hand between the bars and cupped her trembling chin. "You don't do anything halfway, do you? And you don't give up."

"Not when I'm sure of something. Not when I love someone."

He stilled. She loved him? He hadn't expected this. He'd hoped, but… "Come here."

She pressed her face to the bars.

He leaned down and kissed her. It didn't come close to satisfying him. He wanted to hold her. Wanted to make her melt like she had with their kiss. Reluctantly, he pulled away. "I'll do a better job next time."

A wobbly smile appeared. "Always the charmer."

"Only with you. I promise. From now on only with you."

A deep cough behind Abby made him glance over her shoulder.

"Seems I missed a few changes while I was in Barton,"

Ted said, and then stepped forward offering his hand. "Do your best to come back. I'd like you to meet my wife and daughter."

Russ shook firmly. "You're a good friend, Ted. Always have been."

A whistle blew, signaling the Kansas Pacific pulling into the station.

The sheriff walked from behind his desk. "It's time, Carter."

Abby and Teddy stood back while Baniff unlocked his cell door and clapped the handcuffs on him. At least this time he was cuffed in front of his body, not in back. Abby slipped inside the cell and picked his hat up from his cot. She swept his hair back, her hand cool and loving against his brow, and carefully set his hat on his head.

He swallowed, wanting to kiss her again.

"Make sure he has a fair trial, Sheriff. Please. You are our only hope."

Baniff tipped his hat to her and, grabbing Russ by the upper arm, stepped outside.

Abby stood with Teddy and watched the train pull out of the station. She held herself with her arms crossed tight over her middle. She felt numb and helpless.

"He's gone, Abby." Teddy put his arm across her shoulders, and gently urged her to turn back to the newspaper office. "Maybe you can fill me in on what happened while I was gone."

"I fell in love."

"Think I got that part. Let's go have some coffee."

She needed something to keep her occupied. The worst had happened. Now all she could do was wait for news. "I'll make it."

Teddy paused midstep, and then continued. "Right. You'll make it. I'll get busy on the paper."

At noon, Teddy went home for his meal. Abby wasn't

hungry. She climbed the stairs and entered the room Russ had used. It was dark. Like her thoughts.

She walked over to the window and slid the curtains open, tying each side back with their sash. Outside, the sun barely showed itself through a thick layer of snow-filled clouds. Across the street, Mrs. Taylor stood on the boardwalk in front of her husband's barber shop, shaking a small rug.

Abby turned away from the window and stared at the bed's rumpled sheets, the mashed pillow, the blanket. She must get hold of herself. This moodiness wasn't like her. None of her worry and doubt would help Russ. She marched to the bed and pulled off the sheets. She'd take them to the laundry.

She carried them downstairs when a sudden thought stopped her. She could contact the widow! Maybe this Mrs. McCabe knew something—something she was afraid to tell the law there in Barton. Hadn't Teddy said that people were afraid to speak because they were afraid they would be fired at the mine? Maybe Abby could get through to her, woman to woman. Maybe she could convince her to trust Sheriff Baniff. Hope flooded through her. She had to get to the telegraph office immediately.

Chapter Eleven

For eight days Abby had sequestered herself upstairs thinking of Russ. Yesterday, she had gone about in a fog of constantly worrying about Russ and whether he was all right. Teddy had commented on it and wouldn't let her work the press for fear she would smash a finger.

She had to get back to her job. Teddy had been managing too long by himself. Besides, it would keep her mind occupied until she heard word from Russ or the sheriff. Her worries about Russ overshadowed her newspaper work, but she sat down at her desk and started making a list of people she could talk to about advertising space. This one edition of the paper would be the *Gazette*'s Christmas gift to the town of Oak Grove and it would be free of charge. Christmas was about giving and it was time she started doing her part.

After school, Patty stopped in the office. "I have my article. Will you check it?"

Abby sat down at her desk and read the article with a critical eye. Slipping the pencil from over her ear, she made a few minor corrections. "This is wonderful, Patty. You've done an excellent job."

She grabbed the wire basket of the other articles she'd written for the special edition and walked over to the end of the counter where she spread them out. Together, they arranged and rearranged them until they were satisfied with what should be the lead article on the front page and what should be on page two, leaving spaces for advertisements.

Patty thrilled at being part of the entire process. When they were done, she clapped her hands together, her eyes sparkling with anticipation. "People are going to be so surprised! This will be the best Christmas Oak Grove has ever had!"

For the first time in days, Abby smiled. "After our regular edition goes out on Saturday morning, we'll start pulling type for the Christmas edition. Mind you, it will take all day." She rose and slipped on her coat.

"Where are we going?" Patty asked, following her lead and tightening the scarf around her neck.

Abby liked the way Patty jumped right in, ready to take part. It was a good quality for a reporter. "To the restaurant to mark your first officially accepted article with a celebratory piece of pie."

Patty's grin widened. "I like the sound of that!"

Abby laughed. "Me too. After that, we are going to round up some Christmas elves."

That afternoon Abigail and Patty visited neighbors, bartering advertising space in the Christmas edition in return for various gifts hoped for by the townsfolk. For the articles, she had planned only inspiring news that would hopefully bring the community together. The biggest news would be the town project that would be voted on at the Community Christmas Party in two weeks.

Sheriff Baniff arrived from Colorado on the Friday train and strode into the *Gazette* office.

Teddy held up his hand. "Just a minute, Sheriff. Jamie. This is a personal matter. Would you mind stepping out for a few minutes?"

When Jamie had gone, Abigail and Teddy turned back to the sheriff.

"You and Carter were right about that town. Johnson has those workers tied up in knots. I did what I could to assure Carter a fair trial. They are securing a new judge to hear the evidence and I contacted that attorney in Denver."

"It sounds like you may believe Russ is innocent too," Abigail said.

"Innocent until proven guilty. I'll let you know if I hear anything else. The trial is set for Monday."

"Thank you." Teddy shook his hand. "Guess that's all we can do."

"Not quite. Now that that part is done, there is the matter of you two and your involvement."

Oh, dear. Abigail had worried there would be repercussions on her and Teddy's part in helping Russ.

Baniff gave them both a stern look. "This had better be the first and the last time either of you harbor a wanted man in Oak Grove. The way I'm going to log it is that you and your brother were unwitting Good Samaritans. Although the two of you are the least 'unwitting' people I know in Oak Grove, we'll leave it at that."

Abigail breathed a sigh of relief. "Thank you, Sheriff."

Baniff settled his Stetson back on his head, nodded and left the office.

She closed the door behind him. Then, slipping the pencil from her ear, she jotted a note in her notebook. When she finished, she looked up to find Teddy observing her.

"What are you up to?"

"Oh…just keeping a record of elves and unexpected gifts."

Saturday morning, the *Gazette* office was afire with activity. Jamie and Teddy arrived early to bundle the stacks of the regular edition and load them on the wagon. At eight o'clock Abby waved goodbye to Jamie as he snapped the reins and drove his mule away from town. At the same time, she welcomed Patty through the door to begin work on the Christmas edition.

After handing an apron to Patty, she instructed her how to pull the correct size and font of Hamilton type from the upper and lower cases, and how to use the composing stick to arrange the type backward and starting at the bottom of the page they would print to fit it tightly into the large frame.

After two hours of steady work, Patty gladly handed off the composing stick to Teddy, then stretched her fingers and shook out her arms. "I'm glad the edition is only two pages! How do you manage this for one of your longer regular papers!"

Teddy shared a smile with Abby. They both knew the aches and pains of typesetting well.

"Why don't you take a short rest? Look through the Christmas etchings in the drawer and decide which ones you'd like at the top of the page beside the heading."

A steady drizzle throughout the day against the hum of activity inside made the newspaper office feel cozy and warm. The scent of coffee and ink permeated the room. Abby was grateful for the busywork and the camaraderie of her brother, Patty and then Jamie once he returned from his early deliveries.

Still, with any lull, she wondered about Russ. Was he warm? Had the attorney from Denver arrived to help? Did he miss her?

When they were ready to print, Teddy handled the heavy press. It was too dangerous to let Patty manage it. Abby spread ink expertly on the large plate, and then Teddy turned the wheel, pressing the heavy iron plate of type against the sheet of paper. Patty then took up the newsprint and draped it to dry over the rope along the wall. Once dried, the entire process was repeated for the second page. It took the rest of the day and into the evening to finish. Finally, they were done, the papers folded, stacked and ready for distribution.

The next day, the *Gazette*'s Christmas edition went out as scheduled. Patty handed it out after church. Immediately, her friends and family read her article on the front page and congratulated her, which made others stop and do the same. Discussions started up among those lingering on the front steps of the church about which gift made the most sense to start on first. The fishermen argued for benches along the river and the children pestered their parents about a park with swings.

Abby stood back, enjoying the compliments that Patty received. The girl glowed, freckles, ink-stained fingers and all.

Farther down the front page, Abby had listed anonymous wishes. She'd left instructions to contact her should the Spirit of Christmas come over anyone and they wanted to become an elf. She insisted on absolute secrecy. No one was to know the elves' identities, and the elves weren't allowed to divulge who they helped.

By Monday, the box she had placed just inside the *Gazette*'s door was half-full with names of secret elves.

Monday was also the day of reckoning for Russ. The trial started at ten o'clock, and from that moment on she waited in suspense for the outcome. Would it be over in a day? Or take much longer?

At six in the evening, Teddy hung up his apron and shrugged into his coat. "Guess we won't hear anything this late. The trial must still be going on."

"I don't mind waiting as long as the news is good."

Just then the sheriff walked by the front window and entered the office. He held out a telegram to her. "This just came."

Acquitted. Johnson arrested for murder. Back soon. Carter.

Her knees grew weak. "Oh, my!" The words came out barely a whisper. "Oh, my!" She had been afraid to hope.

Teddy took the slip of paper from her. He read it and then gave a big whoop, grabbed her up and swung her around. He set her down and took hold of her shoulders. "I can tell you he's not coming back because of me. Sounds like he might be serious, Abby."

Wonder filled her. How had this happened? She couldn't stop beaming and crying with relief at the same time! The pressed-down worry and frustration of not knowing what was happening had been bottled up inside her ever since Russ had left. The pressure had increased daily. And suddenly it was over! He was a free man and he was coming back!

Chapter Twelve

She watched for Russ daily, keeping her ears tuned for the train whistle. Surely, it would only be a matter of a few days and he would come striding up the main road from the train station. When the number of days stretched into three, and then became four, she started to question what exactly "Back soon" meant to him.

Of course, he had loose ends to tie up. He would have to make sure the mine was operating, and the worker's grievances were addressed. He'd probably want to pay his respects to the widow McCabe. That all took time. Perhaps he'd choose to come by horse rather than by train…although that didn't seem sensible.

Knowing all this didn't make the waiting any easier.

She heard from children and adults alike that wanted to be secret elves and matched them up to the wish list that she and Patty had put together. This lent additional excitement to the holiday season and the town buzzed with an air of mystery and fun.

By Saturday, after five days had passed, Abby wondered if she should send a telegram. No…she couldn't do that. It was much too forward. But why didn't he let her know what was happening? Had she imagined his interest? Maybe it had waned after he realized he was a free man. Or maybe it waned after she had succumbed to his charms. Perhaps the strong emotions had been all on her side. He'd never actually confessed that he loved her—only that he cared. One didn't necessarily mean the other.

Maybe, she was a fool. She shouldn't have let her guard down. She shouldn't have let herself fall in love.

Two more days passed. It was Christmas Eve. If he never returned… No. She wouldn't consider that. She couldn't. That line of reasoning went nowhere and only served to make her frustrated. She bolstered her resolve. There was work to do. The Oak Grove Community Christmas Party would start in one hour.

She took a deep breath and added the finishing touch to her wardrobe—a new maroon velvet hat that sported two black egret feathers that matched her dress. She pinched her cheeks and donned her coat. Gathering the posters that Patty had made, she locked the *Gazette*'s door and headed for the town hall at the far end of the village.

Light spilled from the large front window as she neared, and once inside, the fiddler was already warming up his bow on the small stage. The women in charge of refreshments had the tables covered with festive tablecloths in dark green and gold. Every doorway had large red bows. Quickly, she hung up her coat and hat in the cloakroom and joined Patty.

Together they set up the posters and display for voting. Patty wore a new dress of green-and-red plaid with a red sash around the waist. The girl looked radiant, her green eyes sparkling with excitement.

"You look especially pretty tonight," Abigail said. "Is it for anyone special?"

"Perhaps." Patty grinned. "By the way, Miss Burnett gave me an A on my article."

Abby gave her a quick hug, marveling silently how easy it was for her now when a month ago she wouldn't have considered it. "You worked hard. As a matter of fact, once everyone is here, why don't you explain about the voting process instead of me."

"Really? All right. I can do that." She handed Abigail a small oblong box. "My thanks…for all you've done for me. I wasn't sure you would take me on at first."

"To tell the truth, I wasn't either."

They shared a laugh.

"But you persisted. And I'm glad you did. It has been a pleasure putting out the Christmas edition with you." Abby removed the lid. Nestled on a bed of pretty paper was a MacKinnon ink pencil. "This is lovely!"

"I ordered it the moment you agreed to help me write an article." Patty grinned. "Now, don't rest that on your ear."

Abby laughed. "That would be a sight, should the ink leak. No... I'll keep it for very special letters." For a moment, she thought of Russ.

"In all the time we've spent together, asking others what they wished for Christmas, I never once asked you what your wish was. Do you have one?"

All she had wanted was for Russ to be exonerated. "My wish has already come true."

But wait. There had been another. The one she'd made on the shooting star just after Thanksgiving. "I wished for a true friend. I wanted someone in my life who shared my love of the written word, someone to talk to about writing, a kindred spirit." She teared up suddenly. "And you came along."

"You mean I barreled in."

Abby giggled. "You certainly did!"

Families started arriving and the music started up. To one side of the room, Miss Burnett started games for the younger children. The noise and laughter in the room increased as children and their parents played charades. For a time, Abby watched the game with Patty, and then she took over serving the warm spiced apple cider at the refreshment table.

When she handed off a glass of cider to Angus O'Leary, he leaned toward her and put his gnarled finger to his mouth. "Don't tell a soul. Got those primers ordered. Should be here first of the new year." Then he grinned, winked and walked away with a jaunty spring to his step.

That's right! He was an elf!

A few minutes later, while Abby watched Patty give her speech, Mrs. Gibson approached. Her daughter, Kristine, had wished for help with the milking while her sister recovered from an injury.

"You started something here, Miss White. Ever since the Christmas edition came out, there has been an older pupil from the school waiting at the barn every morning to help with the milking. I offer them breakfast, but they refuse, saying that elves don't get paid. I tell you it's been a blessing."

Abigail grinned. The elves were hard at work! "Many hands make light work," she said, the familiar quote coming easily.

"Indeed, they do." Mrs. Gibson hugged her. "Merry Christmas, dear." She set a bag tied with a red ribbon into Abby's hand.

Another gift? Abby opened the bag just enough to peek inside. Caramels wrapped in wax paper! And oh! That fresh scent!

A blast of cold air suddenly swept through the room. Abby turned toward the door. Gathered in the opening stood a family she had not seen before. They looked tentative and unsure of their welcome. More interesting than that however, were the two women with them… Mrs. Corwin and the widow Eddy. Jamie stepped from behind the group and started gathering their coats.

She walked forward to welcome them.

Jamie grinned at her. "Found out who took the clothes and it wasn't the goat!" He introduced her to the Sturdevant family and explained that their wagon had broken down on the property line between his mother's land and Mrs. Eddy's. "Seems one won't let the other outdo her at being neighborly till they can be on their way."

He walked off with the bundle of coats toward the cloakroom.

Before she could greet the family, the music stopped. Everyone turned to see what the commotion was at the door. There stood Brett Blackwell holding the thick trunk end of a large pine tree! He charged into the room with it. Teddy followed, holding the other end of the tree.

A whoop sounded from two of the town boys and everyone laughed as the two ran over to help carry the tree into the room. The fresh scent of pine permeated everything. Where in the world had it come from? The closest place had to be the Rockies!

Abby's breath caught, and she looked back at the door. It couldn't be! There, with a light dusting of snow on his coat, stood Russ!

He removed his Stetson and scanned the room until he found her. She looked thunderstruck. He couldn't have asked for a better welcome. A grin that had to be the size of Colorado tugged on his face.

"Russ." Her mouth formed his name.

He'd like to bottle this moment. Abby. His little Abby. All grown up and staring back at him like he was the most important man on this earth. Were her insides as jittery as his? Had she missed him as much as he'd missed her?

He walked to her and she slipped her small hand into his. He brought it to his lips, kissing the tops of her ink-smudged fingers gently. Shivers shot through him. He'd never felt this way about a woman before. She had enchanted him. And she'd cared for him, at tremendous risk. Did these people understand how unusual that was? How special she was?

Murmurs around him grew louder. People voiced their curiosity about where the tree had come from. Finally, one youngster cried out, "Elves!" Everyone started laughing.

Abby's eyes sparkled with mirth.

"Blackwell! You got a stand for this thing?" Ted called out.

Ted and the man who had helped Russ with the tree at

the train station stood the pine up in the corner, leaning it against the walls.

Russ looked back at Abby. Her cheeks were flushed and her eyes were bright as she watched the men wrestle with the pine. "I don't think they need us," he whispered into her ear. "Come outside with me. I want to kiss you properly."

Her eyes widened, but she nodded quickly and walked with him through the door and out into the crisp night air.

The kiss he wanted to give her, no one would call proper, but he'd keep it sweet. He wanted more than one kiss with her, more than one moment. He wanted forever.

He stopped on the boardwalk just beyond the window, drawing her into the shadows. Before she took her next breath, he slipped his hand to the small of her back and pulled her to him, kissing her long and hard. His pulse kicked up, his heart thumping against his rib cage. The need to kiss her, to hold her, had been pent up inside him for so long. This was like coming home.

He drew back slightly. "I've wanted to do that ever since the night the sheriff dragged me off to jail."

She hugged him tightly. "Oh, Russ… I've missed you!"

He breathed in the scent of her sweet-smelling hair. Cinnamon. It made him smile. Had she tried baking again?

"What took you so long?"

"Johnson left things in a mess." He didn't want to think about the Barton mine right now, much less talk about it. "Plus, I had to find the perfect tree."

"I can't believe you remembered that! It was one thing out of so many that we talked about."

"I remember everything you said. I couldn't get you out of my mind."

Her eyes clouded over. "Did you try?"

"Not a bit."

"Good." She sighed. "I'm so glad you are free. And I'm so glad you came back."

Always honest, always wide open with her thoughts.

"Your Sheriff Baniff played a big part in making that happen when he contacted the attorney I knew in Denver. Together, they made sure I had a judge and jury that Johnson couldn't sway. You had a big part too. What did you put in that telegram to the foreman's widow?"

"Then it helped? She knew something?"

"She was afraid to come forward because she wanted to protect her son. Turns out he witnessed what happened that day. Your telegram changed her mind."

"I'm so relieved it is over. You've gone through so much."

"I put you in danger, Abby. You and Ted. I didn't realize Johnson had men looking for me. Men not quite as upstanding as your sheriff here. Things could have gone bad. You could have been hurt."

She shrugged one shoulder. "I would do it all again to help the man I love."

He said softly, "Thought I was a bad risk for any girl."

"Not anymore. You've changed." She smiled. "Or maybe I have."

He studied her, smoothing his thumb over her lower lip. "You always lay it out straight. Guess this is one time I want to also. I love you back, Abby. With my whole heart. You're all I've thought about since stumbling into that newspaper office four weeks ago." He leaned in and kissed her once more, this time gently, with a tenderness that said how precious she was to him.

Was this really happening? Had Russ just said he loved her? She was dizzy with wonder. His strong arms, wrapped tightly around her, were the only things keeping her on the ground. His first kiss had claimed her, speaking of his need and want and desire. But this one...this tender one made her melt in a completely different way. It filled her heart and her soul. With him.

He finished the kiss and pulled away a little.

She opened her eyes and almost missed the flash of light that streaked across the sky. She blinked. "A shooting star."

"Did you make a wish?"

She thought for a moment about the past few weeks. She'd wished for a friend for Christmas and she'd discovered many. Patty, who had opened her eyes to the plights of those in Oak Grove. Sheriff Baniff, who had heeded her distress and made sure Russ had a fair trial. And her neighbors, who had rallied to the call of being elves. All she needed to do was open her eyes, open her heart and they were there, waiting and willing to be her friend.

"I don't have one. All my wishes have come true." She gripped his vest, holding him close.

"Then maybe I could have your wish."

"Wasn't getting your life back enough? What more could you want?"

The twinkle in his blue eyes captured her. "Just you. With me. Always."

She swallowed. She had to be sure. "Always… Do you mean…marriage?"

A quick grin flashed as he nodded. "I promise to love you, cherish you and adore equally anything you write or cook…" Then he grew serious. "If you'll have me, Abby."

Her heart spilled over with love for him. "Oh, yes," she said. "To all of it."

He smiled and kissed her once more—a promise, a commitment, a forever.

Epilogue

Oak Grove Gazette
Special Edition 1880
Happy New Year!

The wedding of Russell Carter, owner of Barton Silver Mining Company, and Abigail White, reporter for the *Oak Grove Gazette*, took place on New Year's Day at the Oak Grove Community Church, with Reverend Flaherty officiating.

Theodore White, the bride's brother, escorted her down the aisle and also served as best man. Attending the bride were Patty Owens and Hannah White. Abigail White looked stunning in a deep blue dress with black brocade. The wedding band of gold carried an intricate swirl of silver—the silver coming straight from the groom's mine in Colorado.

After a large reception at the town hall, the newly-weds boarded the Kansas Pacific to make their home in Barton, Colorado. The entire town turned out to see them off and wish them well—including a few elves.

Your Hometown Reporter,
Patricia Owens

* * * * *

*If you enjoyed this story you won't want to miss
these other great full-length reads
by Kathryn Albright:*

The Prairie Doctor's Bride
Wedding at Rocking S Ranch

*And check out the books in her
Heroes of San Diego miniseries,
starting with:*

Familiar Stranger in Clear Springs
Christmas Kiss from the Sheriff

HOME *on the* RANCH

Name _____ (PLEASE PRINT)

Address _____ Apt. #

City _____ State/Prov. _____ Zip/Postal Code

Signature (if under 18, a parent or guardian must sign)

Mail to the **Reader Service:**

IN U.S.A.: P.O. Box 1341, Buffalo, New York 14240-8531
IN CANADA: P.O. Box 603, Fort Erie, Ontario L2A 5X3

HRCBPA18R

Get 4 FREE REWARDS!

We'll send you 2 FREE Books <u>plus</u> 2 FREE Mystery Gifts.

Harlequin® Special Edition books feature heroines finding the balance between their work life and personal life on the way to finding true love.

FREE
Value Over
$20

Get 4 FREE REWARDS!

We'll send you 2 FREE Books plus 2 FREE Mystery Gifts.

Harlequin Presents® books feature a sensational and sophisticated world of international romance where sinfully tempting heroes ignite passion.

FREE Value Over $20

YES! Please send me 2 FREE Harlequin Presents® novels and my 2 FREE gifts (gifts are worth about $10 retail). After receiving them, if I don't wish to receive any more books, I can return the shipping statement marked "cancel." If I don't cancel, I will receive 6 brand-new novels every month and be billed just $4.55 each for the regular-print edition or $5.55 each for the larger-print edition in the U.S., or $5.49 each for the regular-print edition or $5.99 each for the larger-print edition in Canada. That's a savings of at least 11% off the cover price! It's quite a bargain! Shipping and handling is just 50¢ per book in the U.S. and 75¢ per book in Canada*. I understand that accepting the 2 free books and gifts places me under no obligation to buy anything. I can always return a shipment and cancel at any time. The free books and gifts are mine to keep no matter what I decide.

Choose one: ☐ **Harlequin Presents®**
Regular-Print
(106/306 HDN GMYX)

☐ **Harlequin Presents®**
Larger-Print
(176/376 HDN GMYX)

Name (please print)

Address _____ Apt. #

City _____ State/Province _____ Zip/Postal Code

Mail to the **Reader Service:**
IN U.S.A.: P.O. Box 1341, Buffalo, NY 14240-8531
IN CANADA: P.O. Box 603, Fort Erie, Ontario L2A 5X3

Want to try two free books from another series? Call 1-800-873-8635 or visit www.ReaderService.com.

---

*Terms and prices subject to change without notice. Prices do not include applicable taxes. Sales tax applicable in N.Y. Canadian residents will be charged applicable taxes. Offer not valid in Quebec. This offer is limited to one order per household. Books received may not be as shown. Not valid for current subscribers to Harlequin Presents books. All orders subject to approval. Credit or debit balances in a customer's account(s) may be offset by any other outstanding balance owed by or to the customer. Please allow 4 to 6 weeks for delivery. Offer available while quantities last.

Your Privacy—The Reader Service is committed to protecting your privacy. Our Privacy Policy is available online at www.ReaderService.com or upon request from the Reader Service. We make a portion of our mailing list available to reputable third parties that offer products we believe may interest you. If you prefer that we not exchange your name with third parties, or if you wish to clarify or modify your communication preferences, please visit us at www.ReaderService.com/consumerchoice or write to us at Reader Service Preference Service, P.O. Box 9062, Buffalo, NY 14240-9062. Include your complete name and address.

HP18

READERSERVICE.COM

Manage your account online!
- Review your order history
- Manage your payments
- Update your address

> **We've designed the Reader Service website just for you.**

Enjoy all the features!
- Discover new series available to you, and read excerpts from any series.
- Respond to mailings and special monthly offers.
- Browse the Bonus Bucks catalog and online-only exculsives.
- Share your feedback.